# AS THE
# EAGLE
# WALKS

## JIM BADKE

*As The Eagle Walks*, by Jim Badke
©2021, James Badke, First Revision 2024
ISBN 978-1-7777101-0-1

Cover: Aaron Brink, Brass Hand Design, brasshand.ca

The stained-glass image is a detail from the east window, installed in the then-Unitarian chapel of Manchester College, Oxford, designed by Burne Jones and made by Morris & Co. of the pre-Raphaelite school. Photograph by Fr Lawrence Lew OP, used by permission.

Other books by Jim Badke, available on Amazon:

- *The Christian Camp Leader*, 2013
- *The Camp Liverwurst Series*, 2022-24
- *The Island and i: Nelson Dunkin of Copper Island*, 2024

Scripture quotations from the Authorized (King James) Version. Rights in the Authorized Version in the United Kingdom are vested in the Crown. Reproduced by permission of the Crown's patentee, Cambridge University Press.

Where noted, Scripture quotations are from the Holy Bible, New International Version, NIV. Copyright © 1973, 1978, 1984, 2011 by Biblica, Inc.™ Used by permission of Zondervan. All rights reserved worldwide. www.zondervan.com. The "NIV" and "New International Version" are trademarks registered in the United States Patent and Trademark Office by Biblica, Inc.™

As The Eagle Walks *pulled me in from its first page and held me with its richly-drawn characters, vividly-evoked scenes, crisp and often funny dialogue, and mounting tension—all the things we look for in a novel—while exploring real-life matters of faith.*

    - Mark Buchanan, author of *God Walk* and the *David* Trilogy

Peter turned and saw that the disciple whom Jesus loved was following them. (This was the one who had leaned back against Jesus at the supper and had said, "Lord, who is going to betray you?"). When Peter saw him, he asked, "Lord, what about him?"

Jesus answered, "If I want him to remain alive until I return, what is that to you? You must follow me." Because of this, the rumor spread among the believers that this disciple would not die. But Jesus did not say that he would not die; he only said, "If I want him to remain alive until I return, what is that to you?"

This is the disciple who testifies to these things and who wrote them down. We know that his testimony is true.

Jesus did many other things as well. If every one of them were written down, I suppose that even the whole world would not have room for the books that would be written.

- Gospel of John 21:20-25, NIV

# 1

The other island was farther off than I thought. After two hours of paddling, the shore behind me and the yellow hills before me were the same disconcerting distance away. More troubling, heavy swells now lifted the kayak high and dropped it down, down, until aquamarine was all I could see.

I pressed on, pushing away misgivings and common sense in equal measure. The historic island of Patmos was a place I was determined to see, no matter what Jessica said. True, I never thought I would go by kayak. But when I reached the open water that morning and saw the island's golden outline in the distance, I decided it was my only chance. Now that I was more than halfway across, it seemed crucial to succeed and unthinkable to fail. Such obstinacy had taken me to high and low places before. Like now, as I rode waves that felt as tall as haystacks.

On top of one of those haystacks, I turned my head to pick out the cluster of small islets far behind me, the ones the guys at the kayak rental shop suggested I explore. The kayak wobbled beneath me and I had a panicked moment of regaining my balance. My heart raced at the thought of falling out and drifting boatless in the open sea, miles from land. I gripped the paddle harder and corrected my course as I rose to the top of a roller. Patmos drew quickly closer. Some current was propelling me forward, answering the call of the island that beckoned me. The return trip could be even more challenging.

I almost didn't want to return. Why did I think a trip to Europe would save our marriage? If anything, Jessica and I were drifting further apart with each additional tourist attraction we visited. And fighting more. I was so angry that morning, I didn't tell her where I was going as I walked out the door of our suite. I wasn't sure myself until I reached the shore and saw the rental shop and a row of colorful kayaks lapped by the waves. My rage dissipated with each stroke of the paddle. But as I dipped it for the ten thousandth time, I was amazed at how far my anger had propelled me.

I needed to decide where on the island I wanted to land. There was no reason to aim for the uninhabited hills to the left. There was a kind of fortress on top of a rise to the right that looked interesting but was much more distant. The small settlement in the bay in front of me would do as a place to explore and find some lunch. I paddled in earnest, thinking of the time it was taking to travel this far. Jessica would be even less happy if I got back late. I also dared not leave her alone with the nightlife on the isle of Lipsi. Thieves and ruffians didn't worry me; it was my wife I didn't trust.

As hard as I strained toward the bay with the little whitewashed houses, the current bore me toward no-man's-land. If I missed the southernmost point of the island, I could drift out into the open Mediterranean. The thought made me paddle with all my remaining strength. The small craft lost as much headway sideways as it gained forward. At this rate, I would never make it to the island. I imagined myself drifting for days in the open sea. Being discovered by pirates or a skiff full of refugees. Or getting swallowed by a giant fish, as Jonah once was in these waters.

Abruptly, the current was gone. I looked behind me and saw the water moving like a river in the sea. I must have found a back eddy; even the waves were less. Smiling, I paddled a straight course toward shore. The sea surged over the rocks a few hundred yards ahead, and I aimed for a small gravelly bay with smaller waves and a few old sheds. I saw no houses on the rising yellow slope and no roads.

It was glorious to step out of the boat onto firm land, though the beach shifted strangely beneath my feet. When the kayak was out of reach of the waves, I sat on the sand and stretched my aching arms. This wasn't where I wanted to explore. The village must be on the other side of the hill, and tired as I was, I determined to attempt it. A fragrant flowering shrub that didn't yield and threatened to slice my bare legs covered the steep, rocky slope. The top of the hill proved elusive: every summit was a giant step, with another above it. Bird songs I had never heard before filled the bushes. Lizards darted out of my path, and once a sizable snake, to which I gave a wide berth.

It was a full hour's hike before the sea was finally all around me except for one small isthmus to the north. I was exhausted, and disappointed that the view on the other side dissolved into mist not far offshore. The village was as distant below as I had already walked. Remembering the grasping brush (and the snake), I decided to return to my boat and paddle to the village instead. It was almost noon, according to the cell phone I removed from its waterproof bag. The thought of lunch made my stomach growl.

I couldn't tell if I was taking the same route back, as I couldn't yet see the bay where my boat lay. Stones rolled beneath my running shoes and bruised my toes, and it was harder to avoid the brush. In my concentration, I didn't look up until I was near the shore. To my left was the small beach with the old shacks—but no kayak.

Panicked, I scanned up and down the shore. Out of the corner of my eye, I saw movement. On a small trail half a mile away, two men were walking with my kayak between them. I yelled, but the distance and the murmur of the sea were too great. Brambles tore at my legs as I fought my way to the beach. The men were out of sight. Gasping, I sprinted after them along the trail. But at every turn, they weren't there. The path became broader, then a dusty road, and I came across a few whitewashed houses. But no people, no kayak.

Standing at a crossroads, chest heaving, I turned around and around like a man attacked from all sides. It was utterly quiet, apart from the white noise of waves lapping on the beach. The air was breathless, and heat radiated from every surface onto my flushed face. A couple of dogs sniffed in my direction and found the shade again. My kayak—my only transportation—had vanished into the haze. Angry and flustered, I sat on an old barrel out of the sun beside a long shed, eyes closed against the glare of the street until my head stopped pounding.

Small fishing boats lay scattered between me and the shore, and beyond them, a few tall masts. The road took me past a diminutive white stucco church atop a small hill. I stopped and regarded its long, bleached stairway for a moment. At home, this is where I would find help for sure. But what type of church could this be in the Greek islands? Not Baptist, that's for sure.

I needed to call my wife. Not that Jessica would have her cell phone on her. I knew where she spent this day, which is how I ended up paddling by myself. I would be late indeed getting back to the resort on the island of Lipsi, if I could find any way back at all. What would she say when I told her where I was? I had already annoyed Jessica by refusing to join her that morning at the naturist beach she discovered. "You're such a prude, Jason," she told me as I walked out the door. Sometimes I wondered if she was really a Christian.

But no use making things even worse. I could at least leave a message, except my cell read "No Service" as I walked up the steps to the church. No Wi-Fi signal either. Did the village have a payphone? I couldn't recall the last time I used one. I walked the road along the shore toward an area of more houses, seeking a way to make a call.

I found no one who spoke English. The first man I met listened, leaning on a broken oar as I explained about the stolen kayak and my need to return to Lipsi. When I stopped, he shrugged and walked away, muttering something unintelligible. I next came across a group of women carrying baskets of what appeared to be minnows. Not stopping to listen, they waved me off and laughed among themselves. Finally, a young man shook his head as I began and pointed back toward the masts I had passed earlier. "Marina!" he told me, and I thought for a moment that he knew my language; but of course, the word must be the same in Greek. We smiled and shook hands, and I turned and walked toward the masts.

The marina turned out to be small but classy. A handful of expensive yachts gleamed against the cobalt blue of the bay. Deeply tanned men chatted at one of the wooden tables on the patio, drinking wine. The poor bartender and I wrestled in our disparate languages over what I should have. We finally settled on mineral water, which tasted terrible but I was too thirsty to care, and a savory meat and cheese turnover.

It was a good start, but I needed more. When my charades had conveyed my wishes, the bartender indicated the cash register. He wanted money first. I didn't exactly look the part of a wealthy yacht owner, so his insistence was understandable. Being short on euros, I took the phone out of my pocket to grab the credit card I kept inside the case. It wasn't there. What on earth? I immediately remembered—the kayak rental shop had insisted on holding onto my credit card until I returned.

No problem. I opened my phone to my wallet app and held it out to the bartender. He was confused. When he tried to take the phone, I held on and shook my head. He stepped back in surprise and began a lengthy explanation in Greek, which became louder as I continued to shake my head. The men at the table stopped talking and watched the interaction with mild interest.

"Can I help?" A man towered over my shoulder. He seemed amused by my swift perusal of his appearance. A face carved like rich leather, with deep lines and a healthy glow. His hair was long and wavy, blended with gray and tied back in a ponytail, and his beard was full. He wore a rough white cotton shirt and faded worn jeans, sandals hardly covering his chestnut-brown feet. I found myself tongue-tied.

"You speak English!" I managed. "Thank God."

"Amen," he returned.

I explained the dilemma between me and the bartender, and told him about the kayak and how I was stuck on Patmos. The bartender went back to whatever bartenders do. As I talked, the man watched my face with that same bemused expression. I wasn't sure he was listening to me, so I stopped. "Sorry, I should introduce myself. I'm Jason." I held out my hand.

He looked at my hand but didn't shake it. Turning to the bartender, he said something in Greek. The bartender's deference towards this man surprised me, as he also did not appear to be a wealthy yacht owner. The bartender bowed to him and went back to the counter, preparing more food. In minutes, he placed a plate of pasta and a glass of wine in front of me and went back to polishing his cups.

"Bon appetite!" my new friend offered, smiling.

"Thanks," I spluttered, "but I'm not sure I can pay for it. My credit card..."

"I'll take care of it. Enjoy." He turned and walked away.

"Wait! I don't even know your name!"

He smiled back at me but didn't stop. "My name is John. I'm not hard to find." He rounded the corner and was gone.

I sat at the counter, picking at the pasta and amazed at my incredible luck in meeting this generous, English-speaking fellow. He was my ticket off this island—I couldn't let him walk away. I left the wine untouched and the pasta unfinished on the counter. Ignoring the protests of the bartender, I strode across the patio in search of the man named John.

# 2

For all John's assurances, I couldn't find him. He wasn't in the village. I walked the few roads and alleyways, wandered among the fishing boats, and talked with everyone I met. "John?" I asked at first, but no one knew what I was saying. It was well into the afternoon, and I wondered if I had any chance of getting back to Lipsi that day. Jessica would kill me if I didn't.

I stopped one better-dressed elderly gentleman, who looked at me sharply. "*Iohannes*?" he queried, and something twigged in the back of my mind that this might be the name John in Greek.

"Yes, thank you. I'm looking for Johannes!" Well, I tried to say it the way he did. It was the best I could do.

The man's face darkened. He eyed me with suspicion. "Why? Why *Iohannes*?"

I made the mistake of thinking he could understand me. My explanation was beyond his grasp of English, and his face became even less friendly. He stopped me with a finger to my chest. "You... go home." Offended, I stepped back. He came forward, saying something in a tone I didn't appreciate. I held up my hands, which for some reason infuriated him all the more. Finally, I backed away. His sharp words chased me down the street.

Whatever. At least I had the name Johannes to work with. Better, a few more people emerged from whitewashed buildings and shady corners as the heat subsided. I saw no shaggy heads among them that might be my benefactor. But I felt sure, armed with John's name in Greek (or close to it), someone would help me find him.

Again, I was mistaken. My use of the name *Johannes* had an interesting bipolar effect on the people I accosted. Some became immediately angry, not like the man who thumped his finger on my chest, but as if the name itself was a curse. A few of these gave me a thumbs up, but their expression made this a threatening gesture. Most others—all the others— became guarded. Their smile clouded over; they stared at their feet, nodded their head back and clucked their tongue, which I took to be a decisive "no." Word must travel through town because soon, anyone I approached waved me off or walked away.

This felt hopeless. I gave up asking about the elusive John and returned to the marina. I hoped he would return, or I would at least find information on how to return to Lipsi. The cafe was closed, but I discovered a bulletin board leaning precariously over the street. Among posters for fishing guides and items for sale was a faded ferry schedule in Greek and English. If it was still in effect, the various ferries left from a port named Skala, which looked to be more than an hour's walk away. The last boat for the day, even if I had the €9.00 fee in cash, would leave in half that time.

I was to spend the night. At least it wasn't cold. I felt sure I could find a corner with a comfortable bit of grass to lie on. I thought about walking to Skala, but I wanted to see John again. I was curious about people's intriguing reactions to him and hoped for some clues. And I was sure I could beg ferry fare from him—he appeared generous enough. But first, I needed to call Jessica and attempt to explain how I ended up in this wild predicament.

I saw no payphones in the village, and anyway, I was without the means of paying for a call. I thought of the wealthy yacht owners, but found the gate locked at the wharf, and I saw no one out and about. One by one, the boats' lights came on, some illuminating their decks and some warming the lavish cabins that no doubt would offer fine fare later. I was getting hungry again and had little hope of dinner.

Thinking I would find a place to sleep before it became too dark, I walked toward the little church on its hill. The road was lit by one flickering streetlight, and I saw a shadowy figure approaching. When we were twenty feet apart, we both stopped in surprise at the same time and took a step back. It was the finger-on-chest man.

"You...!" he exclaimed, raising that finger again. "Go... home!"

I shook my head, wondering how to communicate why I couldn't do what he wanted. I pulled out my empty pocket and showed him. "No money! See?"

His angry face softened. He contemplated me for a moment, relaxed into a wry grin and shrugged, saying something I didn't understand but that sounded more friendly. "Come!" he offered, waving for me to follow. Having no options, I did. We walked through the village together, my new acquaintance pointing out various features by their Greek names. We ascended a slope and, at one point, stopped to look at the lights and ocean below. Far off, I could see what may have been the lights of Lipsi, where Jessica was likely becoming alarmed. Or else reviewing my extensive life insurance policy.

We were both out of breath, but his was fast and shallow. Time to slow down for the old man, I thought. I held my hand to my ear in that universal symbol of talking on a phone and waved toward Lipsi. "My wife, I need to call," I shouted for no reason. I showed him my phone and pointed to the lack of signal. To my surprise, the man reached into his pocket and pulled out his own cell phone. It was an ancient flip phone, but it showed two bars of reception. I dialed my wife's number and, to my relief, heard it ring.

"Hello?" She sounded irritated, like I was interrupting her. Not a good start. Oh well.

"Jess, it's Jason."

She gasped, "Jason! What in the world... you disappear and don't tell anyone... where are you?"

"Sorry, Babe! I'm on Patmos." She got the short version of my adventures as I glanced up at my Greek friend, who kept looking at his watch. "I should be able to return tomorrow morning if I can figure out how to pay..."

"And what am I supposed to do?" Jessica's voice rose. "Have our one special meal by myself on our holiday? What were you thinking, Jason?" I had forgotten about our dinner reservation.

"Hey, I'll make it up to you." Now the man was tapping one foot. "Gotta go! See you tomorrow." I hung up before she could lay into me more. My predicament was hardly my fault. If anything, it was hers, I told myself.

My friend took the phone back and eyed me with interest. "*Iason?*" he asked, pointing at me.

It took me a moment, but I caught on. "Yes, Jason! My name is Jason."

"Ah! *Iason. Argo!*" I wasn't sure what he meant, so I smiled and nodded. He laid his hand on his chest. "*Manos.*" I was glad for a friend at this point and reached to shake his hand. Before I could react, Manos grabbed my shoulders and kissed me on both cheeks. That was weird, but I felt I was being welcomed. I hoped it would translate into something like food and shelter.

We continued a short way up the hill and came to a metal gate in a flowering hedge. The darkness was complete, and I was glad for the beckoning glow of lights within. Manos ushered me through as we approached a large white stucco house. The scent of blossoms was overwhelming. The door opened, and a woman as tall as Manos greeted us. As we entered, I saw she was in every way like him—fine-boned, dark and handsome. I guessed they were both in their seventies.

Manos introduced me. "Marianna, wife mine!" She looked at me expectantly, and I stepped forward and attempted to do the cheek thing. I say, attempted.

Marianna laughed. "*Amerikanos!*" She kissed my cheeks as an expert, barely touching me, with no wetness whatsoever. I saw my error immediately and laughed as well. Manos explained my dilemma to her, and Marianna looked at me and clucked her tongue. But the way she kept glancing at her husband made me think she was more anxious about him. They had a terse exchange in Greek, Manos shrugging off her words. She settled us both in cushioned wicker chairs on a patio that overlooked the lights on the water below.

Manos sat smiling across from me. I could tell he was full of questions—I had a few myself—but we could make little of one another's language. The glass of wine in Manos' hand emptied slowly, mine slower still. When I first tried it—not wanting to be rude—I found it sweet but harsh, like my grandmother's cough medicine. I was thirsty enough to keep sipping it, and after a while, I did not have to hold it in my mouth as long before I could swallow.

A light went on in Manos' eye. He stood and went to a small bookcase and pulled out a tattered world atlas. "*Pou?*" he asked, pointing to the globe on the cover. I found a map of the USA inside the book and pointed out my drab little town in the Midwest. "Ahh!" he exclaimed, then turned the pages to the Mediterranean and the Greek islands. From the tracings with his finger, I learned he was from Corinth, but his wife was born and raised on Patmos, in a small town to the north called Kampos. The name Corinth was familiar to me from Paul's letters to the Corinthians in the Bible. It was interesting to meet someone who was born there.

I felt comfortable and content. It might have been the wine, but a sudden wave of gratefulness flooded me. I wasn't homeless on some street corner; I was in a home—safe and with new friends. God had some purpose for me being here. I couldn't remember the last time I felt that connection between God and my circumstances. Most of the time, I did my own thing, never considering where God was in it all. It was a curious sensation. Maybe I was there to bring salvation to this man and his wife. If only I could talk to them.

Marianna called us to the table a few feet away. What I remember about that meal was the way they included me in their conversation, though I understood not a word. I laughed with them when they laughed and listened intently to their unintelligible stories. I remember savoring the food, whatever it was, rather than wolfing it down. Again, it may have been the wine, yet it was something more.

I will never forget the moment before we ate. Manos took his wife's hand with a look of adoration, and mine with a grin. Marianna took my other hand, closed her eyes and prayed. She infused her words with joy and gratitude, whatever she said, and I heard the name "*Iason*" as she squeezed my hand. I had done nothing to deserve their friendship—it all started with me insulting her husband—and I did not know what to make of it. She finished with, "...*sto ónoma tou Iisoú, amín.*"

*Iisoú*. Jesus? Could they be Christians? That thought remained in the back of my mind throughout the meal. Their kindness gives it away, I thought. I wouldn't receive such a reception at every door on the island. These are my people.

I finally found the courage as Manos took the plates away and refilled my glass. "*Iisoú?*" I asked, placing my hand on my chest. That confused them. They looked at me with concern, and I tried again. "*Iisoú?*" and I pointed at each of our chests.

This time, comprehension dawned. "Ahh," Marianna put her hand on my shoulder. "*Christianós?*"

"Yes! Yes, I'm a Christian! You—*Christianós?*" I looked at each of them, fully expecting an enthusiastic response. But Marianna sat back with a troubled look. The dark expression returned to Manos' face, and he eyed me warily.

"Why... you... here?" he managed after a moment. "Why *Iohannes?*"

This flabbergasted me. What did me being a Christian have to do with the man named John? Why this sudden change of temperature in the room? They may not be Christians after all, but why this suspicion of me, of my reasons for being there? I closed my eyes, wishing for reassuring words they could understand. I heard dishes clattering and looked up to see Marianna at the sink. Manos stood, eyes down, and beckoned. "Come." He showed me to a small room with a bed made up. As he passed me on the way out the door, his expression was sad, not angry. He said nothing and left me to my thoughts.

I did not sleep well. This puzzle eluded me. I did not know how I had offended my kind hosts or how to set it right. I wondered long about the man named John. Why did everyone react so strangely to his name, and why was Manos protective of him? And I thought about Jessica, eating a fancy dinner alone at the taverna. Hopefully alone. I wouldn't put it past her... I finally drifted off, dreaming I was Jonah in the belly of a whale that lectured me all night in words I couldn't understand.

# 3

The sun streaming through my open window roused me. Six in the morning and bird chatter already filled the air. I could see their bright flits of color go by. From the overwhelming scent of blossoms, I knew exactly upon awakening where I was: on the island of Patmos, with people who may be my friends or might not.

I saw no sign of that incongruity as I entered the kitchen, which was also the dining room and living area in one. Marianna greeted me cheerfully and indicated that Manos was out in the garden. I found him watering the shrubbery from a large, ancient watering tin with a long spout. He nodded to me, set down the watering can and said, "Come." The narrow path towered with vivid pink and purple blooms. An iron gate led to a low stone wall where the Mediterranean gleamed turquoise below us.

Manos sat on a low bench set into the wall and made space for me to join him. We sat in silence for some time. I longed to speak with him, ask my bewildered questions and assure him I was trustworthy. Catching my eye, he reached over and placed his hand on mine. Tears formed in the corner of my eye. I couldn't remember the last time anyone had touched me in such a kindly manner. He squeezed my hand, stood and beckoned me again with the word he had spoken to me most often. "Come."

Breakfast was ready. Something like watermelon, gold rather than red, was to become my favorite. Also laid out for us were eggs scrambled with cheese and chives, a homemade loaf with bits of olive in it, and slices of hard cured sausage. Manos spread his bread with seasoned oil. Marianna was off to the market, if I read my friend's gestures correctly. I tried to ask about the ferry, pointing at myself and over the water. Manos looked flustered, but nodded and held up his watch. He was assuring me I would arrive on time.

Someone came in the door out of sight from where we were sitting. I assumed it was Marianna, but it was not. To my astonishment (and his), it was John. "Well met!" he exclaimed. He took my offered hand this time and sat down at the table with us. Manos looked at him and at me with consternation. Then he gave his characteristic shrug, smiled and grasped John's hand with affection. John smiled into Manos' eyes and said to me, "I see you enjoy the best hospitality this island offers."

John made the room feel small, a larger man than I remembered from my brief encounter at the marina. His hands were massive and weathered, deeply tanned but splotchy. He placed one of those heavy hands on my shoulder. "Tell me, why are you here? What do you seek on the Isle of Patmos?"

It was a relief to speak with someone who knew English. I described our Greek vacation, my desire to visit the island where the Apostle saw his vision, and my imprudence in arriving there by kayak. Again, I wondered if he was listening to me as he picked at the remains of our breakfast. Manos poured him a cup of coffee you could stand a stick up in, which I had declined. John sipped it, watching the sea behind me until I ran out of words.

"Does she love you, this Jessica, your wife?"

His question rattled me. "I... well, of course! We've been married only a few years..."

"Marriage is not an agent of love. Of passion, yes, but that can be short-lived. Love is hard work. In your wife's case, very hard work, I think." He turned his gaze back to Manos, who still admired him. "Our friend Manos doesn't know what we're saying, but he knows love. Both how to give and to receive." He spoke something to him in Greek. Manos looked at me and laughed, and gave his little shrug.

I felt stung by the insult and the inference that I lacked in the matter of love. "You don't know me! How can you imply I don't know about love? I love my wife!"

"And you're anxious to return to her, yes?"

I hesitated too long. In truth, I wasn't anxious to return. Being with Jessica was most often like going to the dentist. Necessary, but not comfortable. "Well, sure!"

"Most convincing. Come, I'll bring you to the ferry in Skala. We'll spare Manos' old legs the journey." He spoke to Manos, who laughed heartily and nodded. I was still steaming inside and would have preferred Manos' cheeriness to John's insults. Manos insisted on taking a photo of us all before we left, fussing over the self-timer on an old film camera. I gave my many thanks (through John) to my host, who kissed me on both cheeks. If only I had something to leave for Manos and Marianna. I felt uncomfortable having nothing to offer.

We set off. At the gate, John retrieved a large basket from a shady spot. "We have a few stops to make on the way," he explained. The basket looked cumbersome, and I offered my help. John looked at me, chuckling, and hoisted the basket to his shoulder. The day was glorious but warm already at 9:00 in the morning. We walked in silence for some time. John was a fast walker, despite his heavy load, and he occasionally stopped so I could catch up.

"Is poverty common where you come from?" he asked as I puffed to the top of the small hill where he waited.

I was about to respond that I lived in the wealthiest nation on earth. Before I could say the words, an image flashed into my mind. Last winter, Jessica's car was in the shop and she needed mine, so I took the bus to work. I had never ridden on a public bus before. College students and moms with young children crowded on hard seats, silent as the grave on that dull, chilly morning. Across from me was a young mother with four small children crammed into the seat beside her. Seeing their inadequate clothing, I wondered if they huddled for warmth. The youngest began to cry. His mother set her finger to his mouth, and he started sucking on it, whimpering softly. Tears ran down the mom's face. I had seen poverty in our town before that day, yet I can't say I had ever noticed it.

"My country has great wealth, but yes, poverty too," I conceded.

He nodded, "Here as well. Our economic crisis deepens, which is to say, more wealth enters fewer pockets." He turned from the road we were walking and followed an overgrown path, which led to a small house in need of new whitewash. John set down his basket and called out a greeting as he opened the door and entered. A squat and elderly woman rose from the table and held out her arms to John. They did the cheek thing and John introduced me. The woman laughed and held out her arms to me as well.

Her small house was tidy and smelled of garlic. One might have called her decor "minimalist," her possessions were so few. John opened his basket and took out some small fish. She was delighted with them, and I think she would have prepared some for us right then if John hadn't remonstrated. They talked for some time in their Greek language, with John asking many questions. I supposed she was a source of information to him, because several times he showed surprise at her answers. She was reluctant to let us go and was profuse in her thanks and cheek-kissing.

"Sophia is forty years a widow. Her sons have sold the family fishing boat and are intent on drinking themselves to death." We walked up a long hill, the sun blazing on our backs.

"You gave her a lot of fish. What will she do with so many?"

"Eat some, trade the rest for the vegetables she can no longer grow." He hoisted the basket to his other shoulder. "I like to go to her house first. That way, I always have enough fish for her. In return, she tells me the local news—whose husband has lost his job, who has had their baby, where the need is greatest."

"You do this often?" I asked, intrigued.

"Always. I have few skills and no more money than they. But I can still fish. Even when the others catch nothing."

I did not like the sound of "no money." I was in the same predicament. "How did you pay for my meal yesterday?"

He grunted. "I did not. Alexander wouldn't dare ask me to pay. He's a bit terrified of me." We reached the top of the hill. A small village sprawled below, with a bright blue harbor alive with boats of every description. "I'll make it up to him. He thinks I'm his lucky charm when he sends me on a fishing tour. Little does he know."

He gave no further explanation as we walked for several minutes in silence. I had to find out if John would help me. "Um, I came with hardly any cash and no credit card, and no one seems to accept payment on my phone." I took it from my pocket and saw I had several texts, which meant I finally had service. "Excuse me." We stopped, and he set down the basket, watching as I scanned my messages. Jessica: "Call me. Important."

She answered immediately. "Jason, where are you? You said you were coming back to Lipsi this morning."

"I'm on my way to the ferry, as a matter of..."

"Listen," she interrupted. "I'm at the airport in Kos. I caught the early ferry. I'm leaving."

"What the...?"

"I had this realization late last night. I'm sorry, Jason, but I've decided we are not meant to be. I've been quite patient..."

"Jessica!" I gasped. "You can't mean this! You're actually going to leave me here?"

"I'm sure you can find your own way home, Jason. And when you return, we can sort this out, okay? I paid for our room at the resort until Monday night, and your flight leaves Tuesday evening from Kos. And by the way, it cost me a ton to get your credit card back from the kayak guys."

I could hardly speak. "Let me get this straight. You're leaving me in Europe, or you're ending our marriage, or both?"

"It's called a divorce, Jason. Happens all the time. I'm moving on, all right? We will be okay. Better for both of us. You'll see." I was speechless for a moment, and she cut in again. "Gotta go, Jason. We'll talk soon, okay?" She was gone.

I stared at the phone, the world a fog around me. I was gradually aware that someone had his arms wrapped tightly around me from behind to keep me from falling to the ground. And he was weeping.

# 4

I stumbled numbly after John as he continued his deliveries of fish on the road to Skala. It wasn't only aged widows we visited. Young families. A man with a cast on his leg. Another who was mentally challenged. Most received John with heartfelt gratitude. Others cursed him, fiercely receiving his fish anyway. One spat at him and would take no fish at all. By the time the sun was overhead, John's basket was empty. The bag at his side filled up with a few gifts of bread and fruit pressed upon us. John and I hardly spoke the entire time. Finally, I could take no more. I sat on a stone bench beside the way, put my head in my hands and wept.

When I looked up after a while, John was watching me, concern etched on his face. I was glad now to have John's company—and his interest—but I did not know what to say. My conversation with Jessica had left me empty. I told him what she had said. "I guess it's over," I shrugged.

He looked at me sharply. "Over? Just like that? Without a fight?"

I stared at the ground. "I can't fight Jessica."

"That's not at all what I mean. Something—or someone—seems to have claimed Jessica as his own. That is unjust. She belongs to you, as surely as you belong to her." He leaned down, so that I had to look him in the eye. "You said you love your wife; are you ready to fight for her?"

"How can you use the words 'love' and 'fight' in the same sentence?" I sat up. "She wants to go. If I love her, I'll let her go."

John snorted. "A fine kind of love that is! I'm not sure you know the meaning of the word. Would you let a child run out into the path of a cart because he wants to?"

"Jessica isn't a child."

"Is she not? When she treats your vows of marriage as secondary to her own whims, is she acting in your best interest? Or her own? Older, wiser heads would say no." My head hung lower, and John sighed. "I shouldn't scold you, Jason. You bear a considerable weight. I would share it with you, not make it more."

"How?" I sighed. "Will you tell me what to do?"

John gave a shake of his head. "That's not my place. I'm not your advisor." He stared at me in thought. "The best I can do is invite you to come and walk with me for a while. We may find your way." He took his bag from his shoulder and removed bread and fruit, along with a small bottle. Below us, a larger boat pulled into the harbor. The ferry. I suddenly had no desire to take it. My only friend within five thousand miles was sitting beside me. Well, and Manos and Marianna. People I had known less than a day.

"You're saying I should stay here longer? With you?"

"You'll be welcome. Much better than waiting out your Greek island vacation at a resort by yourself. I believe a few days with us here would do you good." The more I thought about his offer, the better I felt. I was in no hurry to follow Jessica home so we could talk about our divorce.

"Okay, why not?" I decided. "If you don't mind putting up with me."

John smiled. He handed me the bottle, and I took it with resignation. It was wine of some sort—I was unfamiliar with

24

alcohol—and it wasn't as unpleasant as I expected, but rich and sweet. John explained, "You would call this 'Port.' I thought you might find it easier to swallow. What are you used to drinking?" I tried to explain Dr Pepper, which made my mouth water at the thought, but he shook his head. "I know soda," he said, "and I'm sure one can gain the taste for it. You can become dehydrated in this climate. We need to find you something more helpful."

"John," I wondered, "why do some people on the island love you and others seem to hate you?"

He nibbled a bit of hard bread. "You noticed I have a... polarizing effect on the population of Patmos, yes?" I nodded. "Indeed, I have many friends, few acquaintances, and not a few enemies. I won't tell you why. You may find out as we walk together."

"Well," I bolstered my courage, "who are you?"

John laughed, "Come and see."

I'm sure I had never walked as far as we did that day. We avoided the more populated areas and stuck to small lanes and pathways. Always, always, John discovered random people in obscure corners. Some we helped with chores, such as pruning a bush or moving furniture or mending a boat. Often, I watched. Others wanted conversation or news or had something to slip into John's bag. This was a tour of Patmos I could never have imagined. As we skirted around a large hill, a formidable yellow-gray structure came into view, the one I had seen from the kayak. "What's that?"

"An eyesore," John snorted, "but I'm getting used to it." He offered no further explanation.

"How long have you lived here?"

He didn't meet my eye. "Most of my life, I guess. I've come to like it."

"And before you came to the island?"

John didn't answer right away. We passed a woman sitting on a worn lawn chair in the shade of a small tree. John took bread from his bag and set it on her lap with some kind-sounding words, and I realized she was blind. She grasped his hands with an exclamation of joy and chatted with him for some time. As we left, he placed his hand on my shoulder. "It's not in your best interest—or mine—for me to answer your every question. You'll learn to trust me in this. Soon, I may have more to offer."

We left the road and took a well-worn path of flagstones and steps, down and around a rocky outcropping. The garden was in the theme of large, like its master. Towering shrubs, tended with care, were full of fragrant blossoms that hummed with fat bumblebees. Ancient trees, twisted and gnarled but ever-green, released the scent of heaven. John opened a small gate onto a stone patio and to a modest yet elegant whitewashed house. The Mediterranean sunset was 180 degrees in breadth, and breathtaking.

"This is your home?"

"Yes." He set his bag and basket down on a small table. "It's been long in the making and remains humble, but you're welcome to it all." As with many of the houses I saw on the island, the windows had wooden shutters to protect against winter storms. A few chickens bobbed in the dry grass below us.

I couldn't think of anyplace else on earth where I would rather live. John was watching for my reaction, but I was speechless. "It's amazing, John!" I finally mumbled. "Just incredible."

We ate on the patio as the sun sank into the sea and the world turned scarlet and vermillion. A large bird circled for some time as a dark silhouette against the vibrant colors, hardly moving its wings. Dinner was like eating at a restaurant with an expensive view. I rarely ate fish, but what John prepared was excellent, and I told him so. "How do you make fish taste this good?"

John set another filet on my plate. "I caught them early this morning and roasted them over an open fire. Little more. God doesn't need my help, only my cooperation."

God. Was John a believer? I sat back, full of questions, wondering which of them he would answer. "Were you ever married, John?"

He looked out over the sea as if the distance was farther than the horizon. "Engaged, never married. Long ago. She couldn't wait for me, and I couldn't ask it of her. Sometimes I see the local young women and they remind me of her. But I can't remember her face."

"And you have no picture of her?"

John's eyes grew wide. "Picture? No, I have no pictures. That may be hard for you to imagine when you take a photo of your dinner so you'll remember it." It was true. I had taken a picture of my plate of fish with the sea as a backdrop. "What will you do when all the memories you commit to your phone fade away? When they become deleted or obsolete or buried in a mudslide of images and information?" I found his words unnerving. They brought to mind a podcast I heard that predicted all our digital photos wouldn't survive more than a few decades. "I prefer the library of my mind, thank you, as cluttered as it is."

"John, what is your best—your favorite—memory?"

He sat back in his chair, closed his eyes, and a full, contented smile took over his rough features. I saw deep joy mingled with other emotions hard to read. But that was all. He never answered the question. We sat in silence for a time, darkness falling around us. I realized I was drifting off to sleep when I felt his hand on my shoulder. "Come. The day has been long and full. You can have my bed; I'll be slow to sleep tonight." I didn't argue; I could hardly keep my eyes open. He pointed me to a side room, and I remembered nothing more.

# 5

Pale light came through a small window overlooking the sea. Quiet kitchen noises nearby told me that John was already up. Yet I was reluctant to crawl out from the comfort of the rough wool blanket that covered me. I pulled the phone from my pocket and turned it back on. 5:48 AM. Only 31 percent battery remaining, but I had two bars of reception. I would need to charge my phone soon. Ignoring the 58 emails, I glanced at the many text messages. Only one from Jessica, telling me the number of my locker at the resort and reminding me of my flight details. Cold digits, nothing more. Now that it had finally happened, my heart ached with the loss of her. The screen blurred before my eyes and I turned it off.

John poked his head in the door. "Breakfast, if you like. Sorry to disturb the two of you," he said, nodding at my phone.

"Yeah, coming!" I struggled to set my bare feet on the cold stone floor and was tempted to take the blanket with me. When I arrived at the table, my nose wrinkled with the discovery that breakfast was more fish. "Do you eat fish for every meal, John?"

"This fish is for lunch. I've been smoking it all night." That made me smile. I imagined John puffing on a long, thin sardine cigar. "We'll take it with us. We have much to do today, you and I." He took a pot from a small wood stove and poured its contents into two large bowls. "Oatmeal, not too thick, not runny, sweetened with honey and cinnamon bark. Goat's milk?"

I declined the milk and scowled at the porridge. My grandmother force-fed this stuff to me as a kid, and I always hated it. John noticed my hesitation. "What, you don't like fish, and you don't like oatmeal? You'll starve here!" He set a basket of steaming hard-boiled eggs on the table.

I ate my bowlful and found it better than I remembered. Honey helped the medicine go down. When done, without thinking, I pulled out my phone again. John watched a while and broke in, "It's a strange time when the tools grow smarter, and those who use them grow stupider."

"I'm not sure what you mean," I retorted, feeling insulted again. I returned the phone to my pocket. "A phone may not be necessary on an island where nothing ever happens. Where I come from, a person can't manage without one."

"Oh, I believe you. Why, then, do you consult it when you're on an island where nothing ever happens?"

I had no answer to that. "You tell me."

"Have you considered that your phone can't manage without you? It lusts after your attention and demands your devotion. Your phone maliciously feeds your addiction, as the drug dealers do with the prostitutes in town."

I snorted, but his words again made me uncomfortable. "What's this, a conspiracy theory?"

"It's not a theory. You know it in your heart: your phone plays you like a fish on the line." He stood and stretched. "Which reminds me, it's time to go catch some. Coming?"

We threaded our way down to the sea in deep shadow. I shivered at first, but the fast pace soon warmed me. Fishing turned out to be a simple affair: John took down a small net from where it was hanging and cast it out on the water. He held the end of the line attached to the net and sat down. "I learned long ago that I'm a terrible fisherman," he confessed. "We watch and wait and pray."

That was interesting. Indeed, apart from a miracle, I had a hard time understanding why any fish would wander into his net. "Why don't you use a fishing line and bait? That's what people do back home."

"I have many bellies to fill. Line fishing takes time. For me, fishing is boom or bust, plenty or nothing. He either fills my net, or he doesn't. He knows what he's about."

"Meaning God."

John contemplated this. "Yes, God. You know, it was the fish that first made me realize…" He broke off as he felt a tug on the line. "Come, help me! Why did I not bring the second basket? I should have known." I grabbed a section of the line he was hauling. It was the most peculiar sensation. The rope was alive—jerking, jostling, tugging. As the net neared the shore, John tied the line fast to a bush and waded into the water. I pulled off my shoes and joined him. Dozens and dozens of flashing silver bodies slimed my hands as we dragged the net out onto the shore. Seeing this many fish in one place astonished me.

John flashed me a big grin. "See what a blessing it is to have you with us! He smiles on your being with us." He sat down beside the wriggling pile and laughed. "Thank you, thank you, my friend." But I thought, by the distant look on his face, he wasn't talking to me. John handed me the large basket he brought with him. He asked me to fill it while he climbed back up the hill for a second one. "We may need three baskets!" he called down to me as he ascended.

I didn't remember ever having touched a whole fish before, let alone ones that were still alive. They proved slippery, and several times I had to pounce before an escapee made it back to the sea. When John returned, I was picking them up by the armload, mindless of what they were doing to my T-shirt.

John set an empty basket on its side toward the net and scooped them in. Why had I not thought of that? By the time we filled two and a half baskets, I was the fishier of the two of us.

John stood beaming at the three baskets, then at me. "Come, you'll want to wash that shirt if you're to enter my home again!" I peeled it off, and we went down to the shore to wash. I was conscious of my sickly white skinny torso next to his bronze muscles. John showed me how soft sand worked like soap. But when I pulled on the wet T-shirt, I still smelled like a seafood store.

The sun rose over the hill, and we sat with our backs to it, facing the sea. John occasionally searched out a flat rock and skipped it on the calm water, a skill at which he was talented. Catching the fish felt great. Like I had finally done something authentic and significant. I wondered what time it was and retrieved my phone from the rock where I had stashed it. Eight in the morning. Many days, I woke up at eight in the morning. I saw a notification for a new text from Jessica, but before I could open it, John beckoned with his hand. "Your phone— can I look at it?"

"Sure, I guess." I opened the phone with my thumbprint and handed it to him. John did not seem unfamiliar with a smartphone. I watched as he checked the weather forecast and grunted his skepticism about its predictions. He opened a news app and scrolled down, paused when something caught his interest, and shook his head a lot. Finally, he closed the phone and made to hand it back to me, but stopped.

He looked at me, at my phone, at the sea. I felt a jolt of panic in my stomach, thinking he was going to toss my phone like the flat rocks. "John, don't you..."

"I'm going to set you free. One day, you'll thank me." He put the phone in his pocket. I sighed in relief.

"Just for the day, right? You'll give it back to me tonight, okay?" He said nothing. Not soon will I forget the emotions I felt at that moment. Like John had ripped my lungs out. Denied access. Voiceless. And very alone in the world.

"Why, John? How can you do this?"

He looked unconcerned. "I grow surprisingly fond of you. This is how I'll help you."

"Help me?" My voice rose. "You cutting me off from my entire world! I have no money here, no way to communicate. I don't even remember what time my flight was to return home!"

"Yes," he replied, standing and picking up a basket. "That's precisely what I said."

# 6

Our first stop that day was Manos and Marianna's home, which was closer than I imagined. I discovered that our trek to Skala and back the day before had been a broad loop north, while Manos' house was just a strenuous climb over the hill to the east. I'm not sure what a basket of fish weighs, but I was ready to lie down and die several times before we made it to the top. Thankfully, John had taken a good part of the fish to the smokehouse before we left, so my basket—unlike his—was half full. When we reached the top, he wasn't even breathing hard.

"John, how old are you?" I panted, setting the basket down once again.

He stared off over the sea and said nothing. As I watched him, waiting, I realized this was a question he wouldn't answer. He stood perfectly still. His face seemed as hard as flint, as if waves or storms or other events would break upon him. Admittedly, I admired John, despite how flustered and angry I was with him over the phone. I wanted to know who he was and realized this might take more time than I still had left on the island.

Manos clapped his hands and did a jig when we showed him the baskets of fish. He took a photo and beamed at me as if I had something to do with our catch. I tried Manos' strong coffee—black, upon his insistence—and found it surprisingly refreshing in the heat of the day. They spoke in Greek, of course, with John translating what he thought might interest me. I wondered where John had lived that his English was so articulate, with a slight accent I couldn't place. That would be the next question I would toss his way and see if anything came back.

The rest of that day was like the one before, except we took a different route and met new people. We always discovered folks in need—whether it was fish or help or friendly conversation—and it was exhausting. John, as usual, seemed unfazed. Every time we stopped, I panicked as my hand went to my empty pocket and found no phone. At some point that morning, I realized it had been 24 hours since I began following John everywhere. It felt like ages ago.

As we walked in silence, I missed Jessica. As exasperated as I was with her, I wished she was there with me. How I longed for a second chance with her! I wondered if she had already found someone else. Was this why she left early? I tried to imagine that scenario and it made me feel sick. Like brushing my teeth with a stranger's toothbrush, but far worse. I hadn't realized that the bond of marriage was so intrinsic. What I felt inside told me that marriage was much more than a ceremony and a legal contract. Marriage is a union of body, soul and spirit, and not meant to be "put asunder." Jesus had that right.

I didn't realize I had stopped walking until I looked up and saw John coming back toward me. My eyes filled with tears as we set our baskets down. John said nothing, placed his heavy hand on my shoulder and waited for me to stop shaking. "I feel all torn apart, John! Am I so awful a person that not even my wife wants to be with me anymore?"

"Yes, I suppose that's true. She has not yet learned grace, this Jessica. You might teach her."

I snorted. "Fat chance of that. Our next conversation will be about who gets the TV and what to do with our china set."

"You don't know that. Don't let go of hope, Jason. It's your anchor in a stormy sea." He stood and raised his empty basket. "Come, the day wanes. Time for home. We'll stop on the way and see if Manos can conjure us more coffee."

But Manos was sick, lying in bed with what he claimed was only indigestion. John put his massive head gently on Manos' chest and listened for a long time. When he sat up, his face was grave. John asked questions, and Manos whispered in reply. Marianna stood clutching the doorway, watching and listening. When Manos drifted off to sleep, John rose and motioned us out.

"Is Manos okay?"

John didn't answer. Marianna brought out a beautiful shepherd's pie for us to share before joining us at the table. John held her trembling hands and spoke words that sounded reassuring. Finally, she gave a deep sigh and smiled at us. "Manos endured heart trouble in the past," John explained. "I fear it may have returned. They can afford the doctor, but Manos is stubborn and doesn't want to pay his high fees." He caught Marianna's eye as if to give her courage. "He stopped going last year, but there's a medication that would help him. We'll go tomorrow and see if we can have his prescription filled in Skala."

John stood. "But first, we pray." He beckoned us back to the bedroom. We gathered around Manos, who still slept. His face was far too pale and gray. Marianna handed John a small flask, and he poured oil on Manos' forehead. It ran down his face. His eyes fluttered open, and he found each of us without moving his head. Marianna placed her hand on Manos' chest, and John covered it with his own. When I added my hand, it was so small and white in comparison. I wondered what I was doing in this place where I didn't belong.

They prayed in Greek, yet it sounded to me like the tongues of angels. Passionate words, punctuated by tears and occasional sobs. They weren't questioning God; they were pleading with him, banging at his door. I had often wondered what it was like for Jesus' disciples as they listened to him pray. God speaking to God. It must have been something like this.

They paused, and both looked at me. Flustered, I opened my mouth and prayed. "Um, God, I... just want to thank you for bringing us here... together, and... just ask that you make Manos well again. Um, in-Jesus-name-amen." I was more conscious of my damp T-shirt that I hadn't changed in two days than of having made a fool of myself.

John sighed. Deeply. He prayed again, in English. "Father, you have blessed your servant with a long experience of the abundant life, and to you we're grateful. We love him; we love Manos. My Lord, you have extended grace to our friend and are welcome to take him to yourself at the moment you deem best. Still, we plead with you to heal his faltering heart and give him more days to worship you on earth. Give rhythm to the irregularity I hear in his chest. Keep his heart in time to yours. Do not bring sorrow to our hearts today, but the joy of once again witnessing your power to heal. Whatever happens, to you be all the glory, for you are good and your mercy is measureless."

He went on for what felt like an hour, in Greek or some other dialect, sometimes in English. I admit I drifted off more than once. In the middle of one of those nods, I felt John's hand on my shoulder. "Time to go. It has been a long day." I rose and stumbled after him. "It's okay," he reassured me. "I too have fallen asleep over long-winded prayers." We gave our farewells to Marianna and stepped out into the dark. All I could see was John's white shirt continuing before me. I hardly remembered entering his gate and collapsing on the hard mattress. I slept like the dead.

# 7

Our catch the next morning was less than the day before, a mere basketful of silver bodies. I suggested we split the fish between two baskets, one for each of us, but John had another plan. "No, I'll ask you to go into Skala this morning on your own while I continue my visits with the fish. I'll give you a bag of smoked fish to trade. You'll earn enough money for the medicine our friend needs, some fresh clothing for you, plus your ferry passage."

Objections to his last suggestion came to mind, but I held them back. Every day I felt more ready to remain than to leave the island. John intrigued me; but if I was honest, mostly it was that I wasn't ready to face Jessica. I felt safer here than anywhere. I knew my stay couldn't be indefinite, but somewhere on these dusty white roads, my reasons to remain outnumbered those in favor of going.

But I found John's request alarming: to venture outside the relative security of his presence and his familiarity with my language. "You'll do fine," he assured me. "Word about you has traveled, as happens in island communities. You'll find friends you did not know existed. Even an enemy or two," he laughed. "Be smart like a wolf, as discerning as a dove."

On the way, we stopped at the home of Manos and Marianna. I was relieved and pleased to see Manos at the breakfast table, sipping mango juice. He looked worn, but his smile was broad. "I live another day, my friends!" John translated for me. "Thank you for your words to the Father on my behalf. I'm glad he listens to you."

"And to Marianna, who prays for you without ceasing." John smiled back at him as he repeated this in my language. "How do you think you have lasted this long?" His wife blushed at John's words and looked at Manos so lovingly it made my heart ache with longing. Who on earth cared for me like that?

John wouldn't stay for a second breakfast, and we were soon on the road toward Skala, carrying Manos' prescription and a roll of film he wanted developed. At a path I recognized as leading to the home of the widow woman, we parted ways. John gave many excellent instructions about where to go and who to see, which I had to have repeated several times. Even then, I wasn't sure I had them right, as proved by the solo adventure that followed.

The road to Skala wasn't long. I'm not a shy person, yet I became self-conscious as I encountered more people. Some extended inquisitive glances; others, a warm greeting which John had taught me to return. I found the market I needed without making awkward inquiries. But once there, I was unsure how to find the vendor to whom John told me to take my fish for trade. The name eluded me. I walked along, hoping for some clue or at least a friendly face to go by.

"Come! Sit!" He wasn't the most ruffian-looking of the men in the market, but close to it. His face was half-hidden by the hood on his shirt; his jeans were filthy. The man beckoned me with one hand while pouring the wine with the other. I felt I had no choice but to join him, and his few English words made me hopeful. "*Amerikanos*, yes?"

I nodded and sat down. Since I wasn't the first person to drink from the glass he offered me since it was last washed, I sipped it warily, hoping the alcohol had some disinfectant quality. "Do you speak English?"

He gave a characteristic island shrug. "Some. I am Antonis. What you need?"

I took the bag from my shoulder. "My name's Jason. I have fish to sell. Smoked."

He reached into the bag and sniffed the piece he found. "Is good. Where you get?" He nibbled the bit as he inspected the rest of the bag's contents.

"Do you know John? Lives in the south."

Antonis looked up at me in surprise and laughed. Not the most pleasant laugh. I was ready to go find another buyer, but he put his hand on my arm. "John? *Iohannes*? Only one John here. Always only one. What you do with him?" He said something in Greek that sounded disparaging and laughed again.

I felt offended. "I can sell my fish elsewhere..."

He pressed my arm and prevented my getting up. "No, no. I buy. No thing wrong with fish. But the man..." He made a face that I guess meant John was a crazy man.

I pulled my arm away but hesitated, curious to know his opinion. "What do you know about John?"

Antonis stared into my eyes like I was some idiot child. "He—John—he are... *palavos*. He mad! Devil!" He looked suspiciously at the bag of fish. "Maybe I no buy." He looked afraid for a moment and laughed again. "You maybe steal this, no?"

"No! Nothing like that. John gave me the fish to sell." I stood up to go.

Antonis stood and glared at me. I felt threatened and sat down again, and his face relaxed. "Give you ten for fish, yes?"

I said nothing. The ferry passage alone was nine euros. John must have expected me to receive much more for the fish if I was to buy clothing and medicine for Manos. "Not enough. I need to buy medicine."

He didn't understand me, and it took some exaggerated charades to make my meaning clear. "Drugs?" he guessed finally. "For you?"

"For Manos."

Antonis' face darkened. "Manos. Friend to John. I hate." I couldn't imagine how someone could hate someone as harmless as Manos, and asked why. "He send me to jail, long time. Bad place, that." He spat in the dirt by my feet. I felt the spray.

"Manos was a policeman?"

"No, not police man. *Dikastes*." He took a hammer from a box behind him and banged it hard on the table, making both me and our glasses jump. I took from his pantomime that Manos had been a judge and had sentenced this man to jail.

I stood up again to leave. "Sorry to hear that. I'll go now."

He waved an angry hand in dismissal. When I turned, he called in a voice husky with emotion, "You watch out, man! John no good. Manos no better—he worship him, I think! Both... crazy!"

I stopped. "What do you mean? Who does Manos worship? John?"

Antonis snapped his fingers. "Him. Many others do. All crazy."

"But why? Why would they worship John?"

He looked at me like I was playing some game with him. "You must know. Who they say is John." He poured the rest of my wine into his own glass and gulped it down in one shot.

"I'm afraid I don't."

He shrugged and eased back into his chair. "You are fool. I feel sorry." He gave another wave of dismissal.

But I would let him put me off. "Tell me. What do people say about John?"

He laughed, mocking, and leaned toward me. "They say—John is Apostle. *The Beloved.* Very, very, very old man. Oldest."

I felt something cold in the pit of my stomach. "John, the Apostle? Like, from the Bible?" I couldn't believe what I was hearing. How could anyone think this? And Manos, how could he possibly believe that his friend was John from the days of Jesus? Yet, what would a man like Antonis gain from claiming so?

"You go now. Sell your fish." Antonis spoke more Greek words that sounded less polite while waving me away with both hands. I picked up the bag and walked away.

As someone whose roots are firmly practical and conservative, I dismissed the man's assertion as absurd. But as I walked through the market, I felt perplexed. I saw Manos' face as he gazed at John more devotedly than I've ever seen one human look at another. I did not for a moment think John was two thousand and more years old. Yet it shook me to think Manos might believe this. Did Marianna? And why would John let them believe anything so preposterous? Was there something sinister here, some hold that John was using over his friends?

A small person tugging on the bottom of my shirt interrupted my crazy thoughts. It was a little girl in a brightly colored dress, black curls framing her tiny face. My first thought was that she had some trinket to sell me, but then she used my name. "Jason?" I nodded, surprised, and she took my hand in hers and led me through the vendors. We threaded our way to a table that had a canopy to provide shade from the glaring sun. An elderly woman sat behind it, and at first glance, I thought she could be related to Manos. She gathered the child in her arms and kissed her, then set her down and regarded me with a welcoming smile.

She pointed to the seat beside her. "Jason!" She laid her hand on her chest. "Myrto!" I remembered this as the name John told me, but hadn't realized it would be a woman. Her English was as nonexistent as my Greek. We made our way with gestures, and she exclaimed over the smoked fish, which she deposited in a plastic cooler behind her. The little girl crawled onto my lap, staring up at me until Myrto gave her a piece of mango to distract her. It was soon all over my T-shirt.

I had no apprehensions, as I had with Antonis, about getting paid. A meal was a necessary part of the bargain, as Myrto laid out bread and cheese and the rest of the mango for me. The glass of wine also looked more appealing, though more acidic to my taste. Imagine my having a taste for wine! That would impress Jessica. How I wanted to talk to this woman! I had many questions I couldn't ask. When our gestures ran out of steam, we sat, our smiles wan with the vast verbal distance between us.

Myrto reached into her bag and retrieved a small metal box. She gave me 40 euros for the fish, and I had no idea if the price was fair or she was overpaying me. It was much more than Antonis offered. She knew what I needed to buy and drew me a simple map to a small dispensary and a used clothing store, both nearby in a poorer corner of the town. The proprietors were kind and helpful, and I soon had everything I needed. Jessica would have loved shopping there. It was exactly the type of market she was always seeking.

After dropping off Manos' film and buying the medicine, plus jeans and a shirt like John's, I still had more than enough left for ferry passage. I walked by the ticket office three times but put the money back in my pocket. We were to meet at Manos and Marianna's at the end of the day, so I explored a little more and set off toward home.

# 8

Manos was delighted with the medicine, not knowing of John's intention to buy it. He and I made our way down to the bench overlooking the bay to watch for him. Manos had a book in his hand, which he offered to me after we sat and admired the view in our own languages. It was a Bible in English, King James Version. Manos opened it for me to the Gospel of John, and I felt a jolt in my stomach as I remembered Antonis' words about its author. He motioned for me to read it to him.

It took me a moment to compose myself, and I read out loud:

"In the beginning was the Word, and the Word was with God, and the Word was God. The same was in the beginning with God. All things were made by him; and without him was not any thing made that was made. In him was life; and the life was the light of men. And the light shineth in darkness; and the darkness comprehended it not. There was a man sent from God, whose name was John..."

But not John the Apostle. I paused and Manos glanced at me. This was John the Baptist, I remembered. The forerunner of Jesus. One of my professors used to say that John the Baptist tilled the hearts of the people of Israel so they could receive the words of Jesus. Unlike Patmos, the Bible has more than one John. Such as the one who wrote the words I was reading. God's words, breathed through John the Apostle.

"...The same came for a witness, to bear witness of the Light, that all men through him might believe. He was not that Light, but was sent to bear witness of that Light. That was the true Light, which lighteth every man that cometh into the world. He was in the world, and the world was made by him, and the world knew him not. He came unto his own, and his own received him not. But as many as received him, to them gave he power to become the sons of God, even to them that believe on his name: Which were born, not of blood, nor of the will of the flesh, nor of the will of man, but of God. And the Word was made flesh, and dwelt among us, (and we beheld his glory, the glory as of the only begotten of the Father,) full of grace and truth."

These were beautiful words. I was sure I had never read them out loud before, and doing so—especially on the island of Patmos—made them splendid and grand. I wished I had paid better attention in Bible college. The Apostle John wrote his Revelation on Patmos, I knew. But what about his Gospel? Was it written here also? I couldn't remember. Manos took the book from me and thanked me. *Parakalo*, I replied, and he smiled. I was learning.

I caught a movement below us, and into view came John, swinging his empty basket. He saw us and shouted up a greeting, and we both hollered in reply. Far from posing as a man 2000 years old, John often looked—and acted—like someone younger than me. He danced on the road to some music in his head and bowed as we clapped for him. I relaxed. Why should I pay attention to a man like Antonis? He was wrong about Manos—and John. Antonis was the crazy one.

That evening, John and I sat on his patio, watching the red sky fade to black. The taste of the lamb souvlaki Marianna had insisted on us was still in my mouth. John was nodding in his chair, but I was full of questions. I turned them over in my mind, wondering which one he would most likely answer.

"John, when and where did you learn to speak English?" I thought it best to squeeze in two questions at the same time.

John leveled a single sleepy eye at me. "Say what?"

"Did you spend some time in America? Or where? Your English..."

"Your country? You think I lived there?" He rubbed his eyes and sat up.

His response rattled me a bit, and I felt myself getting annoyed at his noncommittal answers. "Well, you speak perfect English, with just a trace of an accent. Is that your native language, or did the Greek come first?"

He contemplated me, eyes bleary, and stretched to his feet. "It's late. Fish to catch tomorrow. We should sleep."

I wouldn't have it. I stood and confronted him. "Hey, I've been patient! I'd like some answers. Like, I'm on an island with—with, nothing—and you took my phone! And I don't even know who you are!"

His eyebrows furrowed, and it came to mind that I wouldn't want to get on the wrong side of this fellow. After a tense moment, he sighed and his face softened. "We have had a long day. Come, sit down. Sip a little wine to calm yourself. I'll tell you what I can."

I sat, feeling chastened, and accepted a cup of deep red. John stared at his but didn't drink it, and several minutes passed before he responded. "Long ago, when I was young, I once had something urgent and important to say to someone whose language I didn't know. To my amazement, I could understand—and speak—his language." He chuckled when he saw my expression. "Yes, I know it's difficult for you to suspend disbelief. You have little imagination. But what I say is true." He sat back and closed his eyes. "I promise you, I have never lived in your country, and I have never learned your language."

I sat back too, anger surging. "You're joking!"

John sprang up, bright-eyed and smiling. "Joking? No, but I can tell you a joke!" And he told me a funny story about a dog with no legs—and no name. It didn't matter what you called him; he wouldn't come anyway.

"And what am I supposed to make of this?"

John shrugged. "I could suggest you sleep on it, which would be the best of advice. Yet if I can tell you a joke in English, it means I'm fluent in your language. If you don't want to believe how I mastered your language, it's your choice. It makes no difference to me or to my regard for you." He tossed me a wool blanket. "Can we say good night as friends?"

I nodded and accepted the blanket. Without another word, I turned to the mattress he had borrowed for me, which we had set in a corner of the kitchen. I was too upset to sleep for some time, despite the wine.

Twice this day, I had struggled with the impossible: John as a man two millennia old and John as a man who magically knew my language. In both cases, I ended up feeling mocked, first by a rogue and now by my friend. I wrestled with both dilemmas, trying to find reasonable, logical explanations. The more time I spent with John and Manos, the more I respected them. Antonis was unreliable but not irrational. Which meant that everyone was lying to me for reasons I didn't understand. Or that the impossible was true. I could accept neither option.

Finally, I came up with this: John (whose name was probably not John) grew up in an English-speaking family who lived abroad. As a young man, he found himself on Patmos, just like me. He met an older man named John and discovered over time that people on the island thought this man was the Apostle. He began doing what John did, learned Greek, spoke wisdom and fed the poor like his master. And when that John grew old, the new one took his name and took his place. "Only one John. Always only one." That's what

Antonis said. My John was next in a long line, going back to who knows when, perhaps back to the original.

I sat up in bed, my heart pounding. Just like me. I'm like John. I come to Patmos, hang out with this old dude named John, do the stuff he does...

Holy crap. What if I'm being groomed to become the new John?

Or what if I'm on trial, the thought came to mind. I may be a potential candidate, going through my paces to see if I'm worthy of the office. What happens to the rejects in this Apostle School? For that matter, what happens to the dropouts? Because no way on earth am I staying in line to become an apostle. My thoughts crowded in on one another as sleep overtook me. I'm on trial before twelve identical John's, sitting on low benches cut into the sides of a cavern. I am found wanting, and their objections come thick and fast to my becoming one of their order.

An intruding thought jolted me awake again. If my theory about John was correct, he had reason to invite me to stay longer. Did he mean to convince me to give up my life in the US? And the hope of saving my marriage? That didn't seem like something John would do, but I hardly knew him. My reasoning became sluggish, my brain cloudier. And finally, I slept.

# 9

As I watched John cast his net early the next morning, my reconstructions of his life the night before looked feeble in the growing light. I had no track record to question John's intentions. I liked John and wanted to get to know him better, and wasn't about to let a misunderstanding come between us. My fears that he had an agenda for me dissipated like the mist. Nothing John ever did or said gave me a reason to believe I was destined to become his apprentice. But I was more determined than ever to solve the mystery surrounding him.

I was ready to help John with the net. But this day the fish seemed elsewhere occupied. We waited for a while, watching a large hawk or eagle ride the updrafts above us, also fishless. John cast the net again, just in case, and we sat idle, chewing on smoked fish. "John, what do you know about the Apostle John?"

He looked at me gamely. "You ask many questions! I suppose I will reconcile myself to it." He tossed a shower of small pebbles that made an odd sound in the water. "I believe I know him well enough. What would you like to hear?"

"Well, I know the Apostle John wrote the Book of Revelations on Patmos..."

"Revelation, not plural. It's one Revelation."

"Okay, fine. But did he write the Gospel of John here too? And then there's First John and Second John as well."

"And a third. Why does this matter to you?"

"Manos had me read to him yesterday, from the beginning of John's Gospel, in English."

John smiled. "Yes, he would enjoy that. He would like to speak English better."

"Why don't you teach him?"

"Um..." John looked puzzled. "I... it doesn't work that way." He tossed more pebbles—and harder. "You read the Gospel. And what did you see?"

I thought for a moment. "Beauty. Grace. I'm sure I never read it out loud before. It makes the words so..."

"Do you not usually read out loud? What benefit is there in reading in silence, except to the one who reads?"

I had never thought of reading as something to do socially. Seldom had I read to anyone out loud, certainly never to Jessica. "What, do you never read to yourself silently?"

John stood and pulled on the rope leading to his submerged net, finding no wriggling resistance. "I grow a bit weary of your perplexing questions." He sat again. "But I like what you have to say about the Gospel. Beauty and grace. Yes, it was all that." John gazed across the water. His words made me uncomfortable.

"Can you tell me...?"

"Yes, no, probably not!" he laughed, flicking the water on his hands in my face. "Come, let me ask you a question. You say you don't know me, and you speak truly. But neither do I know you. I would be grateful to hear your story."

"Me? Why? I have little to tell you." If one wanted to define the humdrum life, I was it. These days, I rarely did the unexpected; paddling to Patmos was an exception. "You mean, like my testimony?" I told my testimony several times before when I was at camp and once in front of the whole church.

"Testimony? No, no need for that." He looked at me quizzically. "Come, tell me about your life. Start at the beginning," he coaxed me.

Having little reason not to, considering we were still fishless, I began. This is what I told him. It's a story that would go well with a strong cup of coffee.

I was born and raised in a typical small Midwest town. Three-story brick businesses leaned over one main street, and a scattering of old and new homes sprawled on either side. My dad was a web developer and my mom the receptionist for the local dentist. All my siblings were older than me, so I arrived home from school each day to an empty house, made myself a snack and watched TV. All my outside interests were in seasons: baseball season, marbles season, sledding season. Until my conservative parents finally let me play video games, which overtook all other pursuits.

My dad saw me on the computer a lot, and thinking I was a techie like him, suggested I follow him in his lifelong career. What I never told my dad—but now told John—was that most of my screen time involved watching pornography, introduced to me through ads on my video games. I had a nagging feeling I wasn't being a good Christian, but it was an addiction. I didn't know how to stop and wasn't about to ask for help.

I took my dad's career advice and pursued a communications degree. Of course, there were no jobs on the other side of graduation, but I was persistent enough to do well on a free-lance basis. Then I had a few scares and one life-threatening experience overseas. A crazed man held me hostage for an hour, wielding a pitchfork in a barn where I was supervising him. I promised God that if he got me out of it, I would go to a Christian college. He did, and I followed through.

I managed pretty well there until I met Jessica at the beginning of my final year. She was a Bible college "bad girl," and I was the student body president and expected to be the first in my class to become a pastor. I took on Jessica as a project and she returned the favor. By the time we each graduated, Jessica had stopped partying every weekend, and I had stopped wanting to be a pastor. We married because we didn't like being celibate. But we had our difficulties right from the start. Jessica always struggled with the pull of the world. I began each day with the wind already knocked out of me, slaving at a job I hated, often bringing my frustration home to dump on Jessica.

The whole time I was telling my story, John interrupted me. He had questions about parts of my world for which he had no reference. Sledding. Video games. Pornography threw him for a bit of a loop—I could tell the whole idea made him angry. His curiosity made for a convoluted story.

"What do you mean when you say you 'asked Jesus into your heart'?" John had a genuinely puzzled expression.

That confused me, since John seemed to know the Bible. "Well, like, that's how I became a Christian. I asked Jesus into my heart."

"I understand that is what you're saying. But what does this asking mean?"

John's tone intimidated me, and I couldn't think of an answer to his question. What *did* it mean to ask Jesus into my heart? Had anyone ever explained this to me? Or had I done it because it was what I was told to do if I wanted to avoid hell? "Um, I guess it means I asked Jesus to—I don't know— be in my life." I felt my face turning red.

John looked out over the water for a long time. I could tell he was thinking, but I didn't know if I should continue my story or wait for him to say something that would make me feel worse. Finally, he looked at me. "Jessica, your wife—she's a beautiful woman, yes?"

Where was this going? "Well, yes, she is." I pictured her in my mind, and she was lovely.

"I would like to meet her. In fact, I would like to sleep with her, if that's okay with you."

My jaw dropped to the ground. I couldn't believe what I was hearing. "What?? You can't... How could you think...?" I was on my feet, ready to—I don't know what, since John was twice my size. I was furious.

"You don't like this idea! Why? Why can you sleep with her, and I cannot?" John didn't let up. I was ready to hit him with a big rock.

"Well, because!" I blustered. "You're not her husband! I am! You have no right!"

"And what makes her your wife?"

"We... we had a wedding! We said vows to each other." That made me sit down. "We promised..." I took a deep breath. "We committed our lives to one another. Forsaking all others." Ouch. "Till death do us part. We signed papers." Tears formed in the corners of my eyes.

John's tone softened, but he didn't give in. "Then it would not be okay for me to invite her into my bed."

I looked at him. Something was twigging in my brain, but the parallel was blurry. "John, you're going to have to help me out. I don't know what you're getting at."

He put his heavy hand on my shoulder and squeezed it with affection, looking me straight in the eye. "I agree. As a complete stranger who has made no marriage vows to your wife, I cannot invite her into my bed." That was a relief, but John wasn't done. "How could you, then, without any vow of fidelity to him, invite Jesus into your heart?"

Wow. I didn't like his analogy. I was trembling, and not because of the morning chill. Being around John was like walking out in a storm. You didn't know whether to expect a downpour or a lightning strike. "Okay, I understand. But you just took a dump on my entire Christian existence! If my 'asking Jesus into my heart' offends you, what do you suggest? How is a person saved?"

John tugged the line on the net, to no avail. "I see. You think asking Jesus into your heart should save you. I don't know where you got that idea. What does Jesus himself have to say? How would he answer your question?"

"With another question?" That made John laugh. Immediately, a memory verse I learned in Bible club as a child came to mind. "Revelation 3:20. 'Behold, I stand at the door, and knock: if any man hear my voice, and open the door, I will come in to him, and will sup with him, and he with me.'"

"Well said!" John looked pleased. "Though I must assume the strange word 'sup' has something to do with sharing a meal." To be honest, I didn't know what "sup" meant either. "But your quote isn't helpful. Jesus said these words to a church, not to unbelievers. True, these believers were stumbling in the dark, yet he waited patiently for them to hear his voice and regain close fellowship with him."

"Okay, here's another one." I thought back to what I read the day before with Manos, another verse I memorized as a child. "'But as many as received him, to them gave he power to become the sons of God.' John 1, verse... I don't know. There you go—to be saved, you need to receive Jesus as your Lord and Savior."

John was clearly uncomfortable. "And this is what the churches in your country teach? This is their Gospel?" He hauled in the empty net.

"Well, it's what the Bible says! 'As many as received him...'"

"Receiving Jesus is essential, but it does not mean what you make it mean. It's not about Jesus entering one's heart. You would do better to translate it, 'as many as... welcomed him,' or 'recognized him.' Received his message."

"If they receive his message, are they saved?"

"Not likely. Remember the story Jesus told about the sower and the seed? All received the word, but only in one case did this result in salvation. With the others, the word was taken away, or withered, or choked by the cares of this world."

"What was different about the one that was saved?"

"Go back to what Jesus said, but add in the important bit you missed: 'All who received him, who *believed* in his name, were given the power to become children of God.' The one who combines the word of Jesus with faith, that one is saved."

"See? Everyone who asks Jesus into their heart by faith is saved!"

John sighed. "You're stuck on this phrase. Does it not bother you that none of the Apostles spoke this way? Nor did Jesus. Do you not remember his message? I do!" He stood to his feet and called across the water, "The time has come! The kingdom of God is near! Repent and believe the good news!"

The way he spoke these words made a tingle go down my spine. As if the power in them was drawn through the centuries from the very lips of Jesus. I wondered again, who is this guy? "Okay," I admitted, "I can't remember anyone preaching about the kingdom of God. I'm unacquainted with that concept. Please enlighten me."

John looked at me like a child who asks a question the teacher just answered, and hung up his net in the tree. "Really? You take the name 'Christian' on yourself lightly if you're not familiar with the kingdom of the heavens." He sat down beside me. "The good news is that in Jesus, the kingdom of

God has arrived on earth. By our faith in Jesus, we become his subjects. He's the King!"

"If Jesus is the King, why isn't everyone his subject?"

"Because he's a subversive king, like David while Saul still lived—anointed, but another currently has the throne. We gather to Jesus as revolutionaries, setting people free from the oppression of our enemy. In his name, we take over the world, one life at a time." I liked that picture, having never thought of myself that way. A rebel with a cause.

"You quoted several phrases from the Gospels and the Letters," John continued. "Tell me, what writing captures for you the essence of being a child of God? How do you read it, from the words of what you call the Bible?"

I thought for a moment. One verse every Christian knows by heart is John 3:16. I quoted it as I learned it, from the King James Bible. "For God so loved the world, that he gave his only begotten Son, that whosoever believeth in him should not perish, but have everlasting life."

"I can't say I'm unpleased with your choice. These are excellent words. But they aren't what I would choose to represent my faith."

"What verse would you choose?"

"James the elder—the half-brother of Jesus, who sounded much like his brother once his brother lived within him—he put it well. 'Here is religion that is pure and spotless before God the Father: to visit orphans and widows in their distress, and to keep oneself unblemished from the world.'"

I wasn't expecting this from someone like John. "But... but that's *religion*!" I spluttered. "Christianity isn't a religion—it's a relationship!"

"Lord, have mercy!" John closed his eyes, his expression pained. "What is the Gospel, Jason? That Jesus can be your friend? True, he called us his friends and demonstrated the greatest of loves when he laid down his life for us. But he also said, 'You are my friends if you do what I command you.' What kind of relationship is that? Can you imagine your best friend saying, 'You can be my friend if you do everything I tell you?'"

He stood and gathered up our empty baskets. "Come! We have no fish, but we can do other good work today. The morning passes, and our conversation becomes fruitless. Let's go do whatever good we can." Though I hardly considered our discussion "fruitless," I welcomed a break from my frustration with John. We gathered eggs, made lunch and filled our bags with large lemons from an elderly tree that groaned with them in John's garden. Then we walked up the road north in silence.

# 10

"We won't go far today," John explained as we rested at the top of a hill. "We need to be back in time to prepare for the Sabbath."

I had lost all track of days. "Tomorrow is Sunday already?" My mind went to a locker at the resort with my belongings in it. And a plane ticket. Was my flight on Monday or Tuesday? I needed to get my act together. Or... not. What if I didn't? At least for a while. Was that even possible? What would Jessica say?

"Sunday? No, tomorrow is Saturday. Do you not honor God's day of rest?"

I shook my head. "My parents were big on no shopping or playing football on Sunday, but that was about it. These days, everyone shops and does whatever on Sunday."

"As do we. But we're talking about the Sabbath, which begins Friday evening and goes to the end of daylight on Saturday. Do you not keep the Sabbath?"

What? Is John Jewish? I thought he was a Christian. "No, I don't believe Christians have to keep the Sabbath. Aren't we free from the Law?" Here we go again, I moaned inside. John and I spoke different languages when it came to faith. I was more confused than ever about where he was coming from. Especially as he didn't answer.

We visited the home of the most broken man I ever met. Grief and guilt consumed Nikolas because of his wife and daughter, who left him over his abuse of alcohol. Departing from Patmos, they traveled to her homeland, Syria, shortly before the escalation of civil war. As Christians, his wife's family became the target of extremists, who burned down their house with the whole family inside. Nikolas seemed to appreciate our visit and the lemons, but the depth of his suffering was haunting.

We had continued a short distance down the road when John stopped and faced me. "Why does someone die for their faith?" I had no answer. Though I heard many times about the persecution of Christians in some parts of the world, the thought that I could die for my faith never came to mind. "I tell you, it's no small matter to die rather than renounce one's faith in the Messiah. Many turn from him in fear and shame, loving their lives and the world too much to let them go. But I've known some who refused release rather than disown the One who saved them. Why?"

"I don't know, John. This is outside of my experience. No one I know has ever been threatened because of their faith. Well, besides you."

"And that is perhaps why the teaching of the kingdom of God is lacking where you live. When the stakes are not high, the earthly kingdom and the heavenly are easily confused. The two are not the same, not until every knee bows and every tongue confesses that Jesus the Messiah is Lord and King. But those who die for their faith know they belong to a new kingdom. The world isn't worthy of them!"

John stopped and looked at me. "You said earlier that Christian faith is a relationship, not a religion. It's neither. It's devotion. Allegiance. To live as if nothing else matters—not even your own breath—only the kingdom of God. We confess allegiance to our revolutionary King."

That brought back childhood memories. "I understand allegiance—we used to pledge it every morning in school. But you're asking me to revoke my passport and take up a new one."

"Isn't that what Jesus said when asked about the greatest of the commandments? 'Love the Lord your God with all your heart, with all your soul, with all your might.' All. Every part of us. Not one thing held back. We leave everything to follow him."

His words made me feel vaguely guilty. "I've always found it hard to understand how to love a God I can't see and hear," I admitted. "I can imagine giving him priority, but I don't know how to love him with everything I've got."

"Yes, how does one live out this love for God? It's when we 'love our neighbor as we love ourselves'. My life practice as long as I can remember has been to do the most good I can to everyone I can, every day but the Sabbath. And sometimes even then. I seek their best interest, their redemption, their well-being, their perfection in Jesus. And I do it by the power and authority of Jesus, who works mightily in me and through me."

His words knocked me sideways. How is it that no one ever said these things to me before? I had lived my whole Christian life as if it were all about me. I always heard that Jesus loves me and has great plans for me. But I never recognized what it means to love him in return. That to love him means to lay down my life for his cause. To take up his occupation. To devote myself to loving my neighbor.

I asked John if anyone close to him had lost their lives for their faith. "Most of them," he whispered, looking off over the blue sea. "Of those closest to me, all died for their faith. All except me. How many times I longed to join them! How I still long to join them." He looked at me with a wan smile. "Yet, here I am."

We walked on in silence until we reached the tiny home of Sophia, the widow we visited on my first rounds with John.

She greeted us in her warm and smothering way, yet even I could see that something troubled her. We sat at her ancient table as Sophia mumbled her woes into John's ear, head down and hands massaging one another on her lap.

After he had listened awhile, John sat up and looked at me. "One of Sophia's sons is missing. None of the rumors in town are good." I remembered that Sophia's sons were drunkards. John rose to his feet. "I'll go into town and find out what I can. It wouldn't be safe for you to come with me. If you like, Sophia needs companionship right now, even though you can't communicate well with one another. Will you stay?" What else was I to do? I nodded apprehensively. What would a day with Sophia look like? John left with a basket of lemons balanced on each shoulder.

We sat in silence a long while, Sophia buried in her grief and anxiety, me not knowing what to say, what to do or where to look. I despaired the incongruity between me and John, who would know exactly what to do and what to say. My notion that John was coaching me to replace him someday was laughable. I could as readily become an astronaut and fly to the moon, or host my own prime time talk show.

I glanced up to find Sophia looking at me kindly. Her nut-brown face had wrinkles on its wrinkles, and physical pain showed with her every movement. Yet her eyes were as bright as a young girl's. I wondered if she had been handsome in her day. She was handsome still, but now it was in her resilience. She spoke to me for a while. I nodded as if I understood every word. The Greek language is beautiful to listen to, yet elusive. Much of our vocabulary comes from the Greek language, so my mind picked up on words that sounded familiar but with no way to string them together.

She asked what sounded like a question and waited, watching me. I surprised myself by reaching across the table and taking her hands. "I don't have any idea what you're asking me, but my heart goes out to you." She tilted her head like a puppy trying to understand. "How I would love to hear your story! What is it like to live in poverty in your tiny home year after year, your sons going astray? Your already-small world growing smaller as your limbs give way to arthritis? What is it that keeps your eyes alive, that makes you kind when the world has not been kind to you?"

Sophia nodded, squeezed my hands and spoke a word I knew. "*Efcharistó*," she murmured. Thank you. I said the proper reply in Greek, and she smiled. Creaking to her feet, she puttered around her little kitchen. I could see she was making food for me. I wanted to protest because she had so little, but I didn't know how.

It took her a long time. Finally, she set a small wooden tray before me. Five small cubes of cheese, cut so precisely they may have been the same dimension. Two pieces of bread, small enough to have been sliced from a bun, dipped in seasoned olive oil. And something small and withered that might have been a fig, along with a diminutive cup of dark tea. I had no choice, as it was clear she would watch me as I ate.

The sun streamed in through a small window and spotlighted Sophia's chair. She sighed and closed her eyes. She may have arranged her dining room suite for this eventuality, conducive to afternoon naps. It wasn't a bad idea. When I saw her breaths grow deep and regular, I realized how exhausted I was myself. Fishing at six in the morning was taking its toll. My eyelids became heavy, and we napped together for a while.

"She is weeping."

My eyes flew open. Nothing had changed in the room. Sophia still sat with her eyes closed, her chin resting on her ample bosom, fast asleep. Who spoke these words in my language? Did I hear it in my sleep? Why was it a woman's voice?

As I wondered, Sophia gave a start. Without appearing to wake up, she spoke. "There she is, sitting in a window seat, drinking her coffee." My mind reeled. Who was she talking about? And how was it that Sophia spoke in perfect English?

"She is heartbroken. She is having second thoughts, doubting her presumption that divorce would be of little consequence." I stared, open-mouthed, hanging on every word. "Poor child, poor, poor child. So-called friends have done this. They coached her into unreasonable expectations, challenged her to do better for herself. It was all anger and offense. But now she is feeling the loss, the agony of putting asunder what God has joined together. See, she is crying..."

I made some involuntary noise and Sophia awoke, raised her eyebrows and smiled in recognition. I can't imagine the expression that must have been on my face. "Sophia," I gasped, "you spoke to me... in English!" My tone and agitation made her sit back and look at me with a frown. "Sorry, but... do you understand? Do you know what I'm saying? Who were you talking about?" But it was no good—I saw no sign of comprehension on her face. She couldn't follow me. Overwhelmed, my head dropped to my arms on the table.

I became aware of someone rubbing my back, like my mother used to do when the bullies at school upset me and I could no longer hold it in. Sophia murmured words, but in no language I could understand. Had I imagined it? Had I dreamed that Sophia spoke to me in perfect American English? No, it had happened indeed. I sat up. She was ready with an ancient embroidered hankie, which felt like new sandpaper as she dabbed at my tears.

Sophia pushed back from the table and beckoned me out a side door, which led to a small back yard. A large heap of branches took up most of the space, and I saw the beginnings of a pile of broken pieces stacked against the house. She pointed from one to the other, indicating what she wanted me to do. I sighed, pulled a branch from the pile, and broke it without difficulty over my knee. When she seemed satisfied that I understood this therapeutic chore, she creaked her way back inside. I soon warmed to the work, and—as I guessed was Sophia's intent—the knot in my gut eased.

But not my thoughts. I had never before witnessed anything so clearly supernatural. I mean, Manos became well after we prayed, but it might not have been because of our prayers. And the big catch of fish was unusual, yet not extraordinary. But this! How could anyone explain Sophia's clear articulation? In a language she didn't know? And what on earth did it mean? Was she speaking of Jessica, and how, since I had never mentioned her?

As I sweated over the pile of branches, mindless of what a towering stack I was making, a thought occurred to me. I confessed to being a believer, one who believed in a God who made the universe. Why did I find it strange and unnerving to witness the supernatural? If I believed God intervenes in the natural order, like creating the world, why was I surprised to see it happen before my eyes? I realized I had never expected him to do it. Which made me wonder if I believed at all.

I couldn't question or explain away what I had seen and heard. No doubt there was some reason for John's fluency in my language, but I couldn't account for this. If God spoke to me through Sophia, what was he saying? Was he giving me hope for my marriage? I longed to hear more, to put the pieces together. I wanted to learn from John and Manos and Marianna and Myrto and Sophia. To understand who they were, who I could be. This realization flooded me with the hope that my life didn't have to suck after all. If only I could stay longer.

My shirt was damp and my hands burning from the percussion of breaking branches. The sun had gone down behind the house, the pile was complete and John hadn't returned. Sophia stepped out the door and put her hands to her face when she saw the enormous stack of sticks leaning against her house. She took my hands and clucked her sympathy over their ragged condition, then hugged me and kissed me on both cheeks, thanking me over and over.

We sat down at the table for another tiny cup of tea when we heard a shout of greeting outside the door. It was John, all but carrying a man his size. The fellow looked—and smelled—terrible. We had him lie on a pile of blankets near the stove. Sophia took charge. She removed her son's filthy rags, sponged him clean and rummaged clothing from her late husband's wardrobe. He still reeked of alcohol, and his large bones had far too little flesh. From his harsh, shallow breathing, I had small hope he would survive.

"I found him in the garbage dump," John later recounted. "I guess his friends found it more convenient to take him to his grave while he could still move on his own feet." John looked exhausted. "I don't know if he will make it through the night. The local health center can't take him, and a storm prevents his transport to the mainland. But he will find no better care than from his mother. More than once has Sophia brought someone back from the brink of death. And this is her son. She will work and pray tirelessly for him, as little as he deserves it."

John left again and returned in a short time with bread and fruit and a pot still steaming with broth. Sophia nodded her thanks and turned her attention back to her son and to her God. John kissed the back of her head, and we slipped out into the growing dusk. It was strange to me, leaving this little woman with a man who should be in intensive care in a hospital. Darkness overtook us before we stumbled down the path to John's house, both of us spent in body and soul.

# 11

It was a dark and stormy night. Seriously, it was. John fastened all the wooden shutters and moved the furniture inside as soon as we arrived home, eying the dark mass to the west. I chided him for working on the Sabbath, and he grinned. The air was still but breathless as we ate a simple meal and made ready for bed. I felt too exhausted to relate to John the troubling events of my day, and he looked too tired to receive them. He left a candle burning ("for the Sabbath," he explained). The small flame flared straight up, with nothing to disturb it.

I had hardly slept when a violent wind assaulted the small house. It became a loud and droning roar, reminiscent of the old movie *Twister*—the sound of too much wind. The shutters rattled and didn't keep fragments of the storm from rushing through the room. I buried myself in the wool blanket, like a child who believes the monster under the bed can't find him that way.

I couldn't sleep. After an hour I thought, surely it will stop now. But it didn't. I must have dozed, because the next I knew, the light was growing outside and the tempest was as wild as ever. A regular booming accented the roar, and after listening for a while, I realized it was the sound of waves breaking on the rocks below us. God have mercy on any fisherman caught out in that storm!

I could hear John moving about, but I was warm and safe and didn't want to get up. No way would we go fishing today. I remembered it was the Sabbath and wondered what that meant for our schedule. I was dozing off when John brought me the usual oatmeal, steaming hot. I now looked forward to porridge and wondered if the daily bowl explained why I never had an upset stomach any more. That and the absence of donuts and burgers. I thanked John and asked him what this day would look like.

"Windy and wet! I'll not ask you to go anywhere today."

"Meaning you are going somewhere? I thought it was the Sabbath."

"Two somewheres. I must check on Sophia and her son. And the believers will gather at the home of Manos and Marianna tonight." John pulled a heavy wool poncho over his head. "What is lawful on the Sabbath? To do good or to do evil? To save life or destroy?" He selected a stout wooden staff from several by the door. "I wouldn't lift a finger for my own benefit today, but for one in need, I would give my life. If I could." When he opened the door, the sound of wind and waves was terrifying. He closed it again. "If this settles down by evening, I can take you to the gathering tonight. There are many I would like you to meet." Head down, he went out into the storm. I had no opportunity to tell John about my unsettling visit with Sophia.

That was a long day, made longer by the lack of a way to check the time. I seriously missed my phone, as I found it difficult to adjust to time without measure. More, I grew to loathe time without activity and measure. I counted out loud and repeated the alphabet to give myself some sense that time was passing and hadn't stood still. There was little to occupy my mind except for the occasional louder scream of wind. I imagined that, rather than wind rushing over the house, the house itself was moving through the air at an incredible rate.

It may have been desperation that made me seek out pen and paper, which I found in a side table drawer in John's room. It was the regular lined paper with three holes I used all through grade school. The pen was a bit blotchy and bore the embossed name of the marina below Manos' house, where I first met John. I began there—with meeting John—and found the words flowed. Not so much about my story, but rather the people I met and what I had learned and realized since arriving on Patmos. My musings went something like this.

I used to think churches that weren't like mine were off-track and fatally flawed. In my mind, it would be unlikely to find any true believers in these churches. Why would any real Christian stay, since their teachings were weak in theology and smothered in tradition? Some of the doctrines that set them apart made me shake my head. I thought (sometimes out loud), Where did they come up with that idea? That's not in the Bible!

In contrast, my Evangelical stance was, well, correct. Rooted in the word of God, not beset by convention or hedged in liturgy. This was Christian faith as understood and taught by Paul and Peter and John. And Jesus, right? I was ready to defend my set of doctrines against all and any who thought otherwise. Not that I knew many people who believed differently than me.

But my confidence was being rattled on Patmos. Manos and John and Sophia and Myrto were unlike anyone I ever met at church. Yet their faith was authentic and practical; their prayers and kind deeds put me to shame. I was beginning to wonder if the evangelical faith I grew up with was the one that had taken a skid off the road. Now that this self-doubt had entered my mind, I saw it everywhere. At the aging movie theatre in my hometown, the screen has a dark spot near the middle. Once you see it during a movie, you can't un-see it, and it spoils the film. That is what was happening to my faith. More and more dark spots were appearing, ones I never noticed before, and now they were all I could see.

I wrote like this for a long time, then sat back in my chair and became aware again of wind and rain lashing the house.

The floor was littered with pages. As I picked them up and tried to arrange them in order, I noticed that John's usually cozy house was cold and damp. The small wood stove on which he did his cooking was hardly warm. I was fiddling with its various openings, trying to see where to add wood, when the door opened and the storm entered on the heels of my friend John.

He shook his wild mane of hair; the spray hit my face. "My apologies," he muttered, peeling the wet cloak off over his head. He disappeared into his room and came out wearing dry clothes. "It's not a pleasant day. But I'm hopeful its fury is weakening." He showed me how to feed the stove. As the room warmed, John produced two bowls of soup. I realized I hadn't eaten since early morning. I didn't enjoy feeling helpless in John's home and was determined to start earning my keep.

"Sophia's son...?" I began, but stopped as John's face fell.

"He passed in the night. Sophia is heartbroken. Though no one could fault her in doing everything possible to save him." He put his spoon down. "I still find death bewildering, after all these years."

Remembering Sophia's kindness, I felt like crying. With more emotion than intended, I blurted, "John, why is one healed and another isn't? Couldn't God have saved him?"

"God also did everything possible to save him. Far, far more than what he deserved." He stared at his spoonful of soup. "He stands before God and finds all the fault his own. Lord, have mercy."

"That's no comfort for Sophia."

John glanced up at me. "It's her one source of comfort, the mercy of God! We can't always understand what God does, but we can cast ourselves upon who God is. Sophia's life has been tragic, yet the love of God is her constant. Her anchor in the storm."

"I have a hard time reconciling those two realities in my mind: Sophia's tragic life and the love of God."

"It's because your mind is too small." How did John manage to insult me so blithely? "You see everything as if reflected in this old pot—blurry and distorted. How can you understand the riddle of life on earth? It's far beyond you."

"And beyond you?"

"Of course. But my experience of life is more... extensive. I've seen much."

On impulse, I decided to take a chance. "A man in Skala told me that Manos believes you're two thousand years old." As soon as I said it, I wished I hadn't. John was already agitated with our conversation; now he grew angry.

"It would be best to allow Manos to speak for himself. You do wrong to pay attention to gossips and mockers." He stood and clattered our dishes into a pile. "I take it you haven't asked Manos about this?"

"No! I didn't think... Hey, I'm sorry," I stammered.

"Well, don't." His eyes were on fire. "He grows fond of you, and you'll distress him with such a question." Striding to his room, he said over his shoulder, "It's still the Sabbath. We need some time alone with our thoughts. Leave the dishes!" He closed the door.

My face was hot. I felt ashamed, yet bewildered at John's response. I could see why he would be protective of Manos, but this was a bit over the top. Or was Manos the one he was protecting? The words of Antonis at the market enticed me again, and I pushed them away in frustration. I loved the simplicity of life on Patmos. To see it become complicated was annoying.

I didn't enjoy being alone with my thoughts that afternoon. I was weary of the sound of the wind, weary of myself, and chilled to the point of wrapping up in my blanket by the stove. Thoughts crowded in on one another: Sophia and Manos and who is John and why am I drawn to someone who so infuriates me?

John emerged as the dark day grew darker. I realized I must have dozed off for a while, and the sound of wind was gone. He smiled at me in my blanket. "Come, bring your blanket with you. The storm is passing, but it will be cold tonight."

"We're still going to Manos and Marianna's place?"

"We'll gather with them and several others, but it will be at Sophia's. She needs us and is in no condition to travel. I should warn you that it won't be pleasant in her home, yet this is what followers of Jesus bear for one another."

On the way, I told John about my time alone with Sophia and her strange words in her sleep. The story intrigued him, and he asked me to try to remember exactly what she said. "And you hadn't talked with her about Jessica before this happened?"

"No, not at all. She doesn't... well, I didn't think she knew any English."

"She understands more than she lets on. But no, she couldn't have that conversation with you. Strange, I haven't known Sophia to see visions before, as it seems she experienced in her sleep. Did she remember it at all?"

"I don't think so. She seemed bewildered to wake up and find me all freaked out."

We walked in silence for a time. "Jason, it may be time for you to go home to Jessica. Tomorrow, you take the ferry to Lipsi." John's heavy hand rested on my shoulder again. "I'll be sorry to see you go."

I didn't trust myself to reply. At the thought of leaving, a wave of emotions rolled over me—a sense of loss and apprehension. I felt like I was on the edge of something significant here and was far from ready to leave. Nor was I yet the person I wanted to be when I next saw Jessica.

# 12

Marianna was already at Sophia's house when we arrived. She had rearranged Sophia's scant furniture to squeeze us all into her living space. Manos had stayed home. As we walked in, my nose wrinkled at the evidence of suffering and death. I hoped Sophia didn't notice my expression as she kissed my cheeks. I wanted to step back outside, especially when John opened the door to Sophia's bedroom to look at the still form lying covered by a white sheet on her bed.

I always had a strong aversion to anything to do with death. I never attended funerals, not even my grandfather's. Driving by cemeteries gave me the creeps. When I was younger, I became a vegetarian for a time, until I eventually tolerated the idea of meat. To me, the worst smell in the world is something dead. In Sophia's house, it was pervasive, inescapable. As more people arrived, they chatted as if nothing was the matter. I even heard Sophia laugh once. I sat squished in a corner, silent, isolated and wishing I could be anywhere else.

The room became quiet, and I realized everyone was looking at me, like a bug on the wall they had just noticed. John spoke, and I heard my name. There were nods and acknowledgments, so I assumed he was introducing me to the group. About a dozen of us crammed into that warm and airless space. Quite a range of ages; most were working poor, I guessed. Myrto's granddaughter smiled at me and whispered something in her grandmother's ear. They laughed together, and it shouldn't have made me uncomfortable, but it did.

"They want to hear your story, Jason. Would you like me to translate, or should I tell it myself?" I couldn't imagine telling my story in that place—I was trying hard not to breathe—and I gave John the go-ahead. John must have embellished because I heard laughter and sometimes exclamations of surprise. Everyone looked at me and made approving or sympathetic noises. It felt strange. I didn't know how to respond, and I felt more like a bug on the wall all the time.

When John finished, a young man spoke up, and John nodded. "We would like to pray for you, Jason." He didn't ask me for any prayer requests. Instead, they all reached out and put their hands on me, whatever part of me they could reach. They prayed, all of them. All at once. And not quietly either—it was like each one had to speak up so God could hear. I had my head down and eyes closed at first. But as the prayers continued, I glanced up to find several of them looking at me as they prayed. Others called out to the ceiling with their free hands raised. It went on for ten minutes, and by the time it ebbed to silence, I felt immersed in something warm and comfortable. All my objections to being in Sophia's home faded away. They had lifted me up to heaven and placed me in the hands of God.

Myrto began to sing, and all joined in. Sometimes when I'm in church, I've thought that if the power went off, we would hardly hear the worship band, much less the congregation. No need for high tech here—they sang from the bottom of their hearts and at the top of their voices. Myrto's granddaughter may have been the loudest in her high shrill, and the young man beat the time with his foot. Sometimes only the men or the women sang, and always at the volume of a heavy metal band.

They prayed for Sophia, but it differed from when they prayed for me. They wept, holding Sophia as the tears streamed down her face. Some murmured prayers. Once again, I didn't know what to do. I sat watching Sophia and tried to imagine her life. Raising children who had no hope of amounting to anything. Watching them fall to the deadening allure of alcohol and lose their family boat and all they had struggled to achieve...

Everyone had grown quiet, and they were observing me, listening. Words were pouring out of my mouth that I didn't know, but they seemed to understand. The words ended as I was overcome with self-consciousness. John spoke up and encouraged me to continue. "You were telling Sophia to grieve, but not without hope. That she can rest in the eternal mercy of God and sleep well tonight, knowing that... What is she to know? Please continue."

But I could not. I felt the heat of my face and was thankful when everyone resumed their prayers for Sophia, who continued to watch me curiously. What on earth? I didn't believe in this stuff. I always considered speaking in tongues as gibberish to make some people seem more spiritual. Sophia spoke the day before in perfect American English, a language she couldn't understand. But I never expected the same to happen to me.

John was teaching. The group was responsive, expressing their agreement and encouragement. Once, that same young man asked a question, which—to no surprise—John answered with another question. The young man told a story about himself, I assumed from the laughter and teasing he received. I looked across the room and saw that John watched me with a pleased look on his face. Despite understanding nothing in that room, John's affirmation spoke to me and gave me hope.

Of course, we ended with food, brought by everyone. Myrto took charge, sweeping the crowd out of the kitchen into the yard and under a black sky alive with stars. I've never seen them so brilliant, before or since. With no moon, we could see one another by the light of the stars alone. Several of the group sat around me as we ate, practicing their limited English. I enjoyed correcting their errors and adding to their vocabulary. They found interesting the English word "disaster," which in Greek referred to an unfortunate arrangement of the stars. I've rarely had such fun.

As John and I left, we had to hug each person in turn, and many kissed our cheeks for good measure. When I offered a hug to Myrto, she scoffed at my feeble effort and lifted me off the ground in her smothering embrace. John laughed. "Now you know what is a hug and what is not!" We left with satisfied stomachs and the taste of garlic and feta still rich in our mouths. John would be back the next day to help bury Sophia's son, once the local coroner had seen the body. I would be boarding a ferry away from all this, a thought I pushed from my mind.

On the way home, I was full of the experience of John's little church and relieved to speak with someone who understood me. John explained that several more believers would usually come but had stayed away so we could meet at Sophia's house.

I was asking if other groups met in different parts of the island when John grabbed my arm and motioned me to silence. We weren't far from his house, and I could hear the waves on the shore below us—and something else I couldn't make out. John started sprinting down the trail to the water, with me struggling to keep him in sight. We burst onto the narrow beach to a scene of clamor and chaos.

Dozens of people, who appeared to have come up out of the water, staggered in the starlight. They moaned and wailed, and some screamed back over the dark water in a language I didn't recognize. Shouts of despair came back from the darkness. I stood frozen on the sand as I realized the magnitude of what must be a shipwreck. The starlight allowed me to see those immediately in front of me. But by the pandemonium, hundreds struggled in the dark.

John grabbed me by the shoulders. "Run! To Manos! Tell him, refugees on the beach—he will know the word. We need boats, medical help. Tell him many lives are at stake! Go! Now!" He uprooted me with a shove. I ran back up the slope, my legs like lead, scouting the road in the dim light and afraid of not finding my way to Manos' house. As I ran in the direction of the few lights I could see, I wondered how John was managing at the beach. He was the one rescuer in a sea of desperate people. That thought made me run faster. I came to the lights and they were no help at all, only outbuildings on top of a hill. But they looked familiar; I was sure I was on the right path. In moments, I saw more lights below me, and to my great relief, Manos' house perched on the side of the hill. I ran down and pounded on the door.

In a moment, Marianna opened the door, clutching a housecoat around her. She looked bewildered at my outburst, but my urgency was unmistakable. She called out to Manos and ushered me inside. I tried to calm down, thinking of Manos' heart condition, but when he came out of his room, I could still hardly speak. "Refugees! On the... beach! Below John's... many... need help! Boats! Medical!"

Marianna handed Manos his phone, and he jabbed at numbers. His voice was terse, urgent and commanding as he gave instructions. For the moment, he was again a respected leader on the island. Manos made several more calls and stood to his feet. Marianna spoke some words of objection, and they bantered for a moment. Manos sighed and sat down again. "I... not go. Marianna..." he shrugged. I nodded my understanding and headed to the door. Marianna stopped me and went to search in a closet. She came back with flashlights, newspapers and several lighters, which she wrapped in a few blankets. Thrusting these into my arms, she opened the door for me.

It took a while for my eyes to adjust back to starlight. I wanted to save the flashlights for whatever lay ahead and was glad to catch up with someone who had a headlamp. He was surprised I couldn't understand him. Before we reached the trail to John's house, several more had joined us, all saying little, hurrying hard. One had a gigantic lantern that flooded the way ahead like a spotlight.

As we approached the slope down to the water, we saw people coming up, some wrapped in blankets, others with hardly anything on at all. Several of our party took them in hand, forming them into groups and leading them to shelter. The rest of us continued to the beach. The number of people crammed into that space was overwhelming. Men, women and children were shouting, wailing, crying. I nearly stumbled over a child crouched on the ground. I reached to pick her up and a man shoved me away, cursing and pulling her roughly into his arms.

I spotted John right away, a head taller than most of these people. He distributed my blankets and flashlights, and we kindled another fire to add to the several that were already blazing. Driftwood was delivered hand to hand, as it was difficult to move in that crowd. "The storm swamped their boat, and they have been drifting half-submerged for a full day and night," John explained. "When they heard the waves hitting our shore, they panicked and spilled into the sea. Many have died, but many more were saved. Praise God!"

John gave me a flashlight and asked me to help him search for those who needed medical attention. I did, hoping to not find any because I had no idea what to do for them. When I neared the water, a man saw me and shouted, beckoning me. He was trying to assist someone close to shore. I grabbed an arm to help him pull—and gagged. The arm was cold and as stiff as a mannequin. We dragged the body up the beach and I turned away, not able to look. But wherever I looked, the flashlight picked out others lying motionless except for the action of the waves. I continued my search but soon came to realize that all these refugees were either alive and in need of dry clothes and lodging, or they were dead.

Boats arrived, many boats. Some searched the water for survivors, and others came to shore to take people to shelter. I saw another loading corpses and looked away. The refugees were reluctant to board a boat—for fear of the water or fear of the law, I wasn't sure. People were shouting and shoving, which I thought strange on the part of both refugees and rescuers.

The beach emptied of people until a small handful gathered around John at the remaining fire. John knew their language (no surprise), and they talked with him for some time with animation. John explained to me, "They claim they paid their life savings to board an overcrowded boat. The first day, another boat came and took away the crew they had paid, leaving them to fend for themselves. They drifted around for days out of sight of land, with little food and water, afraid to move for fear of capsizing. The storm hit and swept many away, and the boat filled with water. They sat in cold seawater for more than a day, and several died.

"These few still on the beach are afraid of the authorities. Their past records will probably result in deportation, and to return to their home country means death. We must be careful because I suspect that these are desperate and dangerous men and women. I question the truth of their story. But I also won't have them die on the beach. We'll take them home with us and see what tomorrow brings." He explained this to them, and they heartily cheered their benefactor. They hardly noticed me.

But as we wound our way up the hill, one man plucked at my elbow and spoke, to my surprise, in English. "Is good! Thank you!"

"You're welcome," I replied, reaching out to steady him as he stumbled over a rock on the trail.

He pointed ahead to John's towering figure. "Who that man?" he demanded.

"That's my friend. His name is John."

"Is magic, this man? A devil?"

What a strange question. "No, I don't think so. Why do you ask this?"

He was panting from the climb. "Because..." he gasped, "I saw. I come out of water, lie on sand. This man..." he pointed at John, "This man, he walk right by me. He walk out on the water, like sand. He walk out and pull people to shore."

"Well, that's good," I replied kindly, but not understanding his point. "John is a good man..."

"No, no! This man walk on the water—on top of waves!" His voice was full of awe. "He walk on water like it is the ground! Like he is ghost!"

He must be delusional, I thought. Crazy from all the trauma. I didn't reply, and we soon arrived at John's house. It was chaotic for a while—we heated water and pulled out every blanket and dry piece of clothing in the house. John raided his stores of fish and eggs, and soon everyone sat back around the stove, stomachs full and bodies warm. There was raucous laughter and excitement. All expressed amazement at their incredible luck, being alive and whole and free, when so many others had died.

John called me out to the courtyard. He looked exhausted. "I'm getting too old for this," he muttered.

"Tell me about it." I was beginning to notice I ached everywhere from the running and the strain. "What now?"

"Pretty lively group for a bunch of drowning castaways." John watched them while sipping a hot drink from a mug. "Something about them does not sit right with me. Are they truly refugees, or are these more likely the smugglers? They will cause trouble."

I thought so too. "Do you expect it will be hard to make them go? Will they take advantage of your hospitality?"

"It will surprise me if any of them remain by morning. They will drift away and try to make their way to the Mainland. But yes, before they leave, they will take advantage of me."

"But your blankets and your clothes...!"

"Will drift away with them. Not for the first time. We must take care that they don't also take our lives. Come, we go to Manos' house tonight."

"What, you're going to walk away and leave them to do whatever?"

"They will do whatever, whether we're here or not. I would rather not watch." We heard the sound of breaking glass. "Nor join the glassware. We will go."

We slipped away into the night, but all the way up the hill, the din of our guests' wild occupation followed us.

# 13

Manos was furious when we told him. He was certain they were smugglers and wanted to call the police, but John calmed him down. "We'll sleep," he told us, "and see what tomorrow brings." John insisted that I take the guest room, while Marianna placed thick blankets on the floor for John, though he hardly slept that night. I saw his outline against the harbor below as he sat on the patio and watched the lights. Finally, I drifted off and didn't wake again until the sun came up out of the water.

I could see that John was in no hurry to go home. And I was in no rush to remind him I had a ferry to catch. I had almost decided not to go. My reluctance had as much to do with facing Jessica as it was about my desire to stay. I thought of asking Manos to use his phone to call Jessica. I could tell her how I missed her but wasn't ready to come home yet. That is, if I still had a home.

John read my thoughts. "You don't want to leave today, do you." I shrugged. "I'll not make you. I can put up with you a little longer." He reached over and messed up my bedhead hair like I was a little kid. "But if you don't go today, you have some arrangements to make. You mustn't worry Jessica. We'll give Manos money for the use of his phone, yes?"

I felt a considerable weight lift off my shoulders. I don't have to leave, I sighed inside. Such a relief. But complications came to mind. My stuff in a locker at the resort—including my passport, wallet and plane tickets. My flight. My parents. My job. Oh, how I didn't want to go back to my job. The mortgage and other bills to pay. And Jessica, whom I did not want to lose.

But I loved the way I had learned and grown from being here for less than a week. What if I stayed a month? I could go back now and continue as the sorry excuse for a human being I had been all my life. The guy Jessica wanted to leave. What if I stayed longer and returned to her as a new man? Could that happen? It was a gamble, for sure. But I was no longer satisfied with the life I had known before coming to Patmos.

John and Manos had left me to ponder over my now-cold cup of coffee. I found the two of them on the bench in front of the house, watching the sun find its way into the coves and other shadows below us. I sat down. "John, I'd like to stay longer, if that's okay with you." He put his arm around me and squeezed. "I... I believe God isn't done with me here yet. There's much more to learn, more to become."

John turned and explained this to Manos, who smiled at me and clapped his hands. "Good! Good! Is very good. Thank you!" I determined right then to learn as much Greek as I could—the hard way, since I didn't seem to have John's gift for language. I wanted to have actual conversations with these new friends of mine.

The decision made, I was ready to tackle the necessary phone calls. John explained my need, and Manos nodded and went to the house. As he returned with his cell phone, he pointed at the bench on which we were sitting and said, "Best... here best." Manos and John left me to my privacy.

I decided to call Jessica first because she could give me numbers for the resort and airline, or better yet, call them for me. I was about to dial her cell when something twigged in my brain. I was about to blunder in as usual and make a worse mess. I would say the wrong words, and it would turn into a fight on the phone with Jessica. I felt the heat of tears spring to my eyes and closed them tight. I guess I prayed, but with no words, simply a lifting of my heart to God that said something like I was an idiot and please help me. I opened my eyes and dialed.

Two rings, and three and four. I was afraid she wasn't going to answer, then heard a click, but she didn't say anything. I heard breathing, and finally a tentative, "Hello?"

"Jessica! It's Jason."

I heard a gasp. "Jason! I thought you were a telemarketer; the number was so long on my display! It's... like, after midnight. Where are you?"

"I'm still on the island of Patmos. It's been..."

"And your flight is, like, isn't it tomorrow? Shouldn't you be on your way to the airport? What's going on, Jason?"

I took a deep breath, let it out, counted to ten.

"Jason...?"

"Jessica, let me explain, okay? Please—listen and don't interrupt; let me talk, all right?" I had never dared use that assertive tone with her before.

"Um, okay..."

I dove in. Told the whole story. I told her about Manos and Marianna, about John and Sophia and Myrto. In the back of my mind, I was calculating how much smoked fish this call was going to cost. With all my heart, I poured out my story to Jessica—about my hope to change for the better. When I finished, she was silent. "Jessica?"

She sniffed. "I... that's beautiful, Jason! I've never heard you talk like this before, and I'm sure it's been significant to you. But I... I don't know what to think of it all."

"Me neither, Jess. For a long time, I've been an asshole to you and to a lot of people. I'm sorry, and if being on Patmos will make me the man you deserve, I want to stay longer. Because I'm crazy about you, Jessica, and I don't want to come back and be that idiot again that made you want to leave. Will you give me a chance, babe? Can you be patient and wait for me?"

I heard the sound of soft crying at the other end. "I..." she sniffed, "I can't believe you called yourself an asshole! Maybe there's hope for you after all," she laughed. After a moment of silence, she sighed, "Jason, I don't know what to say. I want to believe we can be different, but... I've made bad choices too, and... I don't know, you might not want me anymore. You're a good guy, Jason! I don't want to hurt you."

I closed my eyes. I didn't want to think about what she might mean by bad choices. "Hey, I'm sure we'll need to forgive one another. But I want to, Jessica. I want to make this work."

"I gotta sleep soon, Jason. Up at 6:00. Let's not make any decisions yet, okay? You stay on the island for a while. I'll take care of everything, all right? The resort, your flight. I'll call Gerry at your office and tell him you need medical leave or something. When you're ready, tell me you're coming home, okay? And we'll talk. Until you're back, I promise to not do anything... rash, or stupid. And the same for you. Sound good?"

"Like an answer to prayer, Jess. I love you! Sleep well. See you soon." And I hung up. The screen said the call was 26 minutes; I owed Manos a bundle. I rejoined John and Manos and handed him the phone. "Sorry it was long. It might be a pretty expensive call."

John waved his hand. "A few euros. But was it successful? What does Jessica have to say?"

I couldn't answer right away. My throat grew tight and tears threatened. "She says she'll wait," I managed. "It's more than I deserve. I can't believe what a jerk I've been to her and never noticed."

"Do you know why it was not until now that you had this epiphany?"

I thought for a moment. "It's you. And Manos and Marianna. Everyone here. Next to you, I'm like some creeping thing I wouldn't think twice of stepping on."

John translated this for Manos, who didn't laugh. Instead, he patted my hand and looked at me sadly, bowed his head and spoke. I realized he was praying for me. I felt fervor in the pressure of his hand and the tone of his voice. Though the words were gibberish to me, the meaning was clear. Manos was wrestling for my soul. As his intensity increased, a deep longing grew in me to own what Manos and the others had, and I did not. It wasn't envy or jealousy; it was pure desire to be a man after the heart of God.

As Manos finished his prayers, we heard the distant sound of bells. "The Monastery," John explained, "calling the people to the Holy Liturgy. You remember—the big eyesore at the top of the hill." He stood and rubbed his tired eyes. "You should go sometime. It's like a pond a thousand years stagnant. Yet you'll find signs of life, some dear fathers and mothers, brothers and sisters in the Lord."

"You don't go?"

"I'm not welcome. My presence on the island causes them enough consternation. Were I to go to their service... Well, all hell would break loose, as you say."

"I don't understand."

"Nor will you, because I won't explain." He embraced Manos and Marianna and thanked them for their hospitality. "Can I ask a hard task of you?" He directed this at me.

"Absolutely!"

"You'll find no one there, but will you go to my home and see if it's still standing? I don't ask you to clean up the mess you'll find. Yet I can't be in two places at once. I must go to

Sophia. The coroner will be busy after last night's disaster, and we must bury her son today. And I'll talk with the police about our houseguests, as Manos insists." I nodded, and he smiled at me and left.

I would have lingered with Manos, as it was pleasant in his home and I was afraid of what I would find at ours. But he wouldn't have it. He kindly but firmly showed me to the door, and Marianna handed me a bundle of what I took to be food. I ambled over the hill, and all about me was clear blue sky and water, with no evidence of storm or disaster. The house was quiet as I approached.

I don't know what I expected. The house still standing? Yes, of course. A big mess and signs of a hasty retreat? Doubtless. What I didn't expect was the vileness. John's home was always pristine, his patio spotless and sun-bleached. Now it was strewn with foul, damp clothing, shards of glass and smashed fruit. The stench of urine and vomit was everywhere; someone had defecated in a stone birdbath. It was so bad, I had to walk away. But the smell followed me. I felt as defiled as the house itself. It would take all my nerve to return and make any sense of the chaos left at John's home.

I sat on a large rock looking down the trail to the beach, eating my lunch and watching another large bird circle above the slope. Hopefully, it wasn't a vulture seeking the dead. Glancing down, I saw movement below. Someone was walking up the path. It better not be one of the idiots who betrayed John's hospitality, I thought. I didn't have the strength or skill to do to him what my anger wanted. As the person approached, I saw it was a woman, well dressed, with a large camera bag on her back. A small man followed her with a larger pack and a long tripod under his arm.

They stopped when they saw me, conferring together before they approached. The moment she opened her mouth, I knew she was American. Who else would start a conversation—with an apparent native—by saying, "Hi! How are you?"

Fortunately for her, I spoke American. "I'm good. How can I help you?" She looked startled but pleased. I realized that in the short time I had been on the island, I already looked like I belonged.

"You're American!" She held out her hand. "Tracy Ryan, Boston Herald."

It was tempting to leave her hanging, as John had with me, but I resisted and took her hand. "No kidding! I'm Jason. Glad to meet you."

"What's a good Midwest boy like you doing in a place like this?" I bet she asked questions like that ten times a day. Tracy reminded me of Jessica: mid-length blonde hair, athletic, energetic. It was an excellent time to think about Jess.

"Just visiting a friend."

"Were you here when refugees washed up on shore last night?" She motioned to her companion as she spoke, and he pulled a camera out of its case. What would John think of this?

"I'm not sure I'm at liberty to talk about it," I demurred. "Why have you come? Bodies of dead refugees washing up on shore is old news, isn't it? Happens all the time." I wondered why I was defensive and if I was overdoing it at the same time.

She didn't seem to notice. "I'm looking for a man who, according to the refugees, saved many people last night. Was that you?"

"I doubt it. Most of the people I saw were already dead." My heart started to race.

"They say he was a big man. He spoke their language—which was an obscure Arabic dialect—and he could walk on water."

My face must have gone pale. She smirked as I stammered, "That's ridiculous! Walked on water? They must have been delirious or something..."

She pulled out her cellphone and showed me a video clip. It was jerky and dark and hard to see in the bright sunlight. The clamor of waves, wailing and loud cries were a tinny version of what I had witnessed the night before. People were struggling in the water, reaching out their hands in desperation. Some huge person came from nowhere and seized as many hands as he could and pulled them to shore.

The man moved across the water as if he had pontoons on his feet, which gripped the waves like cleats on turf. He was visible for five seconds, and the video froze to a blurry stop. But in those seconds, I recognized the familiar form of my friend John. I closed my eyes. My head was pounding. When I opened them again, the woman was staring at me, bemused. "Hey, you okay? Where did you go?"

I sat back on my rock and wiped the sweat from my eyes. "Yeah, I'm all right. Give me a minute." I struggled to clear my brain and say the right thing. "That was a pretty traumatic experience. Your video kinda brought it all back."

"I'm sure. Pretty brave of you to go and try to help. But what about the walking on water dude? Did you see him?"

"In the video?" Man, I needed something to drink. I was dying out in the heat. "Hard to tell what's happening. I sure didn't see anything like that last night."

The reporter looked disappointed, and the camera guy set down his gear. "Well, more than one person is talking about it this morning, all over the island. I wouldn't have believed it either, of course, until someone asked if I would buy his video clip. I'm no film analyst, but it looks pretty legit to me." The two of them stuffed equipment into their backpacks. "Hey, call me if you hear anything more about this, okay?" She handed me her card. "Where are you staying?"

"Um, a hostel in Skala," I lied, excusing myself with the protection of my friend.

"Really? What were you doing all the way out here in the middle of the night?" Wow, she was sharp. "For that matter, why are you still here this morning? Couldn't sleep?" I had nothing to say. We stared at one another for thirty long seconds. "Well, whatever." She hoisted her pack. "If you want to talk, give me a call. Drinks are on me, okay?" They departed in the direction of Skala.

John. Walks. On. Water. That's all I could think about as I returned to the house and started moving junk into one sizeable pile outside the gate. That John knew the refugee's Arabic dialect didn't surprise me anymore. But this... this had no possible explanation. I knew of one Person who could walk on water—well, two, but the second one had a struggle. My friend had opened himself up to a whole lot of questions and a pack of trouble.

# 14

It was dusk when John appeared, bearing our dinner of bread, cheese and salad from the funeral. I was glad to hear that many believers had come to support Sophia. As much as I wanted to offer comfort to her as well, I was grateful to have a reason not to go. But John's return was equally troubling to me.

He commended me on my efforts at clean-up, eying with disgust the soggy heap I had created. I didn't tell him how bad it was, scooping the unmentionable onto that pile, which John hoped we could burn in a day or two. I thought the chickens were lost, but they had returned one by one as I cleaned. Most of what was missing in the house was clothing and food. Even the shorts and T-shirt I came to the island with were gone. We were left with the clothes on our backs, but we at least had our lives, John pointed out. We continued cleaning in silence until John approved of our efforts, then washed up and ate dinner.

Our conversation was awkward and strange. I didn't know how to bring up what happened that afternoon and finally said as casually as I could, "We had a couple of visitors today."

That surprised him. "Who?"

"Reporters. American reporters." He didn't reply, and concentrated on bending the tines of his fork back into order. I tried not to sound accusing. "They were looking for you."

He glanced up. "Me? What could they want me for?" His guileless tone wasn't convincing.

"Well, they didn't know you by name. They were looking for a man who helped the refugees last night—the man everyone is talking about."

"Many people helped..."

"It seems this one understood the refugee's obscure language." I held his gaze. "And he could walk on water."

John stood and prodded the tiny fire in the woodstove and set the kettle on to boil. "What did you tell them?"

"I said it was impossible, that the people who saw this were delirious. That's when they showed me the video."

John sat down wearily. "They had a video?"

"It's not clear, not enough to positively identify you. But enough to convince the reporters it's genuine. They want to find the man who can walk on water."

"And what about you?" He gazed at the fading sunset. "What will you do with the man who can walk on water?" I heard a weary sadness in his voice. Like he had been here before.

"I want to remain his friend. Like Manos and Myrto and the others who protect him from prying outsiders." He turned to look at me, relief in his eyes. "But John, I want to know who you are."

Darkness was coming on fast. The patio where we sat faded from sun to pale pink to shadow in moments. Our silence was awkward, but the crickets were real. I was so used to the sound of them, I hardly noticed anymore.

Finally, John spoke. "I'm a fool to tell you. My friend, you could be my downfall. After these many years."

"I have no wish to be your downfall. But I need to know."

It was quiet for so long I thought he had decided against me. Finally, he whispered, "My father's name was Zebedee. My brother and I were about to take over the family business when we left him with the nets to follow a man who was more than a man." He looked at me, and I had to swallow hard. "Is that enough? Do you need more?"

My throat was so constricted, I could hardly say the words. "But John, how...?"

"If you read the Gospel that bears my name, you'll come to a place where the Master tells Peter the way he will die. Flustered, Peter looks back at me and asks Jesus, What about him?"

It was dark and I could no longer see his face. I liked it better that way. The unimaginable was more manageable when I couldn't see him. He continued, "His answer to Peter has sustained and haunted me all these countless years. 'If I would have him remain alive until I come, what is that to you?' I remember I laughed, as was my nature. But when Jesus caught my eye, I did not laugh. I saw in his eyes years of joy and sorrow mingled, years I would endure. How many years, I couldn't have imagined."

My heart pounded. Not fast, but loud in my chest. No one can live for two thousand years. John might be fifty years of age at most. Sometimes he looked in his twenties. Not this. I couldn't suspend my disbelief, not even for John.

But how could I doubt him?

"John, I don't... I don't know what to do with this..."

"Let me suggest some options. You could smile sadly and feel sorry for my delusion. You might have me committed to an asylum. Or you may attempt to kill me and prove me wrong. All these have been tried before." I detected no bitterness in the voice in the dark, though a hint of amusement.

I shook this off. "You say you're two thousand years old."

"More or less. It was a bit astounding when I realized I could round up my age to a couple of millennia."

"And you walked with Jesus."

"Still do. I recommend it."

I glared at him. "This is hard to take from a guy wearing jeans, who speaks perfect English and can lift a hundred-pound basket of fish to his shoulder and carry it up a hill."

"Not a hundred pounds. Would you rather I wore a white bathrobe and blue sash for you? Spoke in Aramaic?"

"How does being John make you fluent in any language, or able to walk on water?" My voice held its incredulous tone. I couldn't help it. Why would he expect me to believe he's the Apostle John? Was this his way of dominating Manos and others on the island? His ruse seemed so wrong, but also out of character from what I had seen in John so far. Was he deluded?

John stood and poured wine into his cup. "Morning won't wait. We need a big catch of fish tomorrow. Sleep well, my friend." And he walked into his room.

Sleep well, I did not. Ever since I met John, he produced in me a kaleidoscope of emotions I seldom experienced before. My mind dodged between rage and shame, indignation and wonder. It was impossible to believe John was the Apostle. Part of me wanted to, for the sake of our friendship. But I could not. This must be a role he was playing, like Aladdin at Disneyland. Yet if this was so, it was unfair to expect me to go along with his posturing. I had half a mind to turn him over to the news cameras and see how he did under their scrutiny.

It felt like I had hardly gone to sleep when John nudged my elbow with a bowl of oatmeal in hand. "The fish are calling us, my friend! Thankfully, our guests weren't interested in oatmeal. But unless we go fishing, oatmeal is all we will eat today!" He was cheery enough. I had a headache upon waking and grumbled a reply. But the oatmeal was warm and comforting, and I soon resigned myself to another day of following the man who called himself John.

We filled both our baskets. I insisted on carrying my own fish up the hill, which was fine for the first thirty yards. My heart was beating hard and fast; I was sure John could hear it. I set the basket down on the patio and collapsed into the nearest chair. John wasn't even breathing hard and was soon busy processing the fish for drying. We didn't talk except when necessary. I was okay with that.

"You struggle with my recent revelation—sorry, poor choice of words—my disclosure that I am the Apostle John." We were threading dozens of small salted and herbed fillets onto a wooden frame where wind and sun would dry them. I nodded my agreement, not trusting my words. "It's what I expected," he continued. "I want you to know I rarely tell anyone. Experience has taught me to wait for the right moment. I don't think it was a mistake to tell you. In time, you'll know if it's true."

"Can I ask you something?"

"Anything at all. But remember, I will answer only if I believe it's in your best interest."

"Why did Jesus call you and your brother the 'Sons of Thunder'?"

John looked at me with a grin, closed his eyes with intent concentration—and gave out an enormous fart.

"You're kidding."

"Ask a foolish question, receive a foolish answer," he laughed. "Really, I said you could ask anything, and you ask this."

I had no more questions. Instead, John affirmed my growing conviction that he was at best play-acting, if not taunting me. Why he would do this, I had no idea. Resentment grew; I wondered if I should leave. Part of me was still intrigued by John. But I was sad he was keeping up this charade. Why couldn't he be straight with me?

The fish were drying on the frames. John stood and stretched, his back cracking with a satisfying sound. He watched as the large bird circled above, and I wondered if our fish racks looked like a display case to it. John's basket still held a few fillets, and these he pan-fried for our lunch with lots of olive oil and spices. But it felt like half a meal. "We should go to town this afternoon," he suggested. "We both need clothes and some food to go with fish."

"I still have the money for the ferry."

He shook his head. "Hang onto it. I have a stash. It will be more than enough, and we'll soon replenish it with our dried fish. The islanders love these, grilled with olive oil and lemon."

"You're not worried about the news cameras?"

"I've evaded them before. They never stay long. Come, the day is passing."

Walking into Skala with John differed from my solo experience. Everyone knew him, and their polarized reaction to his presence was even more pronounced than I observed before. I saw friendship, animosity, awe and angry silence in response to his greeting. People were curious about me, his tagalong. I wondered how many other young charges in the past had to run to keep up with him.

We spent an hour with Myrto, who talked non-stop while John nodded and asked the occasional question. He translated what he thought would interest me. Myrto was another significant source of information for him, and her most important news that day confirmed what the reporter told me. Everyone was talking about the man who walked on water, saving refugees. The stories grew with the telling. Now the man also started beach fires with his gaze and raised a few people from the dead. Others scoffed at believing any tale that refugees would tell. The verdict wasn't unanimous, but some were claiming on sound authority that the man was John of Patmos.

At one point, Myrto scolded John, who kept his head down and received it thoughtfully. She stopped and looked at his shaggy head, looked at me, and shrugged her shoulders. I wasn't the only one to become frustrated with this man. I realized it was because we loved him. And one can't love an anomaly without some measure of frustration. John smiled up at her sudden silence, making Myrto laugh with tears in her eyes, and we all laughed together. It wasn't easy to stay angry at him.

We made our purchases in town, filling our bags with whatever we had lost to the refugees, which wasn't all that much. How I loved this simple island life. Thoughts of my full walk-in closet and overflowing pantry back home embarrassed me. What do I need, really? I could draw a line—which I always exceeded—that would be enough for me. Why is "more" so appealing that I have to fill every nook of my home with possessions I rarely use? How foolish. How selfish, when many don't have enough. This was something I was determined to adjust when I got home.

It was a relief to set out from town without having suffered undue attention. The media scavengers must have left. As we ascended the hill out of Skala, John nodded toward a side road. "Come," he pointed, "I want to show you something." In a few minutes, we descended to a whitewashed building where a sign announced in Greek and (nearly) English that this was the "Cave of the Apokalypsis." That sounded familiar—something to do with the end of the world—but John didn't answer my questioning glance.

We continued along a wall and pathway to a small dark entrance. Above the door was an old mosaic of two men with halos standing outside a cave. John glanced at it and snorted.

A group of tourists was exiting, speaking in low voices, and a man in a white robe was about to close the door when John stepped forward and touched his arm. The man's eyes widened at the sight of John, and he shuffled back inside, holding the door open and gesturing us in.

It was cool and refreshing inside. John led me down sets of stairs to where the bones of the mountain poked through the stucco walls. The rooms we passed had many old drawings and artifacts. I was uncomfortable with it all, like the time I attended a wedding in a Greek Orthodox church. All these religious trappings weren't for me.

John looked at me like I should know why we were there. "What?" I said stupidly, looking around at the walls but not seeing any of it.

"This is The Cave. Well, what's left of it after centuries of interior decorating. You know, The Revelation?"

It finally clicked. "Like, the Book of Revelation?" He nodded. "Angels and dragons and trumpets. It happened here?"

"Yes. For a time, this cave was home. Patmos wasn't always a paradise for me. The island was once my prison cell."

"And how did the Revelation come to you in this cave?" I couldn't take the cynical edge off my words. It felt unkind, and I didn't want to be unkind with John.

But John played along. "Unexpectedly. Traumatically. I was already an old man, or should have been. I wasn't sure in the midst of it all that I would survive." He swiped a hand over his face and was silent for a moment. "Wherever in the Scripture an angel appears, what do they always say? 'Do not be afraid.' I heard those words as I lay at his feet like a dead man. But it was no angel who spoke them."

I waited expectantly because I couldn't remember the details of the account in the Book of Revelation. Finally, I asked, "Who was it?"

John turned to me with a look of astonishment. "It was Jesus."

I almost laughed. "Jesus? But I thought Jesus was supposed to be your best friend or something! You say you hung out with him for three years..."

"You don't understand. Jesus—with whom I once daily walked and slept and shared a bowl—in this cave, he was revealed. *Apokálypse*. Face to face. Creator. The One who holds worlds together. Almighty God. The Great I Am." He sank onto a seat carved into the wall, and I had the sense that the place held for John the ambience of wonder. "True, it was what I had believed about Jesus for many years. But to see him... that way. I fell like a stone. Like I was dead. Perhaps I was dead, and he raised me to life again."

I didn't believe a word, but I wondered. What would it be like if I was hanging out with John and—poof! He's God. The whole world in his hands. All-knowing, everywhere present, all-powerful. John as John was alarming enough. I would not likely survive John as God.

"And next...? What happened then?" I humored him.

John sighed and stood to his feet. "Read it for yourself. I haven't the strength to tell you more. Remembering is exhausting enough." He started up the stairs, and I followed him back out into the fading daylight, more frustrated with him than ever.

If this was an act, John was pretty good. As we arrived back at his house, I realized I couldn't help appreciating John, both the friendship and the challenge. But his invitation to "come and see" tested my skepticism more every day. As I drifted off to sleep, I debated whether it was acceptable to befriend a man who was either a play-actor, a madman or a liar.

When we hauled in another significant catch the next morning, John asked if I would mind returning to Skala. We removed all the now-dried fish from the frames to make room for the fresh, and he dictated to me a list of items we had forgotten to buy. I was glad for the walk but also relieved from the angst of John's presence. I took my time, frequently setting down the heavy bag of dried fish to enjoy the view and the sun on my back. The mornings were getting colder. Fall would soon return to my Midwest home, which felt like a long-past unpleasant dream. I wondered if Jessica was already packing up to leave.

Myrto was jovial and gracious, as always, and burst in delight over my growing collection of Greek words and responses. She set to work coaching me and expanding my vocabulary until my head spun. Of course, she also fed me the entire time until she had stuffed both mind and stomach. I wandered the markets and shops, seeking the items on John's list. I was inspecting avocados when an American voice spoke in my ear, "Hey, I believe I owe you a drink!"

I turned, and there—far too close—was Tracy Ryan of the Boston Herald.

# 15

The bottle of wine we shared looked more expensive than what John served. I can't say it tasted better, but it was headier—it gave me a slight buzz right away. Across a small table from me, Tracy sipped hers while plying me with questions I didn't want to answer.

"Are you ever not at work?" I finally countered in exasperation. "Are you always a reporter?"

She looked at me quizzically. "What do you want from me?"

I felt my face turn red. "I don't know... conversation! There's hardly anyone on the island I can talk with. Can we discuss something other than me and why I'm here?" I was backpedaling and she knew it.

"Fine. Though I'm far from satisfied with your answers and more determined than ever to find out what you're hiding." Tracy sat back in what I took to be her version of relaxed. Like a crouching tiger. "What do you want to talk about?"

"Um, what do you think of the island of Patmos?"

Tracy shrugged. "I've seen more interesting parts of Greece. What's the appeal? I'm not exactly a rookie when it comes to travel, you know."

She couldn't seem to help it—always the interviewer, never the interviewee. I told her about my visit to the Cave of the Apocalypse the day before, skirting around the fact that it was

John who took me there. She didn't have a clue what I was talking about.

"Some guy goes into this cave, and what happens?"

"The entire Book of Revelation! You know, the Bible?"

She held up her hands. "Sorry. I don't go there. Religion is not my field."

"You report from Greece and have no background in religion? How do you manage that?"

"Oh, I'm interested in the supernatural. Anything weird and wonderful. Just not the institution." Her voice took a hard edge. "Are you religious?"

A week ago, I would have had no difficulty answering that question. Now I didn't know what to say. "Maybe. I'm trying to figure that out, I guess." I took a moment to savor the wine. "I follow Jesus, so if that's being religious, I guess I am."

"You're drinking wine."

"Everyone drinks wine in Greece," I shrugged. "Have you tried the water?" I took another sip. "True, back home the Christians I know don't tend to drink alcohol, but in many countries they do."

"Okay, tell me about this cave dude."

I nearly dropped my glass. Thankfully, she was gazing over my right shoulder with a let's-get-this-over-with expression. She didn't notice my alarm. I wondered why I protected John when I couldn't accept his claims about himself. Still, I chose my words carefully.

"John, the guy who wrote Revelation, was a disciple... an apprentice of Jesus. You have heard of Jesus, right?" She rolled her eyes and looked less interested. "He and his brother James and ten other guys..."

"Only guys, huh?" That flared her up. "Old boys' club."

"Young boys. They were all thirty or less, even Jesus."

108

"Really? I always picture him as this middle-aged dude in robes."

I shook my head. "Nope, they were younger than us." I hoped I guessed that right. "Anyway, John and the others hung out with Jesus for three years. He taught them about God, and they went around helping people." Like John, I realized. He's still doing what Jesus taught him. "And then Jesus got in hot water with the authorities, and they executed him."

"The cross," Tracy offered.

"Yeah, the cross. Three days later, his disciples discovered he had risen from the dead, and he appeared to them." Tracy raised her eyebrows at this. She was very cute, and I was trying hard not to notice.

I paused too long. "And then...?" Tracy asked, looking interested again.

"Over the next decades, more and more people believed in Jesus—that he was more than a man. He was God, and his death had a purpose. It meant we could all be forgiven."

"Forgiven by who? God? What did anyone ever do to God? What *can* anyone do to God? Hurt his feelings?"

She was sharp. But I perceived more anger than curiosity behind her question. What's more, I didn't have an answer ready. It was an excellent point and one I hadn't considered. What did God care about our sins? They don't affect him. We hurt each other and ourselves. I had to ask John about that. I deflected with another question. "Do you think Jesus' death was simply tragic, that it had no particular purpose?"

"Sure. People die all the time. I mop up afterward—that's what I do."

"But how do you explain the emergence of the church? Right away after his death, thousands of people drop everything to follow this dead guy, Jesus. All those disciples—

except John—were executed because of what they believed about Jesus. They refused to stop believing in Jesus, even to the point of death. Why?"

"What happened to John?"

Nice deflection. I wished I knew the answer to her question, like, knew for sure. "He was exiled here. Patmos was his prison," I quoted.

"What was apocalyptic about this cave?"

"The last book of the Bible…"

"Let me guess—John wrote it in this cave you visited yesterday. I would like to see that." She made a note on her phone.

"That's right. It was a series of visions the Apostle John saw, lots about heaven and the end of the world. I don't understand much of it." Who was I trying to fool? I had never read more than a few verses of it.

"Hmm, I'll have to dig up a Bible somewhere too," Tracy murmured as she typed on her phone. She set it down and pinned me to my seat with her eyes. "Many of the people I interviewed said the name of the man who can walk on water is John."

I shrugged, feeling the sweat run down my spine. "What are you saying?"

"And that you know him, like you're his latest disciple." I tried not to squirm but did anyway. "One man told me that some islanders believe this man is none other than John, the son of Zebedee. The disciple of Jesus, now two thousand years old."

I glared at her. "You've been playing me. You're not as biblically illiterate as you let on."

"Grew up going to Sunday school, just like you. But, as I said, it's not my thing." She leaned forward, eyes greedy for the inside scoop. "So, what's he like?"

I stood and tossed some euros on the table, but Tracy pushed them back. As I walked away, I realized it was the worst thing I could do. I was telling Tracy I had more intriguing info she hadn't accessed yet, and she wouldn't give up until she extracted it from me. I had put John in a worse predicament than he was before. The woman was relentless.

I finished our shopping and headed home before Tracy could find me again. As I passed the lane to the Cave of the Apocalypse, I thought about what I told Tracy. And other stuff I didn't tell her. My conversation with Tracy made two convictions clear to me. One, I did believe what I told her about Jesus. No, more than that, I believed in Jesus. Second, it was vital for me to protect John from the likes of Tracy Ryan. Which made me question again what I believed about John.

I arrived home as the sun was setting over the Mediterranean. The hues were breathtaking, a thin band of red gold separating the deep indigo of water and azure sky. By the time I descended the hill to John's house, I had to feel my way down the path. He sat facing the dark sea with the warm glow of a candle lighting his face.

He looked up and smiled at my collection of bags. "Success? Do we have everything we need now?" He lit another candle with the first.

"I couldn't find garlic anywhere," I said, placing my bags on the table beside the candles. "Fortunately, Myrto had some cloves in a jar of olive oil, which she said would please you."

"I look forward to the oil more than the garlic!" John inspected the bags and seemed pleased with everything. "Any adventures on the way?" I told him about Tracy Ryan, and he looked troubled. "A persistent reporter. I wonder why." Together, we put away the supplies in cupboards that were no longer empty. "Don't blame yourself. She seems skilled in extracting information. She doesn't know the One she's dealing with." The way he said it capitalized the word "One." He wasn't talking about himself.

I sat down across from him. "Tracy asked a question I couldn't answer. We were talking about Jesus and how his death meant we could be forgiven."

John raised his eyebrows at this. "Well done! What was the question?"

"She said, 'What can a person do to God that God would need to forgive them?' Something like that."

John didn't reply right away. In the dim light of the candle, I saw his eyes close for a time. "David. After his sin of taking advantage of Bathsheba and murdering her husband. A horrible crime. But in the Psalm, he says to God, 'Against you, and you only, have I sinned.' Does that seem a bit odd?"

"For sure! I mean, David basically rapes this woman and kills her husband and writes a song about it, saying his sin was against God? It sounds like he doesn't care about how his actions affected Bathsheba and her husband. Only that he somehow damaged God. It makes no sense."

"So Tracy Ryan would say. Do you think the same?"

I pondered for a moment. "I'm not sure. Like I said, I had no answer for her."

"You seem ill-prepared to defend your faith! Here is no major assault, yet you're a bit staggered by her question. We need to work on your apologetics."

"Remind me what you mean by 'apologetics'."

"This Greek word may be one you don't know in English. *Apologia* is one of the great spiritual disciplines, the art of defending one's beliefs by a system of reason and argument. This discipline was always important to the preservation of the church, but I fear it has become a lost art."

"I remember a guy who came to my church and argued against the theory of evolution." I had to explain that one to John, but when he understood, he shook his head.

"No, that's hardly worth arguing about. Who can prove how God formed the world? Sadly, none of us were there to watch. What I mean are the attacks on the essentials of faith in Jesus the Messiah. I heard them all in my day. Was Jesus all spirit, or all flesh? Created or Creator? Is the God of the old covenant the same as the God of the new? Is the life of the follower a matter of faith alone or harsh discipline? I'm not sure what they argue about today, but it won't be new. It was all proposed and debated long ago. Nothing new under the sun."

I hardly knew what John was talking about. Again, I wish I had taken my studies more seriously. I was hearing significant gaps in my understanding of Christianity, issues I had never considered before. "How would you answer Tracy Ryan?"

"Remind me. Try to tell me exactly what she said."

"Okay. I talked about how we can be forgiven, and she became indignant and said, 'Forgiven by who? God? What did I ever do to God?' That's pretty close to her question."

John's expression changed, and he looked at me as if I were a hurt child crying in a corner. It unnerved me. "Tracy, tell me, why are you angry with God? What did he ever do to you?"

His words, not directed to me and couched in gentle tones, cut unexpectedly deep, deep into some locked closet of my soul. I heard myself saying, "Done to me? What has he done to me? Tell me what he hasn't done!!" Words and passion poured from my mouth. The death of my childhood dog after I prayed and prayed he wouldn't die. My parents' breakup. Weekends at dad's, where he spent all his time on the phone, noticing me only when I had done something to annoy him.

Relentless bullies. Lost loves. Raging lust and inescapable guilt. I don't know how long I went on like this, but when I finally ran out of steam, I was shaking.

I looked up and saw John's eyes full of tears, dripping into the darkness that was the floor. "And all this you blame on a God you have never seen, whose touch you have never felt?" He placed his hand on mine. "Do you not think your wrongs could likewise reach across the universe and wound the God you cannot see?"

My head fell down on our clasped hands. Every few moments, a shiver of emotion ran through my body. John continued. "I know. I saw. I watched his blood flow down the cross and darken the ground. I witnessed the unimaginable anguish on his face. Agony that went far, far beyond physical pain as he bore the iniquity of us all. I heard him when he cried out, '*Eli, Eli, lama sabachthani?*' I know. I saw. I was there."

I couldn't breathe. I felt paralyzed by his description, full of power and authenticity, yet too incredible. I felt drawn and quartered between my deep respect for John and my inability to accept his implausible words.

I'm not sure what happened after that. Small noises came from the kitchen. Soon, he nudged my elbow with a plate of grilled fish and some of the fresh vegetables I had brought. I guess I had drifted in my thoughts. I sat up, rubbing my eyes and wondering why I felt so drained. There he was, smiling at me across the table. John. The wanna-be son of Zebedee. The man was exhausting. I didn't know how much longer I could handle being with him.

# 16

I was no less tired as I struggled to keep up with John the next morning, delivering our baskets of fish to all the usual needful. Our circuit took us to the outskirts of Skala that day. Passing a dark corner, I noticed a figure I recognized as Antonis, and not in the best condition. His long hair was matted and filthy, and the mix of alcohol and urine that emanated from him made me hesitate to draw nearer.

I spoke his name, and he looked up. He sneered at me, sneered more at the sight of John behind me. "Ah, holy mans! Yes, come close. Come, laugh at broken guy..." His voice faded into a mixture of Greek and English degradations on us. I was carrying a large orange given to me that morning by an old man whose garden we passed. I held it out, and Antonis waved it off. But when I peeled it and handed it to him section by section, he devoured it like an animal.

"What happened, Antonis?" When he didn't answer, I sat on the ground beside him and put a hand on his shoulder. John watched us. I wished he would tell me what to do, what to say. But I know he was praying for me because a story came to mind, one I had heard a hundred times in church. Not knowing where I was going with it, I began.

"My friend, there was once a man who had two sons. The younger one said to him one day, 'I want my inheritance now'—you know the word 'inheritance'?" He nodded slightly and waved his hand for me to continue, looking down at his shoes. "'Give me what's coming to me because I'm leaving home.' The father did as asked, and the son took the money and moved to the city. He wasted it on wine and women and wild parties until it was all gone.

"When he was hungry, he found a job, feeding pigs." Antonis grunted a laugh at this. "But he made so little, even the slop the pigs were eating looked tasty to him. Finally, he came to his senses and said to himself, 'Man, what am I doing? Even my father's servants are better off than this. I will go back to him and ask him to take me as his servant. I'm no longer fit to be his son."

Antonis looked up at me, his eyes deep wells of misery. All the mocking cockiness had gone out of them. "The man returned home," I continued. "When he was still a long way off, his father spotted him and came running. Throwing his arms around his son, he held him close and wept over him. The man tried to ask his father to make him his servant, but the father didn't listen. He called on his servants to clean up his son and to prepare a big dinner for him."

He watched me, expecting more. I found myself reluctant to continue the story, tempted to cut it off. But he knew I wasn't done. After a moment, I continued. "The older son heard all the commotion and asked what was going on. When they told him, he went to his father and complained, 'Why do you welcome this loser back? He wasted your money on booze and prostitutes! You never threw a party like this for me!'

"The father replied, 'My son, you're a good man, and everything I have belongs to you. But we need to celebrate. Your brother was dead, and now he's alive! He was lost, and now he's found!"

When I finished, Antonis was silent for a long time, as if dozing. But he looked up at me with sharp eyes. "The young son—he is me, yes?" I nodded. "And you—you are... old son? You wish I never come home?"

His words struck deep in my heart. I swallowed hard. "Yes, Antonis. All my life I've been the other son... your older brother." My throat was tight as I admitted this. "I have no interest in people like you. When I see them lying in the street, I never catch their eye; I always look the other way." Tears welled up in my eyes. "Antonis, I'm sorry, so sorry!" I couldn't help myself. My shoulders shook, and I wept like a baby.

Antonis wrapped his arms around me. The stench was like penance, and it was the most bizarre and beautiful moment of my life to that point, weeping in the gutter with this filthy, smelly man. "*Adelfos! O adelfos mou!*" he cried. My brother. When we finally pulled apart, he smiled at me shyly and gave a classic shrug of his shoulders. John joined us and spoke to him in Greek, Antonis nodding and replying in a tone I had never heard from him before. A meek and respectful one.

We took him to yet another friend of John's in town. Aegeus was an older man who bore the scars from the ravages of alcohol abuse but was now at peace with himself and his God. He would know best how to help Antonis recover. As we left, Antonis took my hand. "You come soon—see me, my brother! You see me get good, yes?"

His odor stayed with me the rest of the morning, a constant reminder to keep him in my thoughts and prayers. My mind spun with the transformation I had just witnessed, not only in Antonis but especially in myself. To me, drunks on the street were a "problem" someone should do something about. I never before thought of one as my brother or longed for their return home.

I asked John what he saw happen with Antonis and me. "I saw Jesus!" he laughed. "Jesus sitting in the dirt at the extremity of misery. Jesus coming and sitting with him to share his pain and bring him hope. 'Whatever you do to the least of these brothers of mine in my name,' Jesus promised, 'you do to me'." John wrapped his arm around my shoulder and ruffled my hair. "Well done!"

"What will happen with Antonis?"

"We'll wait and see, like a farmer giving a less-than-promising tree one more chance to bear fruit. He has a long road ahead, but through your storytelling, the Father showed him he has reached the bottom. That it's time to come home."

"I want to help him."

"That's good, and you will. But be careful not to seek to become his savior. Remember, you were the one to confess your sins, not him. He needs you as a brother, not a benefactor. Your remorse is what moved him, not your charity."

We started up the hill past the Cave of the Apocalypse. "John, what's happening to me? In the short time I've been here, I've experienced more than I can process. I'm not sure what to do with it all."

"Do exactly as you did with Antonis: live out what's occurring within you. The Father had already moved in your heart before you sat down with Antonis. When you chose to be with Antonis in his deepest need, you expressed the metamorphosis already forming inside. You're beginning to experience the presence of the living Messiah."

"I don't understand."

We sat on the bench overlooking Skala and the harbor. John took on the tone of the teacher. "I've considered what you told me days ago about your understanding of the life of a believer: 'It's a relationship, not a religion!' Your words troubled me. It sounds to me like the Gospel adulterated, a heady wine with too much water added.

"After Jesus ascended into the clouds, and we began to understand what our lives would be like from that point, we used language other than this. We realized, as the Spirit came upon us in flames of fire and dwelt within us, that Jesus had never left us. Jesus was in us, and what is more, we were in him. As we spoke and helped and healed and led those around us, our every move was in him. This was what Jesus promised would happen, but we didn't understand until we experienced being in him."

He spoke so naturally and convincingly of a firsthand experience of Jesus. "Sorry, I still don't understand. What does it mean to be 'in Jesus'? This is new to me."

John's eyes widened. "New to you? But I saw..." He stopped and stroked his beard in frustration. "Listen, when you noticed Antonis lying in the dirt, what was your first inclination? What did you feel like doing?"

Embarrassed, I admitted, "Pretend I hadn't seen him and keep walking? I don't know. I'm sure I would have felt guilty about that, but it's what we do. We don't become involved, right?"

"Why then, against your nature, did you speak his name? Why did you join him in his misery? Offer him what you had in your hand? Tell him that particular story? Confess your shortcomings to him and weep with him? Why, Jason?"

I looked down in humiliation. "It wasn't me." I said it so quietly, John had to ask me to repeat myself. "It wasn't me!" I blurted in frustration, glaring up at him. "I don't do things like that, okay! Never! Do you understand? All I care about is me!" I was shaking, angry and ashamed.

John watched me and placed his hand on my shoulder. When I had calmed down, he said, "Yes, that's exactly right. It wasn't you. That was Jesus. Jason—you were *in him*."

We sat in silence. The setting sun turned the white buildings of Skala into rose gold, contrasting with the light indigo of the Mediterranean. I needed this time for John's words to sink in. All my life... how could I miss this? All my life, my "faith" was only efforts to satisfy God. My attempts to do what God required fell far short of the mark. My whole Christian experience was about duty and obligations, resulting in guilt and shame because I could never measure up. All I owned was the very religion I so often denounced! I told myself that if I worked hard on my relationship with Jesus, everything would fall into place. All I needed to do was "spend more time with him." Yet aside from some brief experiences at camp, nothing ever changed.

In Jesus. I could live and move and speak and serve—and be—in Jesus. It was no longer about me, but about him.

"But John," I pondered out loud. "How did this happen? How is it that, after a lifetime of doing everything in my own strength, I did this one thing in Jesus? What made the difference?"

"You think this has never happened before? Or is it that you never before understood what was happening during your most selfless moments? Anyone who loves does not act independently of God, because God is love. The way you describe yourself is true of all humans—we think only of ourselves. Wherever you see someone placing the interests of another person ahead of their own, Jesus is present."

"People who aren't Christians do that."

"And Jesus is there. Do you think his grace extends only to believers? If that were true, we would have hell on earth! No, I tell you, wherever you find true, sacrificial love, God is near."

I thought this over. "John, are you always 'in Jesus'?"

He laughed and shook his head. "No, no, you'll often see John and John alone, marching on like a fool, angels scattering out of his way! Even after all these years, I manage to spout off before I listen and rush in before seeing which way the Spirit is leading." He stretched, and I heard his stomach growl. "Right at this moment, I'm weighing the value of our splendid conversation against the gnawing pains of my empty stomach. What do you say?"

"I say we go home and eat more fish." It was dark by now, and the thinnest crescent of moon hung high above the hill. It was adequate to help us find our way. We walked in silence, each with his own thoughts. I still didn't know what to think of John and who he claimed to be. But one thing I knew: I wanted to be like him. This was how to become the kind of man Jessica could love. I resolved to press him further, find out what made him tick, and follow his example.

# 17

I watched John more carefully the next day. I observed his every act of kindness and listened to the tone of his chatter with everyone we met. I noticed that John always carried with him something to give away, whether fish or money or an item someone else had given him. His kindness was tangible and disarming, remembered well after the fact by whatever article he left behind.

"John, you tell me the life of a believer is one of doing the most good."

"Indeed. And in word! All in the mighty name of the Lord, Jesus the Messiah."

"You're right. I watch you do this every day, with both the deserving and the undeserving."

"We're all undeserving. The most undeserving are the ones who need us the most. Is that not what Jesus taught and lived?"

"Well, I guess. Anyway, if you want to do as much good as possible, why have you stayed on this island? There's what— a few thousand people on Patmos? If you're the Apostle John, why don't you go out into the world and reach millions? Think of how much good you could do!" I waved vaguely out over the water, trying to keep my tone respectful.

As usual, John was silent for a time before answering. When he turned his eyes on me, they were sad. "It's tempting to give you a pious, equivocal answer. Something about Jesus—how that even the Son of God hardly traveled outside the region of Galilee. That it's not about numbers." He grunted as the line in his hand twitched. "I'll be honest with you." He sighed, and we stood to pull in the net. "I'm afraid."

We hauled together. "Afraid? You? What have you to be afraid of?"

"The Tracy Ryan's of the world. Exposure. Scrutiny. Cynicism. A padded cell." It was a medium-sized catch, and we scooped the fish into our baskets. "Even here, they find me. If I'm tired of anything, it's the inevitability that I will once again need to go into hiding until the lions lose heart and seek other game."

I pondered this. In my world, fame and fortune were everyone's dream. Imagine running away from it! I thought of famous people who constantly sought refuge from the press, and how their reticence often made things worse. John must overestimate the risks involved in becoming a public figure.

He continued. "It's not that I'm only afraid of exposure. I'm also afraid of me. Sometimes when I put others ahead of myself, I lack the shrewdness of Jesus. I blunder in like a fool. As I did the other night when I walked out on the water without thinking of the consequences." He inspected a frayed spot in the net as he hung it in its tree with care. A tree that— if he was the Apostle—he had known from a shoot out of the ground, now massive, twisted and gnarled. "They must not find out who I am."

"What would happen if they did?"

"You mean, what has happened when they found out. It has occurred often, and the result has depended on the idiosyncrasies of the day. In some ages, they wanted to venerate me. Others have sought to execute me for heresy or sorcery. I've been a laughingstock; I've been the main feature in the pilgrimage of the faithful. One person not many years ago wanted to take my blood; he thought it would give him everlasting life."

"People are strange," I panted as we climbed up the path with our baskets. "I admit I thought about asking you to teach me how to walk on water."

He chuckled. "Poor Simon! He never lived that one down. I wasn't as heartless as Matthew, who dared to include in his Gospel how Peter sank in the waves. I admired Peter's pluck and later once had the opportunity to follow Jesus out onto the water. But I've only been able to do so in time of need. I have nothing to teach you. Remember, when we first saw Jesus from the boat, we were terrified. Walking on water is hardly a typical occurrence."

"Neither is living two thousand years." John looked back at me, laughed and started up the hill.

After making our rounds to both the deserving and the undeserving, we spent the better part of the day with Manos and Marianna. Manos was again not feeling well. Yet he was hale enough to boss John and me from a cushioned chair on the patio as we caught up on some of his neglected landscaping. Many of the beautiful flowering shrubs also bore long and menacing thorns that reached out and grabbed our clothing and our skin.

John watched ruefully as a dark drop of blood formed on a pricked knuckle. "Thank you for the reminder, my Friend," he said—but not to me. "You were pierced for my transgressions! How the blood flowed down your face when they beat that crown of thorns down over your head. And they laughed. But you forgave them because they did not know what they were doing. Nor who they were doing it to." He shook the blood off into the bushes.

"John, tell me about Jesus."

He glanced at me. "What do you want me to tell?"

"Something I haven't heard before. Something that only you would know as one of his original disciples."

He shook his head. "No, I cannot. I understand you would expect me to be a trove of lost treasure, filled with the secret things of Jesus, which I alone know among the living." John picked up a pile of lopped branches and tossed them over a hedge where Manos did his compost. "That's true, but it's buried treasure. It has been two thousand years, Jason! Most of what I remember are the words I've spoken over and over again, the events of importance."

We sat down in the shade of scarlet blossoms high over our heads. "I sometimes think I remember his face, but I'm not sure. As the prophet predicted, it wasn't his dashing looks that drew people to him. He indeed became one of us. Jesus looked like any average Jewish man. What made the crowds follow him everywhere? It was everything he said and did, which was unlike anything they had ever seen or heard before."

"If I ever saw Jesus, I would never forget his face!" I protested.

John looked surprised at my outburst. "I disappoint you in my inability to recall the details after these centuries! I tell you, I wrote at the end of my Gospel that if I put to pen and ink everything Jesus did, the world couldn't contain the books required. Do you think I wrote that because I was planning a sequel or a series? No, because sixty-something years later, I was already beginning to forget. This was why I wrote down what I could before I lost something important." His tone was that of a student defending his homework assignment. "It was with good reason that Jesus gave us the cup and the bread to remember him. Hardly a day goes by and we begin to forget."

We both turned as Marianna's voice called us to lunch. John laid his hand on my arm when I started up from the bench. "Be grateful you at least have my Gospel, Jason, preserved through fire and water all these years. At times, even the written word was threatened. But he's faithful."

We were soon all laughing together at the lunch table as Manos and I tried to speak one another's language. We heard a knock at the door and we all looked up, surprised. Marianna went to see who it was. It was unusual to knock on someone's door on the island—most people just... With a start, I leaped to my feet, apprehending who it might be. When I came to the door, Marianna and Tracy Ryan were in an awkward standoff. Tracy struggled to use her less-than-adequate Greek, and Marianna pretended to not understand.

Tracy's eyes went wide when she saw me. "You! What are you doing here?"

"Having lunch with friends. How about you?" My tone was less than friendly. Marianna bowed out, trusting me to handle this.

"Why should I answer your questions?" she replied haughtily. "You don't answer mine."

"What do you want to know?"

"I want to find this guy John who everyone talks about. He seems invisible! I'm told he sometimes comes to this house."

"Well, I'm not sure who told you that, but..." I started.

"I'm John. How can I help you?" John materialized behind me and filled the doorway.

Tracy gasped as she took in his imposing figure. "You? I... There must be a mistake. You're not what I expected!"

John smiled. "Again, how can I be of service?"

She looked like she was about to ask a reporter-type question, but stopped. I could imagine her reluctance to ask someone as youthful as John, "Are you really two thousand years old?"

When she hesitated to reply, John did the unthinkable. He invited her in.

My coldness, Manos' dark looks and Marianna's forced politeness would have been enough to daunt the most seasoned reporter. But for the graciousness of John. He already had Tracy chatting over a glass of wine and a plate of bread and cheese. Listening in, I discovered she hated fish, was twice divorced and traveled ten months of the year. How John drew all this out of her when I failed to stop her asking questions, I couldn't fathom. It might be because John cared, and I didn't.

Several times, Tracy tried to turn the questioning back to John, but he gave her no satisfaction. Where was he from? I had to smile when John told Tracy he had enjoyed living on Patmos for some time, and what is it like to travel so much, and where do you most feel at home? I relaxed. Tracy would only learn that John was an interesting long-term emigrant with skill in the art of conversation.

So I wasn't ready for it when Tracy tossed out, "People tell me you can walk on water."

John laughed. "That's a bit of a bizarre statement, is it not?" I could tell the rest of us were holding our breath as John paused. "I have friends on Patmos, I have enemies. It's inevitable with such a small community. Which do you think are the ones who make this claim about me?"

Tracy held his gaze, pulled out her phone and showed him the video. He took her phone and watched it a couple of times and handed the phone back. "It's hard to make out what's happening. It was a chaotic night."

"You were there?"

"Of course! It took place near my home. Many came to help, and we saved many lives." He gave Tracy one of his most piercing looks. "When I invited some of these who claimed to be refugees to my home, they ransacked my place. Do you think it wise to trust such a source?"

The atmosphere in the room was tense, the silence strained. John broke it with a laugh. "It's a beautiful day, and we sit inside! Come! We'll go see if I sink or float!"

Tracy and I found ourselves following John out the door and up the hill toward his house. When I looked back, Manos and Marianna were standing at their gate, watching us. What was John thinking? I have to say, when we reached the top of the hill and started down toward the sea, Tracy was panting and I wasn't at all. Walking up slopes with heavy baskets every day had its benefits. Tracy puffed beside me. "What's he going to do? And why are we following him?"

I laughed. "I assume he's going to test out your theory that he can walk on water. As for why we're following him, I've asked myself that question often since my arrival. He's a pretty charismatic character, isn't he?"

"Is he going to walk on water for us?"

"Perhaps he will! He might even invite you to join him." I hoped that wasn't what John had in mind.

Tracy lapsed back into uncharacteristic silence. We passed the path to John's home and reached the spot where I first met Tracy. "Where's your cameraman these days?"

"Back to the States." Tracy stopped and stared down the trail sloping to the beach. "This is where the refugees came to shore!" She glanced around. "Your friend John lives somewhere nearby," Tracy glared. "You lied to me about where you were staying. That's why you were here the night the boat sank—you were staying with John!"

"Guilty as charged," I replied sheepishly.

"Why are you protecting him? What is there to protect?"

"Tracy, I..."

"Don't bother! I'll find out for myself." She jogged down the path where John had disappeared. I followed slowly with a sigh.

# 18

When I reached the shore, John was explaining something to Tracy, waving his hands. The beach bore no sign of the trauma and tragedy that had occurred there recently. The tide had wiped clean the life jackets, discarded clothing and charred wood. But there was still something dreadful about this place where many died. It was no longer a beach where I would sit in a lounge chair, drinking a Coke.

Tracy laughed as I joined them. "Slowpoke! It's about time!"

I smiled wryly. "Getting a quick tutorial on water-walking, are we?"

"No, I told John he doesn't need to prove himself. I'm beginning to like him very much. You were right—he is charming."

"Well, be careful, or you might find yourself staying longer than you intended and eating a whole lot of fish."

John laughed as Tracy made a disgusted face. "That's a good idea! We'll see if we can catch us some dinner." He walked over to one of the few trees on the beach and produced a long fishing rod. "I'm determined to make you a lover of fish, Tracy."

"Good luck," she retorted, glaring at the rod as if it were some instrument of torture. "My first husband would rather go fishing than have sex. One reason I left him, among many, is that I could no longer bear the smell of the fish he was poaching on my stove."

"He did what to his fish?" John untangled the tackle at the end of his line and attached the meat of a clam he had broken. He waded (didn't walk) out into the water past his knees and cast the tackle far, far out to where it landed with a splash. After wading back, he buried the handle of the rod in the sand and propped it upright with a couple of forked sticks. "We'll see what the Lord provides."

Tracy looked at him. "You believe that, don't you. You think God pays attention to you, a speck of dust standing on a slightly bigger speck of dust in the middle of a massive universe?"

I could tell Tracy's tone was teasing, but John was sincere. "I do. He has paid such close attention to me, all my life, that I can't ignore him as many of us do." He looked out over the water, closed his eyes and stood expectantly.

We watched him, waiting for... I don't know what. That huge bird—it must be the same one, I decided—hovered out where his line must be, as if watching his lure. Minutes passed, and the fishing rod started twitching. Tracy was closest; she grabbed the rod as it left the ground and began pulling her down the beach. I raced to her and we joined forces, but even with the two of us, it was all we could do to hold our ground. I glanced back at John, and he was still standing with his eyes closed, now with a smile on his face.

Neither of us could spare a hand to reel in the line. Instead, we walked backward, a hard-earned step at a time. It wasn't until we ran out of beach that John came to our rescue. Seizing the rod from us, he reeled the line as he walked toward the water. At one point, something monstrous and shiny leaped from the sea and fell back with a splash.

John wrestled with the fish for a long time. Finally he called out, "Jason, the gaff—that big hook hanging in the tree." He nodded with his head. It was an ugly-looking claw with a stout handle. I ran it down to him, and he took the gaff while handing me the rod. "Hang on! It won't be as bad now, but hold on tight in case she lunges." John ran into the water with his hand on the line and plunged with the gaff. The line went slack. John struggled backward out of the water, dragging the scariest fish I've ever seen. Its teeth were daggers and still snapping, and John warned us not to come close.

"She's the *sinagrida*—the Queen of the Sea! We'll eat well tonight, my friends! We'll roast her over charcoal, and you'll never again abhor fish!" John brought its life to a merciful end with a blow. Tracy stared with her mouth open as if John had just killed a lion with his bare hands. I doubted she would touch a morsel of our catch at dinnertime.

I was wrong. After the first tentative bite of roasted *sinagrida*, Tracy couldn't get enough. It was, without a doubt, the best fish ever. John cooked it over a special wood fire that I didn't understand. Something about burning the wood so you could burn it over again. That plus some spice mix created by Myrto made for a gourmet meal on John's patio overlooking the sunset. Tracy was like a changed woman, laughing and carefree and chatty. Some part of me still didn't trust her. I hoped John's long experience with people would give him the upper hand with Tracy's insatiable curiosity. She did not seem a candidate for the little circle of people who believed in John.

"John, you seem such a capable fellow. Why do you live on this little island?" Tracy toyed with her wine.

"Jason asked me that question this very morning. Meaning, of course, I have much to offer but choose to spend it all on this island of a few thousand. Is that your question?"

"I suppose. What do you think you have to offer?"

John held out his hands. "These. My hands are the hands of Jesus, my voice his voice, my feet are also his. He left this earth so I could carry on his work in his name. 'Greater things,' he promised I would do. Why should I not be the presence of Jesus on the island of Patmos?"

"What do you think, Jason?"

I thought we were treading on dangerous territory. But what I said was, "I've watched him. Every day, John brings food and help and compassionate care to many needy people. Including some that you or I may think aren't worth the trouble. Every day—except the Sabbath, and sometimes even then. John does what each of us should do in our own community."

"You're Jewish, John?" Tracy looked confused. "You keep the Sabbath! But you talk about Jesus. How do you manage to be both Jewish and Christian? One is all about the Law and the other is all about... well, I'm not sure, but not the Law."

"You forget that Jesus was Jewish. Is he not the one to whom every Jewish prophet pointed, hundreds of years before he was born? 'Certainly he bore our sorrows... By his wounds, we are healed.'" John lit a candle, as we could hardly see one another in the dying light. "And this 'Christian' side of us (and by the way, the term 'Christian' was historically—and is still today—a derogatory term), what is it all about? Jason, what would you say to this?"

I didn't skip a beat. "Love. We're all about love."

Tracy snorted. "Sure, that's a nice sentiment, but it's not true—historically or otherwise. What about the Crusades? TV evangelists? My second mother-in-law? You can't tell me they're all about love!"

"People who take the name of Jesus don't always represent him," I countered. "Don't you have a disclaimer in your newspaper? 'The views and opinions of the author are not necessarily those of the Boston Herald.' None of us represent Jesus perfectly, and some show by their actions that they don't represent him at all. But this doesn't change the fact that love—pure, sacrificial love—is what Jesus is all about. Love is what drives true Christianity in the world." My passion shocked me as I said this. John looked on, smiling.

We were silent, staring at the candle. Tracy sighed, stretched and pushed her chair back. "It's late, and I have a ton of work when I return to my hotel. Which of you fine gentlemen will escort me home?"

John and I looked at each other, but Tracy was looking at me. "Um, I guess...," I hesitated. "I guess that will be me." John looked at me narrowly but didn't say anything. We all stood.

Tracy thanked John for the excellent meal and company. "Let me know when you start your school of waterwalking. I'm in!"

"It will be about the same time you grow weary of your empty way of life and follow Jesus." John said this kindly, and Tracy gave him a quick hug.

We walked in silence for a while, the stars lighting our way. The outline of the hills stood in dark contrast, and the sea was a vague something below us. It felt natural when our hands met, and we walked along that way.

"Your friend John is quite something." Her statement didn't need an answer. I didn't offer one. She tried again. "How long have you known him?"

I had to think about that one. How long? It felt interminable, but I had been here not two Sabbaths yet. "Not even a couple of weeks, I guess. Time is weird in this place."

"Which means you've lost track. I would love to lose track of time. It sounds dreamy."

I was going to say they were the best two weeks of my life but instead offered, "It's like... like my life started a couple of weeks ago. Meeting John and being with him—it's changed me. I can never be the same again."

"In a good way, right? I know what you mean. Makes you wonder what's his story…" She squeezed my hand and spun in front of me. "Sorry! I didn't mean that as a reporter." She turned, and we walked again. "Like, what makes John so… deep, like when he turns those eyes on you, and he's looking right into your very soul. How did he become that way?"

I could think of no safe reply to her question. "That's how you feel with John? Like he can see right through you?"

"And you! You're becoming like him. That's exactly what John would do—he would answer my question with another question. In less than two weeks, he has that effect on you!"

"How can you know what effect he's having? You met me a few days ago. I might be already like this."

"Well, for one, you told me you've changed. And for another, I know guys like you. Lots of them. And they're not like John, not one bit."

"You have me. True enough."

"How long are you staying, Jason?"

"That's a good question. How about you?"

Tracy was quiet for a long time. She sighed. "John is right about me. My way of life is empty." She stopped and we looked out over the harbor, where the lights of the town reflected on the water. "I know, being an international reporter sounds pretty sexy. I admit it's a rush to see my name in small letters at the bottom of an article and think of the millions reading my stuff. But in one day it's gone, a swirl in the water."

She held my arm and put her head on my shoulder. I didn't like how it made me feel. Alarms went off in my brain. It was such a beautiful night. If it were Jessica walking with me, I wouldn't have the uneasiness I felt with this woman. She continued, "I'd give anything for a simple life, like John, every day the same. Nothing to do but make a few people's day brighter."

"It's not always easy for him. Tragedy happens here too, as you know. That's why you came."

"I guess. I think I'm just... weary of it all. What I do makes no sense. Half the time, what I write is half-true, speculative. 'Is the Apostle John still alive on the island of Patmos?' That's what I would have written, all so enough people will click on my article, get wowed, and I collect my check. And I go off someplace else and do it again. I don't even do it for the money. Our accountant has to keep reminding me to cash my checks."

"Why don't you quit?"

"Why don't you give me a reason to?" she answered, looking up at me.

I knew what she meant, but I didn't take the bait. At that moment, I wished I was somewhere else in the sea, especially as I felt my resolve dissolving. "Do you have your story? You'll be leaving soon?"

Again we walked in silence, hand in hand. When she answered, I heard a level of desperation in her voice. "I have no story. It's a dead end. John turns out to be some American dude who has lived on the island for an exceptionally long time. So why do I not want to leave?"

We arrived at Tracy's little three-story hotel, and I delivered her to the door. She turned but didn't surrender my hand. "Stay with me tonight—please! Don't go." Her eyes were half-teasing, half-pleading.

As I looked at her, I gasped. The face that I saw—wanting me, desiring me—was not Tracy, but Jessica. I made a spontaneous move toward her and then caught myself at the last moment as I recognized where I was, who she was. I stood there, holding her hand, with I'm not sure what kind of expression on my face. Tears began pouring silently down my face.

Tracy looked at me with concern, the welcoming smile fading from her face. "Jason, I'm so sorry! I'm not sure what just happened there, but I'm so out of line." She fumbled for the pass-card in her bag, reached up, kissed me lightly on the cheek and opened her door. "Good night, Jason. I'm glad you're a saint. Thank you." And she was gone.

As I walked back up the hill, all the tension eased out of my body. The exam was over, and the holidays were starting. I was in no rush to return home and stopped to watch the reflection of the lights on the water. John was still up and sitting in the dark when I arrived. He lit the candle and looked at me like a proud coach with a prized protege. "You have overcome, by the blood of the Lamb and the word of your confession!" He poured me a glass of wine. "What did she say when you didn't take advantage of her weakness?"

I laughed. "She called me a saint!"

"Most appropriate! He has called you out of the pattern of this world, as shown by your self-control—not a human trait but evidence of the Spirit's presence."

"Hey, I don't deserve your praise. A part of me could have caved in. But all I could think about was Jessica." I told him what happened at the door, and the real reason I avoided a terrible mistake.

"Yes, that's what I prayed! That all your thoughts would be for Jessica." John chuckled. "But this minor miracle I didn't expect—the superimposing of Jessica's face. Very clever!"

"You think I actually saw her, not just some trick of the mind?"

"Yes, no, what does it matter? Here you are, there Tracy is, both safe from one another." John stood and stretched. Whenever he did that, I realized what a massive man he was.

His shadow on the wall was that of a giant. "But you must be careful. Our faithful God provided you a way of escape. Don't take his mercy for granted next time you get yourself in such a pickle!"

After such a long day, I thought I would drop off to sleep the moment I lay down. But I stared into the darkness a long time, watching the three stars I could see through the window. I wasn't wondering about John as much as I wondered about myself. I came to this island self-satisfied, oblivious to the consequences of my attitude and words and actions toward those around me. Especially Jessica. I thought about my audacity in asking her to wait for me while I tried to get my act together. And tonight—how close I came to doing something rash and stupid. John was right that God's mercy saved me from Tracy. How can I become the man Jessica needs me to be, I despaired. Who am I, and how did I spend so many years feeling so sure of myself? I weighed myself on the scale named John and was found wanting.

# 19

John left before dawn the next morning to crew a fishing tour at the marina, which was an occasional source of income for him. At first, I wasn't sure what to do with myself but remembered an idea I had the day before. I wanted to read everything the Apostle John wrote in the New Testament, so I decided to visit Manos and Marianna and ask to borrow his English Bible.

It was a gorgeous day. The morning air was fresh, the sun bright, the sea dazzling as I topped the hill and descended toward their house. Of course, the visit included strong coffee, along with a hard sweet biscuit I hadn't tried before. The conversation was awkward but not impossible. Manos practiced his English on me and appreciated my coaching. In turn, my Greek vocabulary was broadening nicely.

To my surprise, Marianna wanted to join me in my reading of John, though I hadn't intended to read out loud and she would understand few of the words. "Is good, any tongue," Manos explained as he left us on the little bench overlooking the sea. I began—reading slowly, stopping often—but the silences weren't awkward. Marianna understood the need to savor the words, chew them well, swallow when ready.

I reached that most famous verse, John 3:16, which wasn't John's first choice to describe the Gospel. It was beautiful, just the same: "...should not perish, but have everlasting life." The scheme of God, born out of love, to solve the mess we made.

I let the words sink in for a few minutes. The extreme cost of God's love made me realize how much he values us, values me.

I didn't remember ever reading the verses immediately following. To my surprise, they were about judgment and condemnation. It seems Jesus came not to condemn but to save. The reason we need to be saved is that our default position is condemnation. I never liked the idea that God sends people to hell. According to this, he doesn't. People are in hell already—condemned—and God is in the business of saving them through faith in his Son Jesus. That idea was revolutionary for me because it meant this was also my business. To join him in his work of saving the condemned.

Marianna thanked me with a smile and went back to the house, but I decided to keep reading out loud. It was unclear whose words I was reading—was Jesus or John speaking? If it was Jesus, he was talking about himself in the third person, which was peculiar. If it was John, his words were full of meaning and I could scarcely take them in. I had never found the Bible so rich, like a big chocolate brownie with ice cream, which sounded pretty good on a hot day like this.

John liked to draw contrasts; I had noticed a few already. I found one especially interesting because it had to do with our conversation the day before. "For every one that doeth evil hateth the light, neither cometh to the light, lest his deeds should be reproved. But he that doeth truth cometh to the light, that his deeds may be made manifest, that they are wrought in God."

The King James English was a bit formidable, but I saw that bad guys avoid the light because it shows how bad they are. Good guys love the light, not to show off their goodness but to show off how good is God. There was that little word "in" that I was coming to understand. Good deeds wrought in God. Which means doing the most good I can "in God," so it becomes clear that it was not me but him. Like what happened with Antonis and me. Like what I saw my friend John do every day.

"What... where you read?" Manos asked, sitting on the bench beside me.

"*Iohannes*," I answered, showing him the Gospel. "Here, and I want to read *Iohannes* one, two and three. And Revelation." I pointed to each in turn.

"Ah, *Apokálypsi*." He leafed through the pages. "Why *Iohannes*?" I thought of the first time he asked me that question, upon my arrival on Patmos when he poked me in the chest. His tone was different now—kind and interested.

"Because..." I thought about how to phrase this. "I want to know..." He nodded his understanding. "...who is *Iohannes*."

Manos gazed steadily at me for several long moments, as if weighing me on the scale I imagined the night before. He closed his eyes, murmuring something under his breath, then motioned for me to follow him inside. He pointed to the couch and left the room. When he came back, he had a large old leather photo album in his hand, and he settled onto the couch beside me. Manos opened the album from the back cover and began to show me the photos, giving explanations I tried to understand.

As with most photo albums, the majority of the pictures were of special occasions: birthdays, christenings, weddings, Christmas. They featured Manos and Marianna, and others whom I understood to be their adult sons and daughter and their families. There was his sister Myrto and her granddaughter, others I did or didn't recognize, and often John. At first, I had no idea why Manos was showing me this, but as we continued back in time, my heart started beating harder and I found it more difficult to breathe.

Many pages in, I saw a younger Manos and Marianna, and the grandchildren disappeared. Their kids became teens,

Myrto's hair was no longer gray but long and dark. Halfway through, there were pictures of a beautiful young couple in a wedding celebration who could only be Manos and Marianna. Next, photos of each of them as a handsome young man, young woman. Then back, back to pictures of their parents and siblings, photos of Manos and Marianna as teens, as children, as infants. Finally, several more pages of family photos, some of them old enough to be in a museum.

John was in them all.

Not every photo, but nearly every page. Every Christmas. All the weddings. The familiar figure of John in his jeans and cotton shirt, long hair tied back, the sandals. In the photo of Marianna's christening as a baby, John looked exactly as I saw him earlier that morning. I gazed with wide eyes at Manos as he smiled at me, a sense of fear and wonder overwhelming my whole being. I put my head back on the couch and closed my eyes.

John. The dude in blue jeans who liked to rumple my hair. He had aged not a day in the span of Manos' lifetime of more than seventy years. In desperation, I grasped at explanations—the photos were digitally manipulated, or they were of John's father who looked just like him—but it was no use. The photo record was there, year after year. John had never grown old, and there was no telling how far back. I could only conclude that John was indeed who he said he was.

My mind slowly unfolded the implications. This is the Apostle John. Not one in a long line of people who took on the name and role, but the genuine article. These hands once touched Jesus, the Son of God. His ears heard him; his eyes had seen. He took the cup from Jesus' hand and drank from it, dipped the bread in the same dish. John received his grace; he grappled with his words. He wrote it all down in a scroll, which I had just read so indifferently, breezing over many of the words. Now the weight of the book on my lap was so massive, it pinned me to my seat.

Manos reached over and patted me on the knee. To be honest, I was lost in wonder and forgot he was beside me. He called to Marianna, who was at the sink with our coffee cups. She came over, drying her hands on a towel, sat across from me and grabbed both my hands with a warm, motherly smile that made me melt. Manos translated her words as best as he was able. "Is good, very happy! Yes?" I felt initiated into a secret sect and would have been terrified had I not loved these people so very much.

Manos' look became earnest. He struggled, searching for words. "We... ah, *prostatévo*..." He looked helplessly at Marianna, but she knew less of my language than he did. She took the tall pepper grinder from the counter, set it on the coffee table in front of me and cupped her hands around it. Manos did the same, eyes pleading for me to understand. He pointed at the grinder. "*Iohannes.*"

"Yes," I nodded my comprehension. "We protect John... *Iohannes.*" They sighed together in relief as I joined their hands around Grinder John. We broke into laughter at the ridiculousness of our language barrier—we who had such understanding and affection for one another. Laughing was a relief to my overwhelmed mind. Manos wiped his eyes with his sleeve and patted my hand, still shaking in amusement. I wished for John's gift of language at that moment. He stood, took up the photo album with careful hands and removed it to its place of safekeeping.

Marianna left soon after, likely off doing good deeds in the name of Jesus. Manos rejoined me on the couch and looked at me as if I were one of his sons. I loved these people, and I told Manos so. I'm not sure if he understood, but he smiled and patted my knee again. He rose and gestured for me to follow. "Come, come." Talk was over, I guess. Time for action. I stood on unsteady feet and followed him out the door.

Manos took me to a place where a low retaining wall was starting to tumble onto the path. The earth behind the wall made the rocks bulge, and it would soon collapse. I understood that Manos wanted me to dig behind the wall, refit the rocks into place and fill the earth back in. If I built the wall the way he showed me, the earth wouldn't push through again. I told him I would be glad to take on the project.

As I assessed what I needed for the job, I thought about the timing of his request. Like with Sophia, when her vision of Jessica overwhelmed me, Manos was offering me a means of processing what I just learned. But also, as soon as I told Manos that I loved him and Marianna, he gave me this work to do. It was like he couldn't separate words and actions. If you profess love for someone, the next step is to provide a way to live out what you said. You love me? That's wonderful! Here are some rocks and dirt I need you to move.

I started to dig, piling the dirt on a big tarp Manos brought me, laying out the rocks as they came loose from the soil. The work was wonderfully therapeutic to my shell-shocked soul. As I shoveled dirt, I realized my understanding of John as the Apostle had been moving in that direction for some time already, simply by watching him day by day. Manos' photo album was the tipping point, but in time, I might have come to this place anyway. Still, it made my head spin to know that John was the ancient Apostle he claimed to be. And to realize that he loved me, despite my doubt and disrespectful cynicism.

As I worked, Jessica came to mind and the day I first told her I loved her. What impertinence! I was 25, fresh out of Bible college and unemployed at the time. The primary way I expressed this "love" was to make out with her behind the hedge by her dorm. I didn't help her find the books she needed for her research papers, or change the oil in her car so she wouldn't have to pay a shop to do it. I could have said, "I love you" in any number of ways. The one I most often chose showed that all I loved was myself.

Life didn't change after we married, beyond the fact we could go all the way. That soon lost its edge. She looked after herself; I looked after me. I usually managed to remember our anniversary, and I planned a few good dates for us. Where was the love? I mean the authentic, get-your-hands-dirty love? Was I ever the living presence of Jesus to her? Why did I keep bumbling along, oblivious to the fact I was doing more damage than good? All this time, I could have been "in Jesus" with her, pouring out my life for her, seeking her best interest with actions, not only words. How I longed for a second chance at that kind of love.

It was hot. I would have loved to take my shirt off, and I missed having shorts to wear. But I had learned that modesty was a higher value on the island than comfort. What would Jessica think of that? What would she think of any of this? If she was with me, would her perspective change like mine? When I arrived home, how would I communicate what happened on Patmos and what was different for me?

The answer came to me like a wave of realization. I would have to live it out. Not preach to Jessica about my new faith, new values, new ways of seeing. I would have to live my faith. John and Manos and Marianna and Sophia and Myrto lived out their faith in front of me until I grasped it and wanted it and sought it with all my heart. Not with many words, but with active love and truth. And prayer. Lots of prayer. That part was hardest for me, but I was learning.

I had an impressive pile of dirt on the tarp and a sizable collection of rocks. Manos came to check on me and invite me in for lunch. When he saw my piles, he gave me a fist pump of excitement. "*Dén tó pistévo!*" He exclaimed. "How? Is amaze! Thank you, my friend!" Manos had his camera with him and made me pose with my work. He showed me how to build the rocks back up again, following the pattern of the wall that was still intact. The wall needed to be broad at the bottom, narrow at the top, but perpendicular on the side facing the path. Manos took my shovel from my hand and we started up the path to the house.

I hadn't planned to stay so long, but the wall was going to take the better part of the day, including breaks for coffee and Greek/English lessons. Marianna was most helpful in expanding my Greek vocabulary. She never attempted English and would persist until my pronunciation was perfect. "*Psygeío,*" she would say, pointing to their small refrigerator. "*Psygeío,*" I would repeat (so I thought), but she would shake her head and have me try again until she was satisfied with my diction.

I saw her set an extra plate for lunch, and sure enough, John arrived as we were sitting down. He had a metal pole on his shoulder, with several large fish dangling from either end. "I'll never understand!" He shook his head as he laid his burden down in a large washbasin Marianna provided. "Why do they go fishing when they don't want the fish? Oh well, we lowly islanders will enjoy them!" He and Manos packed the fish away in his large freezer, which John had bought for him several years before. Manos spoke to him earnestly, and I saw John glance over at me. They washed up and joined us at the table.

I couldn't take my eyes off him, as much as I tried to keep up with the banter around the table. John lifted his hands and face to heaven as Manos gave thanks for our dinner. "And thank you, my friends. You're far too generous with me." I responded little as John described the men he had taken out in the boat and told stories of the fish that got away. He was the same person I had known since arriving here, but he was also not. How does one get to know a man two thousand years old?

John glanced at me with concern occasionally but said nothing to me directly until we had finished eating. "I saw a friend of yours this morning, Jason."

"Antonis?" I replied weakly.

"No!" John laughed. "Though we should go visit him soon." He looked around the table. "I was walking out of the marina when Tracy Ryan called after me from the cafe." My face clouded over. Manos made a disapproving cluck of the tongue.

"Hey," John laughed. "No making faces! Tracy became a believer this morning. And she wants to be baptized tomorrow evening." My jaw dropped to my chest. When John translated for Manos, he threw his napkin on his plate, rose from the table and stormed outside.

# 20

I'm not sure I could have put Manos' rock wall back together again without the aid of John's undying energy. I wasn't helpful since I was in genuine shock, mostly from the photo album but also from his announcement about Tracy. John glanced at me questioningly, yet I couldn't put into words the avalanche of consternation I felt inside. Nor rise from the pile of dirt where I sat mindlessly holding a large stone in my hands.

I was full-out staring at him. The implications of that morning's epiphany replayed in my mind. With his own eyes, John—my John—saw the glory of the Son of God, full of grace and truth. He witnessed the embodied essence of the person and character of God day after day for three years. They shared meals; Jesus washed his calloused feet. I didn't know what to do with my new understanding, whether to seize on John's every word and action or to cower away in awe and dismay.

"John, I..."

"I'm a man, Jason, like you," he interrupted, patting down the earth between two rocks. "Don't worship me; worship God alone. It's not my doing that I've lived all these long years. If I gained any wisdom along the way, it's not as great as one might expect from a man of my age." He carefully selected another stone and set it into the wall. "What is it you want to know?"

What did I want to know? A million things, but not one came to mind. None that I was sure he would answer, anyway.

That morning, I woke up presuming the whole 2000-year-old notion was a foolish game. Now, I knew it was true. The implications came at me like a stampede of wild animals until I didn't know my right hand from my left. I said nothing in reply.

"Come, time to finish this. The Sabbath is approaching." At John's insistence, I rose from the dirt pile and started handing him rocks again to fit into the wall. In the end, it was a satisfying project. The rock face looked perfect and blended in well with the wall on either side of our repair. As I smoothed out the last shovelful of dirt behind the wall, John dragged the tarp away and dumped the remaining dust. Manos was happy with our efforts, but his manner was strained and overcourteous. He was still upset about Tracy. Marianna didn't ask us to dinner. She knew John wanted to be home for the start of the Sabbath. As we arrived, the sun was a half red-gold disc on the edge of the sea.

John lit the Sabbath candle. We ate a simple and silent supper of bread and cheese, cold vegetables and a bowl of fish broth. Finally, John regained my attention. "You have doubts about Tracy's confession of faith." I didn't reply right away. "You're not behaving like Jonah, are you? Did you hope to see fire and brimstone fall on Tracy Ryan, and now you're disappointed? It's wisdom to wait and see, yet it's uncharitable to not give her the benefit of the doubt. You and Manos both. I seem to have more hope for Tracy than the two of you combined."

"You might be too charitable," I muttered.

"Perhaps. Time will tell. Still, I would rather err on the side of grace than prejudice." Again, I had no answer to this. "We will wait and see, Jason. But in the meantime, we should encourage, not dishearten her. Okay?"

"Okay," I replied. But I did not feel okay. John's lack of discernment raised some serious questions for me. Not about

John himself—even an old man can be duped—but why did God not clue him in to what was happening? Was it a test? I resented Tracy and her agenda as she tried to worm her way into John's circle. All for fleeting notoriety. My motives weren't perfect, but I felt genuine stirrings in my soul, changes in my perspectives, actions and faith that I hoped to never lose. Especially now, as stories from a long-ago past came to life in my friend John. I was becoming a new man indeed. I had reasonable doubt about Tracy becoming a new woman.

The Sabbath dawned gently. I slept in, if waking when there is enough light to read can be called sleeping in. Wrapped in my blanket against the morning chill, I sat on the patio and devoured the rest of the Gospel of John, then went back to reread the bits I liked best. The Writer (in person) was nowhere to be seen or heard. But his written words intrigued me like never before.

I was interested in John's anonymity throughout his Gospel. He never names himself among the other disciples but is namelessly present just the same. When Jesus begins to call people to follow him and become his disciples, the first two are already disciples of John the Baptist. The Gospel records the name of one of them—Andrew, who will immediately invite his famous brother Peter to join—but the other isn't named. My guess is that this is John. Is he just being humble? Posing as the anonymous watcher?

I tried to imagine John the Apostle as once a disciple of John the Baptist. If disciple becomes like master, was my John becoming like the other John? Had he developed a taste for honey and grasshoppers? Traded his linen cloak for camel's hair? Also, I realized that when Jesus called John to follow him, it wasn't the first time John had left his father with the nets to follow someone. He left the shores of Galilee once before to join himself to John the Baptist on the shores of the Jordan, several days' journey from home. What did his family think of his piety? Supportive or not? I wondered if John would answer the question.

I found him sitting on the beach. He wasn't asleep, but it took so long to grab his attention, he seemed not exactly awake either. It was as if I pulled him back to this world from some considerable distance. The light returned to his eyes; with a gasp, he shook his shaggy head, looked at me in recognition and smiled. It felt disrespectful to rouse him from whatever realm he was traveling, but he waved off my apologies.

I handed him a bowl of the oatmeal I prepared for our breakfast. He received it gladly while chiding me for taking the trouble on a Sabbath. We sat on the sand, warming our insides with creamy goodness (yes, I now loved oatmeal porridge). The sun behind the hill at our backs turned the sea from slate to a warm cobalt. The hawk or whatever cruised close to the crest of the waves. I loved sitting with John in companionable silence. How different from the silence on a city bus or in a room full of people looking at their phones. I felt connected with this ancient man, though we said not a word.

Finally, I remembered my question about his family. "John," I ventured, "when you left everything to follow Jesus—and to follow John the Baptist before that—what did your family think? Were they supportive of your quest?"

He turned to me, looking both surprised and pleased. "How did you know I followed the Baptizer before I followed the Messiah?"

I pulled Manos' King James Bible from the bag I now carried everywhere. I showed him the first chapter of John, but he waved it away. "Read to me, please. The gift doesn't go so far that I can read as well." Of course. I read the part about John standing with two of his disciples and proclaiming Jesus to be the Lamb of God, who taketh away the sins of the world.

"See? It says one of the two disciples was Andrew, who right away finds his brother Peter and takes him to Jesus. But the other disciple isn't named. That was you, wasn't it?"

John looked impressed. "Well done! But what if I wish to remain ambiguous? What do you gain by knowing it was me?"

"It's interesting, I guess. What made you leave town and travel—I don't know—a few days to the Jordan River to hang out with the guy who ate grasshoppers?"

"Everyone went to see John. You must understand, this wasn't only me and my friend Andrew and a handful of others. Whole towns emptied to go and hear the Baptizer! We were hundreds, thousands, camped for miles around the Jordan."

"Okay, but they weren't all his disciples, were they? How did it happen with you?"

John looked sheepish. "I had... a bit of an advantage. You see, John was a celebrity in our family."

I raised my eyebrows at this. "What? How?"

"My mother and John's mother were cousins."

Wow. "Making you his second cousin."

"I guess that's what it's called." He looked a bit uncomfortable as I sat and processed this information.

"Your folks were pretty supportive of you leaving the family business to be John's disciple, true?" He nodded. "But while you're away, you take up with a perfect stranger named Jesus..." I trailed off as he shook his head.

"No. Not a stranger." He started tossing little stones in the water, one by one, each falling precisely in the middle of the ripples formed by the one before. "Think. Who does Mary, the mother of Jesus, visit when she becomes pregnant?"

Hmm. This wasn't typical Christmas pageant stuff, which usually begins with shepherds abiding in the fields by night.

Who? The light came on. "The mother of John the Baptist! Who was..." My jaw dropped once again. "No way...!"

John smiled and made little piles with the gravel. "Yes, you have made the connection."

I blustered. "You... your mom and Mary were... sisters! You and Jesus were..."

"Cousins. Yes. The ushering in of the kingdom of God was a bit of a family business." John stood to his feet and stretched, yawning. "My family was more than supportive. My mother was Salome, also called Mary (which was confusing to some). She often traveled with Jesus and his men, as did other women, supplying from their family's means to look after Jesus' needs. Which were never much, yet they were ever faithful to him, generous with us. Far more than we deserved with all the trouble we caused."

We started walking back up the hill. My head spun with this information—new to me but clear for anyone with eyes to see. He continued, "My mother was also at Golgotha. We took her sister Mary into our home after that, as Jesus kindly bid us while he was on the cross." His eyes were deep wells as he said this, remembering a vision he had relived and retold for thousands of years. "It took my mother some time to accept that the kingdom for which she had such high ambitions wasn't the kingdom that had come. This was a kingdom of the heart, not of palaces."

John retrieved some cold tea he had made the day before. We sipped it, sitting on the patio with our feet on the railing, the Mediterranean glistening endlessly below. It was enough that John lived in the time of Jesus; I could hardly wrap my head around the idea that he was Jesus' cousin. That he shared his DNA. "You say that you grew up with Jesus?"

"We didn't live in the same town. But we shared family gatherings, yearly journeys to Jerusalem for Passover..."

"Where Jesus stayed behind at the Temple at the age of 12, dialoguing with the scholars."

"So I heard. I was a young child."

"Well, what was he like as a cousin?" I was bursting with curiosity.

He shrugged. "He was a cousin. I don't remember anything extraordinary about him, beyond the Temple story. I heard he wasn't cut out for carpentry, his father's trade. His brothers resented his absences from the shop. He took to wandering alone in desolate places, sometimes for days. And then John the Baptizer happened."

"Why did you go?"

"John was family, for one. And like I said, everyone went to see him. Israel was without a prophet for four hundred years! When one showed up, we all went. Some sought him out of curiosity—John was always a bit of a strange duck—but many of us young guys attached ourselves to him as disciples. Even Jesus."

"Whoa, hang on. You're saying Jesus was a disciple of John the Baptist?"

He looked surprised. "This is common knowledge. Most of the Gospel writers say so. 'He who comes after me is mightier than me,' the Baptizer cried out to the crowds. In other words, the one now following me—my disciple—will prove to be mightier than me. It was unheard of, a paradox, that a disciple would supersede their master."

"And when John identified your cousin Jesus as that One..."

"We believed him. It made sense to leave John and attach ourselves to Jesus. John practically told us to, telling us Jesus was the One for whom he prepared the way."

"And you followed him from that day on."

John pulled at his beard. "Oh no, not constantly. That came later. We ran out of money and welcome at the Jordan, and returned home to Capernaum. Our father could afford a few hired men, but they were often unreliable. We went back to our nets."

I loved this. John wasn't unveiling anything beyond the written Gospels, yet he made sense of it all. More than that, his words made the story authentic. Not like ancient schoolbook history; indeed, not myth. John was there when it all happened. I wanted to ask further, but I couldn't think of what. Besides, I had business to take care of before I arrived at John's little church in the home of Manos and Marianna at sundown.

"John, you don't mind if I go for a walk this afternoon, do you? Do we need anything in town?"

He scrutinized me for several moments before answering. "No, we have no urgent need, nothing that can't wait until after the Sabbath. Why today? Do I need to worry?"

"No, no, it's something I need to do. I'll meet you at Manos' house. That's where Tracy's baptism will be, right?"

Again, he looked at me questioningly. "Well, yes, but not in his house. We'll walk together to the beach."

"Okay, I'll see you at his house. Or the beach. Sound good?"

"Sounds intriguing. I'm curious, but I will respect your autonomy. Do you need money?"

"Not at all. I'll be fine. See you tonight." If I had my way, the next time we met, it would be without Tracy.

# 21

As I made my way down the hill toward Skala, I realized it might be challenging to find Tracy. Would she be at her hotel or wandering the streets, trying to glean more dirt on John? It made sense to try the hotel first.

I was about to walk away as no one answered my knock. The door opened a crack, and there she was, still in pajamas. She smirked, "Changed your mind, did you? All hot to trot? Well, I'm sure not busy this morning." She opened the door wide and gestured me in.

I stood my ground. "We need to talk, Tracy. Can I buy you coffee? The stuff Manos makes is so thick it goes straight to my brain."

She closed the door and I waited for five minutes, wondering. Tracy stepped out wearing a colorful summer dress and straw hat. Very cute, but I wasn't in the mood for cute.

She grabbed my hand as we walked, and I held her's stiffly. "What's got your shorts in a knot this morning?" she queried. I didn't answer and steered us well away from Myrto's place toward a sidewalk cafe that I knew served decent enough coffee.

I took a slow sip of mine before speaking. "Tracy, you can't do this."

She set her cup down and scowled. "The word 'can't' happens to be my least favorite word. What is it that I 'can't' do?"

"Get baptized tonight."

She laughed. "I would expect a good Christian boy like you to be excited to see me get baptized."

"These are good people, Tracy. It's not right to play them like this. I know what you're up to."

She raised her eyebrows. "Really? What am I up to?"

I tried to keep my voice level, not accusatory. "You hope to access firsthand information about John by worming your way into their circle. You have about as much faith in Jesus as the coaster under my coffee cup. I'm not going to let you do this."

Danger flickered in her eyes. "And how do you propose to stop me?"

"Some unpleasant ways came to mind on my walk here. But John suspects I came to see you. If I tell him you admitted to faking it, he will believe me."

She relaxed and sat back in her chair with a wry smile on her face. "You won't do that."

"Yeah, I will. Why do you think I won't?"

She was enjoying the coffee. When she set her cup down, she leaned forward. "In your travels, did you ever run across a journalist by the name of Elise Marillier?"

I felt a flutter of panic, tried not to let it show, and failed. Tracy smiled knowingly. Collecting myself, I countered, "Why would l meet a journalist?"

"Because you are a journalist."

We maintained a long silence while we stared one another down. "Enlighten me. I seem to have forgotten the details."

Tracy took her phone from her pocket and tapped an app. "Well, your name is indeed Jason. I don't suppose you offered your last name to John since it seems unnecessary here, but it's 'Kiesling.' And your claim to fame is an article on the abuse of mentally ill patients in a Russian institution, where you got yourself hired as an aide." She scrolled down. "Oh, well done! You received the Karpoor Chandra Kulish award for that one. Nice!" She looked further. "And then you settled down—or simply settled. Currently, you work as Features Editor for a company that produces a rash of small-town newspapers." She looked up. "And I bet you always hope to land one more big story someday."

All the blood in my body had rushed somewhere below the level of the table. Tracy enjoyed my discomfort. She wasn't a person I trusted with this information. I guess I shouldn't have walked out on Elise, nearly ten years ago.

"What more did Elise tell you?"

"Oh, I'll save the rest for a rainy day. I don't like to spend all my money in one place." I had no doubt she had enough collateral to do me significant damage. I had never told Jessica about Elise, which I greatly regretted. And what would happen if John found out I was a journalist, even if only a small-town newspaper guy these days? I was still the very type of person John feared the most. Damn Elise!

I tried to finish my coffee without showing that my hand was shaking. "So, now what?"

"For the most part, you play your game, I'll play mine. If either of us spills, we have the means and motivation to hurt each other." She smiled brightly. "In the meantime, you will let me collect this story." Not likely. I was mulling over in my mind the nastier options for dealing with Tracy that occurred to me on my walk. As if she read my mind—or expression— she continued. "And if you decide to bump me off, remember it wouldn't be the Christian thing to do, nor worth it for something as petty as a tabloid article. Besides, I already told Elise I planned to expose you."

"Thanks."

"You're welcome." She set her cup down. "So tell me, did you come here intending to write about John?"

"Not at all. Like I told you from the start, I'm a tourist. I'm on—or was on—vacation with my wife and got stuck here quite by accident." I didn't want to tell her that Jessica was asking for a divorce. "I can hardly call myself a journalist anymore. I chase down exciting interviews with college presidents and farmers repurposing their acreages."

"But you haven't told John you're in the business of publishing news stories. You're no different from me."

"No, I think you're wrong, Tracy. There is one big difference between what I'm doing and what you're trying to do. I came to Patmos with no objective and a nominal evangelical faith that I tried to ignore. But through my time living with John, I've started to follow Jesus in a new way. I see things very differently than I did before. The entire experience is genuine for me."

"But you're not being real with John."

I passed my hand over my face. "No, I don't want him to know I work for a newspaper."

"Are you going to let me get baptized, then?"

I sighed. "I find that the charlatan's life is the life for me, and I couldn't be happier," I said dejectedly as I gathered our cups together.

"You're going to let me go through with this."

"Reluctantly, yes. And if we're going to make it to Manos and Marianna's on time, we need to go."

"No time for a tumble in bed?"

"Give it up, Tracy. This is a charlatan with a sense of dignity."

"I can respect that. But it is disappointing." All the same, I stood well outside her door while she gathered her things.

The walk to Manos' house was stunning. To our right, the sky glowed crimson over the sea; on the left, the pale crescent moon rode high over the deep indigo of twilight. We didn't hold hands, nor had I the intention of ever doing so again. Instead, I yearned for Jessica to be walking with me, seeing what I was seeing, on our way to introduce her to my island family. My heart ached at the thought of adding Tracy's duplicity to my own with my new friends.

"Tracy, I'm surprised that the Boston Herald lets you stay this long. Don't you have other assignments?"

"Still trying to get rid of me? I'm on holiday too. Some people go on vacation to lie on the beach and work on their tan. I go to chase down a story I'm interested in. You must understand, as a former freelancer who got to choose his own story."

"I guess. But what about family, friends? Don't you want to be with them?"

She brushed my hand and I didn't respond. After a while, she sighed, "I'm all I've got. My family are strangers, and I don't do friends well."

Nuts. I did not want to feel sorry for Tracy. Especially now that she held all the cards. "And the guy you're trying to hold hands with right now is the one you just blackmailed."

"Sorry. You can see why I don't have any friends."

Already, a dozen or more people gathered at Manos' house, including several I hadn't met before. They all welcomed us with a hug and congratulated Tracy for her upcoming baptism. Our deception grated on me, but my hands were tied. John arrived last and soon herded us down toward the shore. I could see from the dark looks on his expressive face that Manos was still not convinced. Marianna took Tracy's arm and escorted her down the road, calling out to the others around them and laughing. We were a noisy party in that quiet neighborhood, yet no one was concerned. Only the slight moon lit our way, and it was more than enough, but the cool glow made our journey surreal.

When we reached the water, John took Tracy's hand and led her to the center of the half-circle our gathering formed. He whispered something to her, and she looked a bit stunned at what he said. She shook her head, but I could see that John was insistent. Tracy faced us all, cleared her throat and spoke, with John translating every sentence or two.

"Thank you... for welcoming us... me, warmly. I realize you don't know me, and John has asked me to tell you a bit about my story." She paused with a stricken look at me. I raised my eyebrows and smiled. I wanted to laugh, but it would have been unkind and out of place.

"Um, when I was a child, my father took me to Sunday school..." John stopped her with a whispered question, and he gave an explanation in Greek. "I remember enjoying the Bible stories, and I believed them as any child would at that age, whether it was the Bible or a fairy tale. When I became older and my parents finally split up, I grew angry at the God who hadn't prevented their divorce. I wouldn't say I stopped believing in him, but I didn't want anything to do with him."

She had such a look of concentration that I was sure she wasn't making this up—she was remembering. I also guessed that the memories were tugging at the edges of her emotions. It was a struggle to not let them show. As John translated, the crowd murmured in prayer and sighed about Tracy's misfortunate family. She talked about bouncing back and forth between parents, often being left alone, and finally striking off on her own when she was 17. If Tracy's lifestyle and messed-up relationships shocked the group, the murmurs continued unabated.

"...And I came to Patmos. My purpose in being here is to write up a sensational news story about John." Whoa, Tracy,

I thought. Why are you throwing yourself under the bus? "I wanted to make people think he's the Apostle John from the days of the Bible—or expose him as a fraud." John translated this without hesitation, and all the murmurs grew silent. "I'm sorry. Now that I've come to know him and have seen what he means to you, I know that would be wrong." I heard the believers' collective sigh of relief as John relayed this.

I wondered where Tracy was going with her confession. Was it a miracle, or was she still lying her head off? I couldn't tell. But why would she tell them of her intentions with John when she didn't need to? Was she trying to win their confidence, and she would go ahead and write the story anyway? Or was this God's answer to the murmured prayers of these dear people?

And, was the bomb still coming—the news that I was a journalist too?

"Yesterday, I ran into John at the marina and we chatted for a while. He talked with me about Jesus in a way I had never heard before. Like he was—like Jesus *is*—a real person. As he talked, I realized if what he told me was true, this was the most important news on earth. All the stories I ever chased down are nothing compared to this one." She paused and looked down. I thought she might be shaking a bit. "He said Jesus is the Messiah, the Son of God, and he came to take away the sin of the world." In a quiet voice, looking straight at John, she concluded, "And I believe him."

The group on the beach was quiet for a moment as they took this in. Myrto came forward and gathered Tracy in her arms, and the rest drew close and placed hands on her and prayed aloud together. "Alleluiah" was the word I heard the most. After a bit of hesitation, I joined them, placed my hand on her shoulder and prayed. John had once laughed at me for closing my eyes when I prayed, so I looked straight at Tracy and she looked right back at me.

I prayed words that weren't my own. "Father, you have always been present with Tracy, all through these lonely years when in anger she turned her face from you. I'm grateful you brought her to Patmos and into John's circle. She has confessed faith in you, Jesus, and I have no choice but to believe her confession and receive her as a fellow child of God. If she's lying, I will try hard to forgive her and not hold it against her. I trust in you, the Judge of all the earth. In the name of Jesus, I say this. Amen."

The way she smiled made me wonder. It wasn't triumphant or mocking. Her smile was shy, like I had caught her singing to herself. I wanted to believe her, but the stakes were high for me, and much higher for John. Still, she hadn't ratted on me. So far, I was safe. What's more, despite spilling her own intentions with John, the community surrounded and embraced her. I was now the one on the outside, the guy with a secret. I returned her smile with a half-hearted one.

John led Tracy into the water. They stood chest-deep, the brilliant reflection of the crescent moon framing them in gold and silver. John placed his hand on her head and spoke words in Greek, then took her hand and lowered her backward into the sea. She came up gasping, arms held high. It was a remarkably beautiful scene. Too bad it was probably all a farce.

# 22

The gathering at Manos and Marianna's house was boisterous and celebratory, in stark contrast to the solemn tone the week before at Sophia's. Manos was entertaining, and the group laughed long and loud at his interjections. John looked on and tried to explain it to Tracy and me, but the humor was lost in translation. We smiled and nodded. Manos brought out his ancient camera to record the event with a photo of Tracy and John, and for some reason, me.

I was especially missing Jessica tonight. If she was still one island away, I would bring her here and she would love it like me. We would quit our jobs and never leave. When we were still in college, we would dream this kind of dream. Live simply. Few possessions. Eat great food. Always on some warm island with many beaches. And then we got married and got practical.

John finally had everyone settle down, and we made ourselves comfortable on chairs and cushions on the floor. "Welcome, Tracy, to our gathering, where we have everything in common and no one remains in need."

As John translated for the rest, the group murmured their agreement and regarded Tracy with welcoming eyes. Tracy whispered in my ear, "Sounds like communism."

"Or community," I whispered back. "You'll find this is nothing like church back home. You need to pay attention." John related the goings and comings of the community, aided by others who confirmed or added in. At least, that's what I guessed he was doing.

"Why? Everything is in Greek. How am I supposed to..." She stopped, realizing everyone was looking at her. "Um, did I miss something?"

John stepped around and placed his hands on Manos and Marianna's shoulders. "As your new family, Tracy, we're not happy with leaving you alone in a hotel room. Manos and Marianna will be pleased to have you stay with them." The two smiled brightly at Tracy. "Tomorrow, we will help bring your luggage. At your convenience."

I could see the conflict. Loss of privacy and independence versus getting further inside this circle than she already was. She quickly dissembled, "Oh! Wow! That would be awesome. Uh, thanks." Her look as she smoothed back her hair told me that opportunism had won out marginally. The group congratulated her new hosts with enthusiasm. To me, Tracy whispered, "What did I just do?"

John continued into what sounded like the beginnings of a sermon, and I whispered back, "My guess is, they're offering you more than hospitality. They will take you in to show and teach you the way of Jesus. You have become a disciple, a protégé."

Her eyes went wide. "Yikes, they don't waste time, do they."

John's sermon continued for some time. I could follow bits of what he said, more from his tone and expression than the words. I was starting to lose interest when I noticed Tracy listening intently. "Are you following this?" I whispered.

She put her hand on my arm but didn't turn her attention from John. "Yes, some," she whispered back. "But I don't know how..." She went back to focusing on John's discourse in Greek. I wondered if God was gifting her the ability to understand, which by now wouldn't have surprised me. Except for the fact that it would happen with a person like Tracy.

When John paused to ask the group a question, Tracy's hand shot up. John looked at her with surprise. "Yes, Tracy? What are your thoughts on this? Why did Jesus not speak on his own authority during his time on earth?"

"Um, because. The whole idea was to be one of us, right? If he lived here using his own power all the time, it would be hard for us to relate to him or, like, follow his example. Right?"

John looked pleased. He translated this for the others, and they murmured their assent. Tracy's insight dumbfounded me, and more, her interest. The young guy who liked raising questions at these meetings spoke up. John thanked him and turned his inquiry to Tracy. "Stephen wants to know if there is more to this authority question. Was Jesus dependent on the Father only for our benefit? Thoughts?"

Tracy sat back. "No idea. What do you think, Jason?"

I've never appreciated being put on the spot. Give it to a fellow journalist to do this to me. Fortunately, an answer formed in my head. "Obedience. For some reason, it was important for Jesus to come under the authority of his Father. Doesn't the Bible say that Jesus was obedient to the point of death on a cross? But I'm not sure why."

John brought this back to the group, and Marianna spoke up. "Another time, two people had the opportunity to obey," John translated, "and both Eve and Adam failed. Jesus obeyed to set things right. His obedience as a man achieved his glory as God. He defeated sin and death as Conqueror and King."

"What great theologians we are this evening!" John exclaimed. "Let's consider what to do with our new understanding. How will this make a difference in how we speak and act tomorrow morning?"

The conversation went back to Greek, and I could see that Tracy could no longer follow it. "How fascinating!" Tracy whispered. "I'm not sure what this all means, but it was like something took over! I understood what he was saying. Like, not all the words but the general idea, and I knew how to respond." She rubbed her eyes. "It's made me giddy. Anything like this ever happen to you?"

I thought back over the previous week and the several times I experienced "anything like this." And how "this" precipitated my move from skepticism to faith. "You could say so, yes."

"Do you understand what John is talking about?"

"No, I can't. Not like you." She looked smug about this, and I felt the tiniest sensation of resentment. I realized it might not be easy to share John and everyone else with someone like Tracy.

John wrapped up his sermon with questions and comments from the group. "Anything to ask or add, Tracy?" He didn't ask me. Tracy declined, and Myrto began the singing. Tracy was enraptured by it all, eyes closed, humming along when she could. But I couldn't decide if her newfound faith was genuine or if Tracy was just a pro at experiential journalism.

Everyone wanted to pray for Tracy. They set her in the middle and placed their many hands on her; it must have been a workout to remain upright. She doesn't have a chance, I thought to myself. How can she resist everything these dear folk earnestly plead for her? If God gives heed to a fraction of their petitions, she will become a changed woman by morning. I offered nothing—I couldn't pray in good conscience when my own duplicity still weighed on me.

Stuffed on the moussaka that Myrto prepared for our gathering, we gave our hugs and farewells. I was getting better at a willing suspension of personal space. I hugged and cheek-kissed like anything. Except for Tracy, whom I navigated to keep my distance. I was relieved when Myrto insisted on escorting Tracy to her hotel.

Walking home with John, I asked, "Are you convinced? Is Tracy sincerely a believer?"

As usual, John took a few moments to answer. "What reason do I have to think otherwise? How sincere am I? Or you, for that matter?" But I was sincere. Except for not telling him about my line of work, I was sure I was genuine. Every day (was it two weeks yet?), I was learning and growing in my faith. John continued, "Our Father has offered grace to Tracy, and so will I. And so will you."

Interesting. John had never told me what to do before. His authority over me, up to that point, was that of influence and respect. This was no suggestion; it was a command: be kind to Tracy. I pushed down a twinge of resentment. Surely, I needed this—to know what it is to be a disciple, even when it rankled. "Um, I'm okay with that. I'll do my best to be gracious to Tracy."

"I realize that you—and Manos—want to protect me, and I appreciate it. I remember telling you that people like Tracy Ryan are my greatest fear." How my heart sank. I couldn't do this anymore; I needed to tell him about me soon and warn him further about Tracy. We topped the hill, and the glow of the moon behind us made the darkness at our feet complete. "I won't allow fear to kidnap love and hold it for ransom," he continued. "Tracy is innocent of deceit until proven guilty. She needs our nurture, not our scrutiny."

"I hope you're right."

John grunted his annoyance at my lack of conviction. "Simon made the good confession, saying Jesus is the Messiah, the Son of the living God. In turn, Jesus affirmed his new identity as 'Peter,' one of the foundation stones of his church. And he stated that the gates of Hades would not prevail against his church. Think of that! The church of Jesus lays siege to the gates of hell, and breaches the gates again and again!" His voice rose in the quiet of the evening. "In we rush, through the gates and into the very City of Hades to save the likes of Tracy Ryan! No one can stop us!"

This was another paradigm shift for me. I had heard of the gates of hell, of course. But I always pictured the church in defensive mode, holding back against the attack of Satan. How foolish of me! We're not the ones under siege—we're the attackers, the invaders. Not only that, but we're also the victors! The gates of the city of hell will fall, and we will enter in and set the prisoners free from their doom.

Jesus promised this, and I missed it. Instead, my fellow believers and I sat in a blanket fort of our own making, fortified with candy and comic books, hiding in fear of I-don't-know-what. And here was John, with good reason to be afraid of what damage Tracy might do to him. Instead, he storms into her life with hope and confidence while I stand watching and wavering. I felt ashamed.

We walked home in silence and went each to our bed with our own thoughts. If I learned anything from John, it was that the life of a follower of Jesus is not about talk but about faith and love in action. I was done with talk and wanted in on the action. Had I known where that determination would take me, I might have remained a mere talker. For now, I went to sleep with hopes of winning Jessica's affection all over again. I wanted to love her, not with big words and impressive speech, but in truth and action. But that night I dreamed that, when I got home, the house was empty with not one stick of furniture left behind.

Early the next morning, John and I set our empty oatmeal bowls on the table, ready to clean up and go fishing. A sudden whoosh of wind blasted over my head. I yelled and dove for cover as an enormous bird landed with perfect balance on the back of John's chair. It closed its massive wings and regarded

John with sharp, baleful eyes. John swiveled in his chair until he and the bird were nose to beak. They appeared to be acquainted with one another. The bird, which I took to be a predator, nibbled John's nose while he stroked the feathers under its razor-sharp beak.

"Jason, meet Zesi. She's a Bonelli, a type of eagle." She turned her head and pinned me with her golden eye. "Zesi, this is Jason. Please don't eat him. He wouldn't agree with you." Zesi stretched out her neck and hissed, six inches from my face. I froze as I felt her cold breath. Seldom have I been more terrified. "Relax," John tried to reassure me. "She won't eat you." He went back to stroking her throat. "Probably."

I sat back as far as I could, my heart racing. The bird was magnificent but intimidating, with a wingspan that must have been six feet or more. Her chest and open wings were dappled white, her head and back chocolate brown. Long, white-feathered legs ended in serious black talons. She was breathtakingly beautiful.

I finally managed to splutter, "She's... she's yours? Why have I never seen her before?"

"Mine? No, Zesi is independent. Only a friend. And you have seen her before, but from a distance. She has been weighing your worthiness, I suppose. The bigger question is why she has come now." John inquired that of her as he stared into her eyes and made noises. She replied with a long, slow *criii*. That freaked me out. I wasn't comfortable with this bird's intrusive visit.

I rose slowly from the table and reached to gather our bowls. That was a mistake. Zesi screeched, flapped her wings and shot out one set of talons at my hand. She missed only because she wouldn't relinquish her perch with her other foot. I leaped back, knocking over my chair. John tried to calm her, placing one hand over her eyes and the other on her chest. "I'm sorry, Jason. She doesn't seem to take to you well. You should step inside." I did so gladly, but watched out the open window. John, wincing, took the eagle on his hand, stood and tossed her in the air. Zesi dropped down and out of sight, then immediately returned with a rush of wings and landed on the railing.

"She says the visit isn't yet over, Jason. Would you like to try again?"

"No thanks, I'm good." I leaned on the windowsill, ready to jump back if needed. "How long have you been, um, friends?"

"Zesi's mother brought her to me when she first learned to fly. And her mother's mother did the same before that. An eagle has been with me as long as I remember." John took a thick leather glove from where it was hanging and pulled it on over his right forearm. The bird immediately flapped up and glided to John's hand. He handled her like she was weightless. "She's still immature, about two years old. She will soon bring me a young one of her own, I expect."

How bizarre. I had never heard of anything like this. "But why do they come to you?"

"I don't know. They have been an agreeable companion, especially for the long periods I live alone. Occasionally, they gift me with a small carcass of some kind—a pigeon or rabbit—which is a welcome change of diet. And they're protective of me. Sometimes, I hear a commotion and watch as one chases away some unwanted pest—human or otherwise. These birds never lose their wildness or become domesticated. I have scars enough to prove my occasional indiscretion with them."

Our "guest" remained the better part of the morning, most often watching me. John went to do the nets on his own, cautioning me to stay inside. He left me to be supervised by a malevolent babysitter. Every time I moved away from the window, Zesi became agitated. The one time I approached the door, she immediately rose up and swooped toward me, talons first. I wondered if she considered me an unwanted pest of the human kind, and if I ventured out, would chase me clear across the island. I did not want to discover the answer to that question. Finally, Zesi sent another loud *criii* in my direction, dropped silently off the railing and didn't return. John came up the path moments later. His basket of fish was so heavy, even he was panting.

"You can come out now, Jason! Your jailkeeper has left the building." He set the basket down on the patio and reached for a second one to share the load. "Come, the day is passing and we have much to do. Fish to give, news to learn, good deeds in the power and name of Jesus. We will also pass by the home of Aegeus and see how he's faring with your friend Antonis. And of course, we promised to help Tracy with her luggage and see her settle in with Manos and Marianna. A full day! A good day. Praise God!"

# 23

A full day. A good day. An exhausting day. When we started out, my neck was already sore from tensing under Zesi's malevolent custody. The basket of fish John gave me to carry turned my pain into a constant burn that soon stretched all down my right side. But I wasn't about to tell John. By the time we reached Aegeus' house, I regretted my pride. At least I had emptied my basket at our previous stop.

When Aegeus saw us, he lifted his hands in a rueful shrug. John explained their conversation. Antonis had left during his second night with Aegeus, along with every valuable item he could find in the house. When I heard this, anger and resentment flared up in me. "How dare he! After giving him a chance like that! Of all the ungrateful..." I was ready to find the guy and tear off some hide.

John calmed me. "Aegeus tells me it was no great loss, nothing our small community can't restore. And don't even think of confronting Antonis. He's a dangerous man, and with his companions, more so."

"I was an idiot, helping him that day." I rubbed my sore neck in annoyance.

"No, you mustn't think this. When we're faithful and do what is right, trusting and following the Spirit's call, the results are God's responsibility, not our own. The success is in our obedience, not in our accomplishment. Otherwise, what glory will go to God when events turn out as we hope? Or what frustration or indignation will we bear when they don't?" John thanked Aegeus and left him some fish, and we went our way. "What will be your next steps with Antonis?" he asked me.

"Next steps? You told me not to confront him!"

"Yes, because that would be an unfortunate next step. You can do better."

"You think I should still try to help the guy."

"Of course. How many chances has God given you in your life? We will love Antonis as we find him. But we will also love him too much to leave him in that condition."

"That's crazy."

"That's grace," John countered. "Indeed, it can seem reckless. This love has nothing to do with what one deserves. It's the domain of a holy, changeless, all-sufficient God who is free to love before he has any reason to love. His grace has no prerequisites, no methods of achieving worthiness, no expectancy. He loves us while we shake our puny fist at him and spit in his face. To love like this requires long-suffering patience. More than either of us has on his own."

We didn't find Antonis that day. No one had seen him. One fellow ruffian thought he might have gone north to the town of Kampos. As we walked to Tracy's hotel, I thought about the way John loved me. I sometimes wondered if he saw any potential in me and if he weighed my motives. I would never know it by the way he treated me. He welcomed me unconditionally into his world. All the same, living with John was never comfortable. He was often hard on me—pushing, prodding, raising questions I didn't want to think about. But it was working. As much as he accepted me as I was, I was no longer the man I was. Praise God.

Except I hadn't yet told him about my career or about my conversation with Tracy. You don't hide who you are from people you love, people you admire. But I desperately wanted John's approval. I was reluctant to tell him everything. I told myself I didn't want to hurt him, but if I was honest with myself, it was me I didn't want to see hurt.

Tracy wasn't home. The note on her door said she was at the market to pick up a few items and would be back shortly. As we waited, John struck up a conversation with the proprietor of the little hotel. I gathered that she was not happy to lose Tracy's business to the hospitality of Manos and Marianna. As John listened to her rant, replying with gentle words, her tone changed, her expression softened and tears ran down her cheeks. For some time, the woman poured out her woes to John. In the end, whatever he said to her made her eyes light up with hope. She kissed his cheeks and said *efcharistó*—thank you—over and over.

I hadn't noticed this woman until John talked with her. As I thought about that, I realized I seldom noticed people unless I had some business with them, something I needed from them. The time I approached Antonis was a rare exception. To John, this was his lifestyle—seeing, caring, doing—day after day for two thousand years. Without leaving this island, how many lives had he influenced through these small interactions every day? He was like a virus that starts with one person and infects the whole world. But in a good way. Is that not how Jesus said his kingdom would grow, a tiny seed developing over time into the largest of plants in the garden?

How much had I influenced the world? I wanted to, which is why I chose journalism. I hoped that some people would read my stuff, which might shape them in some slight way. But all day long, in every circumstance, I drifted by many people without eye contact. People for whom I might make a difference if I took notice of them, gave them time and offered kindness and the hope of Jesus. I wondered where John learned his trick of carrying things to give away. From Jesus? I couldn't think of an example in the Gospels. Mind you, when you can heal the sick, give sight to the blind and raise the dead, what more do you need, right?

A cheerful greeting interrupted my meditation. "Hey! Good afternoon! You came—I was starting to wonder!" Tracy set down her bags and hugged us both. "I'm all packed. Just need to settle up with the landlady—she's not too happy about me leaving, by the way—and we can be off!" She was more enthusiastic than I expected. Tracy seemed resolved to see this thing through. When she came back, she looked dazed. "That was weird—the landlady acted like I was her own daughter, leaving home! She packed me a lunch and gave me a gift!" It was a tacky picture frame with seagulls, a few glued-on seashells and a "Patmos" sticker. But it's the thought that counts. Tracy was touched. John said nothing, so I also didn't tell her what transpired with her landlady before she arrived home.

Tracy's luggage was standard professional traveler gear. It was reliable, compact and precisely 50 pounds for the suitcase and 22 for her camera bag. John shouldered the heavy one, despite Tracy's protests that she could roll it along those bumpy roads. I did my best with the other, but 22 pounds in the heat soon felt like 100. Tracy puffed along with her other bags and purchases. "Can I hail us a taxi, please?" she pleaded. John laughed and adjusted the bag on his shoulder. We marched on up the hill out of Skala.

When we came to the lane by the Cave, we stopped to catch our breath. "Tracy, this is the way to the Cave I mentioned. Have you seen it yet?" She shook her head. "John, can we take a detour?"

He shrugged. "Why not? But we can't take this luggage with us. You may show her, Jason. I'll be content under this tree." He sat on a small bench at the base of a flowering tree, and we handed him the rest of our stuff. "Don't worry about me. I've seen the place before." I laughed; Tracy didn't. We walked the short distance to the Cave of the Apocalypse. I was on my guard, which made our conversation awkward.

The young monk who was doorkeeper and guide that day was asleep at the entrance. I hesitated to wake him, but Tracy stepped forward and put a hand on his shoulder. "Excuse me..."

He startled awake and jumped to his feet. "Many apologies," he stuttered. "The warm sun..." he shrugged. I wondered who he thought we were as he looked us over. Vacationing couple, I guessed. As he reached for the door, he offered, "Do you require a guide?"

"No, thanks," Tracy replied. "My friend knows the way." He stepped back, and we entered the coolness of the Cave. I led us down the stairs and straight to the place John took me. Tracy touched the rock walls, smoothed by many hands before hers. "It looks like people have been here for a long time. Do you believe that John, who is waiting outside in his blue jeans, was a prisoner in this cave a couple of thousand years ago?"

I thought about that for a while. Not many days ago, I couldn't have left a silence pregnant for that long. John's example helped me resist the urge to fill every gap in a conversation. In the quiet, I heard water dripping someplace. "When I first met John, I asked him the bold question, 'Who are you?' He laughed and replied, 'Come and see!' That's what I've been doing ever since—following him about, watching, listening. I have come to see that what he does and says, and what he knows, are extraordinary. Extra. Ordinary. I can't give you proof of who he is. But if he claims he's the Apostle John, the last couple of weeks of 'coming and seeing' would lead me to believe him."

"You realize how bizarre that sounds, right?"

"Yeah, like I'm a crazy man." We started through the rooms and up the stairs. "I don't know what this means for me, except my life will never be the same again."

As we stepped out into the bright sun, she stopped me. "Listen, I've decided not to hijack your story about John. Okay? If you want it, it's yours. You'll have to decide for yourself what is the right thing to do." That floored me. I was grateful for her offer but wondered at her openhandedness. I still didn't trust her. We found John dozing in the shade, not aiding some troubled passerby.

For the rest of the journey to Manos' house, John and Tracy walked ahead of me, talking the whole time. I felt left out of the conversation and heard them talking about me. To my amazement, John told Tracy about Zesi the eagle and how that vicious bird trapped me in the house. Their laughter didn't help my growing sense of exclusion. I suppose it was unreasonable of me, but I resented Tracy treating John as a friend when he was likely still her project.

I wasn't in a great mood when we arrived at the home of Manos and Marianna. I should have been happy for Tracy, the way they drew her into their home and their lives. But I was not. It didn't help that she had a room to herself, with a comfortable bed and a view of the sea. John and I walked home in silence, and it was like we were walking farther and farther apart. If I was honest, I was to blame. My resentment of Tracy created the distance between us. I was also afraid of hurting John and possibly losing him altogether.

The next morning, as we brought our half-full baskets of fish up the hill, we found Tracy waiting for us on the patio. She was wearing clothing I was sure couldn't be her own, a Marianna-style long skirt and puffy-sleeved white blouse. But the same sensible reporter-on-the-run shoes, so Marianna didn't entirely have her way. She stood and did a curtsy when she saw us. "What do you think? Do I pass for a local?"

"The lessons begin!" laughed John. "Do you know why Marianna gently insisted on this change in attire?"

"I guess because good Christian girls don't dress the way I usually do? Is that it?"

"Not at all. What would you say, Jason?"

I surveyed what she was wearing and felt that I could be slightly less on my guard with this version of Tracy. "I don't think the lesson is about modesty, Tracy," I offered. "It's that, well—you're not in California, where I'm sure many good Christian girls dress like you. You're in a culture with a different take on clothing. Marianna is saying, 'Be with us, not distanced from us by the way you dress.'"

"Well said!" John's praise felt good. "Jason is right. To quibble about modesty would be petty, and Marianna is not petty. But to respect the culture in which you find yourself— that is love."

"Love," Tracy pondered. "I wouldn't have expected the lesson to be about love or respect. I'm afraid I'm inexperienced with what she's teaching."

"I don't hold that against you," John replied. "I would know nothing of love if Love himself didn't take me under his wing."

"We're going to talk about Jesus now, right?"

"You make this sound tiresome. Why?"

"I grew up learning about Jesus. But not about love. I don't think the people who taught me offered particularly good samples of what they were selling. They were well-meaning, I suppose. But I remember leaving Sunday school feeling bored, confused and vaguely guilty."

"I'm sad this is your story, and it sheds light on your reticence. Why should you think well of Jesus if he wasn't well represented to you?"

"I know, right? Which is why I'm pumped about hanging out with you and the others for a while. I want a clearer picture of who Jesus was. How could I do that better than with someone who knew him personally?"

That made me jump. John looked at her for a moment and replied, "Good. I'm glad your goal is to know and understand Jesus. You'll find that we're imperfect representations of him, yet I believe you will learn from us." John stood. "If you don't have any big plans today, how would you like to come along with us on our rounds? You can watch what we do as we seek to follow the Messiah."

"I'd like nothing better!" Tracy chirped. It was the very thing she wanted to do. I was pretty torn between wanting her company and doubting her promise to back off John's story. I mustered what enthusiasm I could for the idea and handed her my basket of fish. She staggered a bit and gave it back. "Um, I'm watching, remember? I'll let you carry that." Fine.

As John was bagging up some dried fish and a few other items for Tracy to carry, a terrifying flurry of giant wings announced Zesi as she lighted on the railing. She gave me a prolonged hiss while I backed toward the door, and she inspected John's bag. He drew it away and tossed her a small fish from his basket, which she tore and devoured messily. "Zesi, meet Tracy."

Tracy was ecstatic. "Ohhhh!! She's beautiful!" She reached out toward the bird, but John held her back.

"No, not while she's eating. An eagle knows no difference between fish and fingers."

I was glad Zesi had the fish to lacerate instead of me. When the eagle finished, to my amazement John let Tracy hold her. He handed Tracy the leather glove (it went up past her elbow), and Zesi stepped out onto her extended wrist. The eagle bobbed at her, fluffed its head feathers and made chirring noises. I couldn't understand why Zesi didn't tear Tracy's face off. It wasn't fair.

"She weighs less than I would have expected." Tracy stroked its breast feathers while Zesi made sounds not unlike purring.

"I've rarely seen her take to anyone this readily." At John's words, the eagle flapped once and transferred to John's shoulder. He winced under her claws and took the leather glove back from Tracy. "I see I might need a second glove. Ow." Zesi stepped onto John's gloved hand, turned and once again hissed in my direction. "Strange. I've usually found these birds to be a good judge of character. But this one for some reason has a decided dislike for you, Jason. I'm sorry." He tossed the bird into the air, and it drifted out of view. Only then did I venture from the shelter of the doorway.

"The feeling is mutual." I searched the sky, but Zesi wasn't in sight.

"Maybe Jason has something to hide." Tracy gave me a wicked smile. To my relief, John didn't take the bait. He was in a hurry to have us organized and away for a full day of seeking to do the most good. I can't say my heart was in it on our way up the hill.

# 24

As we walked, John told a story. "There was once a woman who was well known in the community for her kindness and thoughtful acts of service. She had a neighbor who was quite the opposite—spiteful, complaining and exacting in all her dealings. An apple tree grew on the border of their properties, with branches hanging over each of their yards. Faithfully every season, the tree bore a heavy burden of crisp, delicious apples.

"Each year, the spiteful woman picked the apples on her side, measuring her property boundary to ensure she missed not one that was hers by right. But, jealous of the unpicked beauties hanging over the other property, each year she shook the branches. Every apple that was her neighbor's fell to the ground.

"Gloating in anticipation, she would watch out her window for her neighbor to come and inspect the damage. With vicious glee, she watched as the kind woman surveyed the apples strewn in the yard, looked toward the cruel woman's house and wept. The kind woman would go to her knees and begin filling boxes with the fallen apples.

"After many years of receiving this injustice, the kind woman died. Because of the promise of a lunch served after the funeral, the cruel woman attended. To her surprise, one person after another came and thanked the cruel woman for her unfailing kindness toward her neighbor. Astounded, she finally asked one of them what he meant by it.

"'Why, it was the apples, of course! You know, the tree you shared,' the man explained. 'You were aware she was terribly afraid of heights, so each year you shook the apples from the tree for her so she could juice them. Many of us enjoyed the fruits of your labor. She often spoke with tears about how much it meant to her!'"

John stopped and looked at us. "Tell me, where do you find love in my story?"

We walked in silence, thinking. Tracy spoke up first. "I don't know. I'm looking but not finding it. I couldn't consider the cruel woman's actions to be love. She didn't know she was doing the other woman a kindness."

"True," I countered, "but I remember you telling me, John, wherever you find love, Jesus is present even when the giver of love isn't aware of him." I stopped, partly as an excuse to set down my basket, still heavy with fish. "Her actions might be acts of love, even if she intended to be cruel."

"Tracy? Thoughts?"

"No, I don't agree. Kind actions aren't necessarily love. She intended to be spiteful, not loving. No one who knew her heart would consider her actions thoughtful."

"John, we're at an impasse. Tell us, what's the point of your story?" I laughed.

"You won't get away that easily. I'm not going to tell you my point. But on our journey today, bring the story to mind as we encounter those in need of what we offer, whether fish or bread or a kind word."

And that was it. I hated it when John refused to explain himself. I was conditioned to instant answers, counting on the first page of Google to be the authority on every perplexing question. Here, I had to think for myself. I found my mind too sluggish to arrive at any satisfactory conclusion. I trudged along behind the two of them like the day before, once again left out of their conversation.

By the time we reached Sophia's house, I had a headache and the beginnings of a bad attitude. The heavy smell of garlic—compounded with unwashed clothing and some obvious problem in the toilet—made me nauseous. I groaned inside as John announced we would spend the better part of the day here. Sophia's aching hips had kept her from her usual fastidious cleaning and laundry, and the untidiness embarrassed her. John assured her we would have her house and wardrobe clean and fresh before we went anywhere that day.

John gave Tracy a lesson on using a washboard and tub. She plunged in with enthusiasm, sending spray and soap suds flying. John tackled the bathroom problem, leaving me to do what I could with a broom, less exuberantly than the others. Sophia kept pointing out the spots I missed. Twice she took the broom from me to attack some corner with vengeance. I couldn't wait to leave. I liked Sophia, but she was demanding. When I had swept to her satisfaction, she took me to the back yard. My previous neat pile of broken branches was already starting to diminish. To my despair, she pointed to a fresh heap ready for me to process. I sighed and made a start to what was a never-ending job.

As I snapped branches over my knee and piled them, I wondered where they came from and how they arrived in her yard. When we took a break to share our lunch with Sophia, I asked John about the branches, and he in turn asked Sophia. "She says she picks them up on her wanderings around the neighborhood. I've seen her do this, one branch at a time, moving at a painful snail's pace."

My heart sank. How could I have such a bad attitude about breaking branches for her—branches that had taken Sophia days to gather? I immediately wanted to go out and collect as many branches as I could find and make a massive pile for her. I asked John about my idea, but he shook his head. "Gathering the branches is something she can still do, and her pace matches the scarcity of firewood. Don't take that from her. The breaking of them is something she can't do, so she's grateful for your help."

He turned to ask Sophia a question, which I guessed was about the day's local gossip. I watched her expressions—animated, excited, angry, tearful—all about stuff she could likely do nothing about. Or could she? Passing this information on to John was doing something. I didn't doubt she would also spend this day in prayer about the news she was telling him. Even with her limitations, Sophia knew how to love in actions and in truth. As for me, I had more to learn.

After lunch, I finished up the branches while Tracy hung the laundry on the line. In the warm breeze that wafted over the hill, the dresses and underwear wouldn't take long to dry. Sophia would be comfortable again, with a clean house and fresh clothing. Tracy set down her basket and sat on my pile of sticks. I smiled at her Marianna wardrobe, hair sticking out of the hasty bun on top of her head and sweaty smudges on her face. She could be any young villager doing a few household tasks. I thought the look was becoming and told her so.

She laughed, "This is your idea of domestic bliss, is it? You the lumberjack and me the homely housewife?"

Oops. "That's not what I meant... I..." Yah, I didn't know what to say. You have to be so careful with your words.

"It's okay; I'm enjoying this. Chores around the house are a novelty to me. At home, I have a lady who comes in once a week, whether the condo needs it or not. Crazy, huh?" She made room for me to sit down, but I sat on a box across from her. "Have you done what John asked? Have you thought about his story and what it means?"

My face fell. "Yes. It means I'm the cruel neighbor."

"Why's that?"

"Because all morning, I didn't want to be here. Sure, I was acting kindly by helping Sophia. But that's just it—everything I did was an act. I felt no kindness in my heart, only resentment." I wanted to tell her that part of the problem came from feeling left out as she got to know John, yet I couldn't do it. "And when I wanted to do something for her that I thought was motivated by love, John told me no. He pointed out that my idea would take something away from Sophia, even when I intended to give." I wiped the sweat from my forehead. "This love thing is way too complicated."

"Well, who says you have to be good at it right away? John has been practicing for two thousand years!"

I couldn't tell if she was serious. I let it pass. "Whatever. He makes me feel like an idiot sometimes."

"Grumpy, grumpy! What's up?"

I didn't reply for a while, sitting and breaking little sticks with my fingers before answering. "John likes you. Everyone likes you, even that stupid bird."

"And this is a problem?" I didn't reply, and after a moment, she continued. "Well, sir, if I didn't know better, I would say you seem to be indulging in some childish self-pity." I sighed and still didn't say anything. Tracy stood. "What do you want me to do about it? Leave?"

I couldn't answer that question.

"Jason, what's going on? Is this about me, or about you?"

"I would have to say yes to both options. It's about you, but it's more about me trying to deal with your arrival in my happy little world."

"Please explain." Tracy's tone was less than friendly.

"Okay. I'm settling into life on Patmos and learning tons from John and the others. It's challenging, but I'm loving it. Then you show up. You try to seduce me; you threaten me with exposure and force me to go along with your pretense. And what's more, I feel left out, and I'm conflicted about not being upfront with John, and I'm proving worse at being a disciple than you. Call it self-pity if you want, but my little world is not happy right now."

"Well, get over it. I'm not ready to go yet. And there are things you're still hiding from me too. I'm going to find out what they are, whether you cooperate or not."

"Hey, loafers!" John breezed around the corner of the house like a zephyr and caught us scowling at one another. "Are we all wrapped up here? Time to move the rest of our fish!" Sophia shuffled into the yard behind him and exclaimed over the firewood pile and full clothesline. We all received double cheek kisses and some small wrapped candies of questionable vintage.

The rest of the afternoon passed pleasantly enough. It was satisfying to recognize the people I had met before and to offer a few words in their language. Tracy was welcomed, kissed and hugged until she looked a bit affection-fatigued. I got over my frustration enough to rejoin the conversation, realizing three could walk together on that road. We must have been quite the sight, the two of us with John towering between. John asked Tracy about her experiences that day as they related to the story he challenged us with earlier.

"I determined right from the start to not do anything that wasn't motivated by love," Tracy told us. "At first—when we arrived at Sophia's house—I didn't think I could do it. I felt degraded and stereotyped when she chose me to do the laundry. Then I... I prayed. I told God how I felt. And right away, a story came to mind from Sunday school days: Jesus washing his disciples' feet. And I figured if the Son of God could lower himself to do that, surely I could..."

She paused because John had stopped on the road and stood with tears pouring down his face. We didn't know what to do. Tracy wrapped her arms around him, and I put a hand on his shoulder. He shook with emotion for several minutes, took in a great breath and let it out slowly.

"My apologies," he sniffed. "Sometimes, memories come back to me vividly..." I could see he was in danger of more tears, so I steered us over to a stone wall where we could sit. When the storm subsided, John told us the memory that triggered his emotions.

"It was Passover. My fellow disciples and I should have been in a merry mood as we looked forward to the feast. But on the way, our ongoing argument bested us again. I may have been the worst, arguing for executive status for myself and my brother when—any day now—Jesus brought in his kingdom. We arrived at the house, and the servant girl was too busy to provide water for our filthy feet. But not one of us would reduce himself to that menial service. We went upstairs, sandals on, feet stinking. Even Jesus. We jostled to the best places around the table. I pulled Judas back to worm my way to Jesus' right side.

"We reclined in silence, glaring at one another and waiting to be served the meal. Jesus stood up and left the table, and we watched in alarm. When he came back upstairs, he was struggling under the weight of a jar of water in one arm and a basin in the other, a towel over his shoulder. He came back to his spot at the table, set them down and asked my brother James for his feet.

"Dead silence filled the room. This was a mockery, a great humiliation. Rabbi Jesus—washing our feet! This was a service not expected of the most base slave, who would only be expected to provide the water and the towel. When Jesus came to Peter, he covered up his legs and voiced what we were all thinking: 'You will never wash my feet!'

"I remember my resentment as Jesus held the feet of Judas, removed his worn sandals and placed his feet in the basin. Judas was a scoundrel—we had no idea how much of one until later—whom we suspected of misappropriating our communal moneybag. In my mind, he was the least deserving of us all. But Jesus took special care with his feet. He looked full in the face of Judas, who sat rigid as a stone, cold and hard as the thirty pieces of silver in his pouch.

"Jesus came last to me. As I looked up at his face, mine fell. Last. I was last. Is this not what he told us often? In my pursuit of being first, I had earned last place. He worked at my sandals, which were all in a knot. Cousin John had said he was unworthy to untie this man's sandals, and now that One was patiently untying mine! Last of all, yet not forsaken. A bruised reed he would not break, a smoldering candle he would not snuff out.

"He took my callused, stinking fisherman's feet in his hands and said nothing. But he looked deep into my eyes, trusting his hands to see for themselves as he washed me. No words passed between us, yet his actions spoke of love unspeakable, even for an ambitious little punk like me. These are the words his eyes said, as near as I can recite them:

"'You will find it hardest tomorrow, young Son of Thunder. You will look on me suspended between earth and heaven and watch my life-giving blood flow down for you. I want you to grow to be an old man, John. Your children will be as many as the stars in the sky, and you will be father to sons and daughters from every nation. You have heard me, you have seen me with your eyes, you have looked upon me and touched me with your hands. You will tell of me again and again and again and again.'"

John's account captivated us. Tears streamed unchecked down Tracy's face, and my own tears were too hot to hold inside. He looked at each of us in turn. "Who can resist such audacious love? That God would become one of us, not to be served as was his right, but to serve and give his life as a ransom for the many..." Tracy took his big fisherman's hand and kissed it. He smiled affectionately at us. "I'm blessed to have such children as you." He stood and beckoned us to follow.

# 25

I was up before dawn the next morning, having not slept well. I was determined to talk with John about my career as a journalist that morning, come what may. It was hardly light enough to see the rain slanting sideways against the house when I brought John a steaming bowl of oatmeal. He rose to fasten the shutters over the windows, which I hadn't thought to do, then wrapped a blanket around him to eat his breakfast.

"I feel the first hints of the coming winter in my old bones," he murmured over his bowl. "It can be unpleasant when the storms arrive."

I sat across from him and poured goat's milk on my porridge. "I believe you. Though I'm sure it's nothing compared to what I'm used to at home. You never have to use a side door because a snowdrift blocks the front one. Or feel your nostrils sticking together as you breathe in the icy air."

"Really? No, that's hard to imagine. I remember seeing snow on the mountains where I grew up. But only a handful of times has snow fallen on Patmos, to my memory." John sat on the edge of the bed, still wrapped in the blanket. "But the damp wind off the sea can find its way to your very heart at times." After we ate in silence for a while, John asked, "What are your plans for the blustery days ahead? When do you return to your snow and ice?"

I let out a long breath. "Soon, I suppose. I'm feeling more ready to get back to Jessica and see what we can work out. But I don't want to leave."

"So I've observed. Neither you nor Tracy have spoken of leaving." My heart raced at his words, but I didn't reply. "There seems to be a quarrel between you."

This was it. The ripe moment to come clean with John. I didn't know how or where to begin. Words burned in my heart, but it was hard to move them to my lips. I needed a moment. "Why do you think that is?"

"She knows you don't trust her. I said we should give her a chance, and I want to offer that same courtesy to you. Tell me, what are your reasons for doubting Tracy's sincerity?"

I took a few moments to form the words. "I do have reasons. But I can't give them to you until I explain why you have reason not to trust me." He glanced up at me. "I haven't been entirely honest with my story." I filled in the gaps, including all the leverage Tracy had against me. Elise. My former career as a freelancer and my current job with the newspaper. The temptation it was to write about John and my experiences here. I ran my hands through my hair and realized I was tense. "I'm what you told me is your worst nightmare."

John didn't say anything, yet I could feel his eyes boring right through me. Exposed. I couldn't believe I did this to myself. Finally, John responded, "I have two questions only. One, why have you not told me this before, and two, why are you telling me now?"

What to say and not do more damage? John wasn't letting me see how he felt about my confession. I decided the best route was straight forward. "On the first day I met you, if I said, 'Hi, I'm Jason. I'm a journalist, and I'd love to write a news article about you,' would you have invited me to 'come and see'?"

"It's never helpful to dwell on what might have happened. I can guess that as you came to know me, you realized your mistake in concealing that part of your identity. You were ashamed to tell me."

"I guess. I told myself I was afraid of hurting you. But honestly, I was afraid of hurting myself."

"And what if I told you that the day I met you at the marina, I sensed you could be a danger to me?" I raised my eyebrows. "I chose to take the risk. My reason for doing this was a stirring of the Holy Spirit of God, who saw you and said to me, 'This one is mine!'"

I closed my eyes. All this time I could have... no, that wasn't fair. All this time, I would have impressed him more with honesty than deception. Looking up, I threw his questions back at him. "Tell me, why have you not told me this before, and why are you telling me now?"

John laughed, which marginally made me feel better. "Well put! What can I say? That your need for redemption outweighed the risk of your discomfiture? For you to come to this point of confession was worth putting up with your pretense these two weeks. It's not been easy for either of us. But this—this is what love does." He held out his hand. "Now we can start over—no more secrets, friends forever. What do you say?"

As I grasped his hand, I felt a surge of freshness, goodness—I'm not sure how to describe it. A tall glass of cold lemonade on a hot, thirsty day. I also found myself pulled from my seat onto the rug on the hard floor. Wrestling John was like wrestling a grizzly bear without the fangs and claws. He let me pin him, only to lift me clear off the ground with one arm and ruffle my hair with the other. We fell back laughing and happily regarded one another.

My eyes dropped. "John, I want you to know—I want to make certain you know—that despite all the lies, I've learned so much here. I was... shallow in my faith, skeptical of you, ignorant of love and what it means to follow Jesus. I have a long way to go, but I'm ever grateful for your patience and all you have taught me, by word and deed."

"You're welcome. Of course, I knew this to be true. Otherwise, I would have sent you packing long ago!" I thought he might be joking. Or not. Anyway, I wasn't going to dwell on what might have happened.

"John, I also want you to know that I'm not going to write about you. You have nothing to fear from me. I'm not here as a journalist, but as your friend."

John shrugged. "Wait and see about that. You may still have something to write. I won't ask you to be someone other than what you are. I'll only love you too much to leave you there."

We were late getting down to the water, and John had doubts about filling our nets. He was right. The few fish we dragged up, John dumped back into the sea. "It seems this day will have a different purpose. We'll give our friends a break from fresh fish." We hung his nets and started back up the hill. I was glad to see that Tracy wasn't waiting for us on the patio, and that I could keep John to myself this day.

"Would you like to do some walking, Jason? I have in mind to make the trek to Kampos, the smaller village to the north. I'm concerned for our friend Antonis. We should confront him and assure him that our offer of help still stands. Should we try it?" I was still pretty mad at Antonis but agreed this was a good plan. We packed our lunch, along with some dried fish and a bag of lemons to give away, and warm cloaks to ward off the drizzle that continued after the storm.

Patmos was a different island on a misty day. The sea and hills were reduced to monochromatic shades. It brought to mind an old *Calvin and Hobbes* cartoon: Calvin's dad is trying to convince him that old photos are in black and white because the world didn't turn color until the 1930s. This was the island we traversed—a world of black and white and gray. We hardly saw Skala as we bypassed the edge of town, and it soon disappeared behind us.

We were in territory new to me. The entire island was seven miles from north to south, less than I drove to church when at home. But walking, this was a long journey, a full day's commitment there and back. I asked, "John, do you ever take a ride in someone's car?" Several had passed us, some with drivers smiling and waving.

"I like walking. It's what I do best. It's good for me, good for this tired earth. I might outlast the world's temporary insanity of burning so much petrol."

That was a thought—to view the era of gas engines as a fad. "You've seen many changes in these past one hundred years."

John shrugged. "Less here than elsewhere, I suppose. Some of it I found fascinating, such as the first time I saw an airplane roar over the island. Of course, I soon learned they were also used to drop explosives on innocent people, and I was less fascinated and more appalled. It's the same with all the creativity of humans. At first, our inventions reflect the awesomeness of our Creator. But the world, the flesh and the devil find a way to twist them to cruel, greedy and perverse purposes. We shouldn't expect otherwise, but it's sometimes disheartening."

"Many innovations have made the world a better place."

"Oh, I don't refute the fact that we cure diseases, increase knowledge and achieve efficiency. It's by the grace of God. Yet I wish the cost of these accomplishments wasn't so disproportionate. We haven't acted as wise stewards of the earth nor represented the values of our Master well. Human suffering increases on a massive scale. Creation groans more deeply than ever before. I sometimes fear her sickness is incurable."

"So, should we give up? Keep exploiting and abusing our planet because it's too late to save it?" I remembered discussions like these in Bible college. "I know many people in my country who believe that all this talk about preserving the environment and fighting climate change is of the devil."

"Who is it that comes to steal, kill and destroy? If these actions are necessary to maintain our lifestyle, we simply emulate the enemy of our souls." John took a detour down a path where we found a young woman toiling in her garden, baby on her back and two more young children piling up the weeds she pulled. She stopped to welcome us and gratefully accepted dried fish and lemons. The children eyed me from a safe distance. But they crawled all over John, examining the contents of his pockets, exclaiming over the treasures they found.

As we continued on our journey, I asked, "Are you saying that our Western lifestyle is of the devil? That's pretty harsh!"

"That is what I know of the history of the West. You appropriate resources that are not your own. You murder or suppress the original inhabitants and destroy their homeland. You seek lower costs for goods by depriving those who produce them for you. You force them into unlivable conditions, polluting their land and sea as well as your own." His voice was bitter. "If that's not Satan's handiwork, I don't know him as well as I thought."

"It's... I don't know; it's how the economy works. I don't see how any of us can change it."

"No, the problem isn't that people are unable to change; it's that they're unwilling to change. What if changing the economic system of the world meant for the West that everything cost more and was less convenient and more complicated?"

"Those wouldn't be strong selling points for most products in my country." Imagine! I smiled as I added, "Starbucks would be an exception." He didn't ask; I didn't explain.

Instead, he continued, "What if you had to lower your standard of living to raise the standard of others? Would you be willing?" I didn't know what to say to that, not honestly. "When your plate is full and the plate across the table from you is empty, there is but one solution. You must take food from your plate and put it on theirs. Our resources are not unlimited. We can be stewards only of what we have."

"I have to admit, I never saw it that way. The solution is...?"

"Love." I guess my reaction showed that I thought his solution idealistic and simplistic. In any case, he was quick to qualify his one-word remedy for the disease of civilization. "Yes, love! Don't scoff. Keep in mind that love is the title at the top of a long list of godly qualities: Compassion. Patience. Consideration. Sacrifice. Mercy. Peace. Kindness. Forgiveness. Self-control. Perseverance. Goodness. Joy. Reliability. Meekness. Tell me that these qualities, in increasing measure, wouldn't make a difference."

"In an ideal world, the meek might inherit the earth. But in the real world, they're eaten alive."

"No doubt. But in the real world, it's the eaten, not the eaters, who ultimately generate true change."

I took a break on a bench by the side of the road. John joined me. "Think of my fellow apostles—every one of them gave their life defending the Gospel. My brother James was the first of us to follow Jesus in that way. Yet through us, the course of history was altered. How? We were 120 simple men and women hiding in an upper room in Jerusalem, fifty days after the death and resurrection of the Messiah. What else were we to do? We watched and prayed—as Jesus instructed us— yet we hardly knew for what we were waiting.

"Suddenly, a noise like a great rushing wind filled the house where we had gathered. Flames, like the fire of Moses' burning bush, rested on each of us, and we proclaimed the good news of Jesus in languages we had never learned."

"The Holy Spirit." Why did saying this make me feel immediately uncomfortable? "I'm not well versed in this concept. I come from a conservative church."

"Concept? The Holy Spirit isn't a concept! He is... well, he is who he is! Like Jesus and the Father, he is God. You and I—we are his temple. Within us he resides, the One-Who-Comes-Alongside. However, it's not surprising when you say you don't know him well. He works patiently within, drawing attention not to himself but to Jesus, the King of kings. But by him, from faith to faith, love flows out of us in all its various forms. His presence is quiet, but his voice is loud." We walked again, and I noticed the fog was lifting through hints of blue sky. "This is the kingdom of God! This is how Jesus will take over the world. How surprised we hotheads were to realize we would be among the first in a kingdom of love!"

How my concept of love was shifting, I realized as we continued in silence. When I first met John, I wouldn't have imagined him to be a man of love. I realized now it was because my idea of love was flawed. Daily I watched this giant of a man—in size and presence—bear my doubts and flaws with great patience. I watched as he gently lifted Myrto's granddaughter to his shoulder, yet he wrested a dying man from the garbage dump. His laughter often erupted from his deep well of joy. He carried heavy baskets of fish, along with mercy and grace, to the most unlikely recipients. He spoke the truth of God into their lives and prayed for them without ceasing. In every way, he gave hands and feet and voice to the love of Jesus for a hurting world. When I first met John, I felt insulted by his insinuation that I was lacking in my understanding of love. But he was so right.

"John," I ventured, "what holds me back? Why am I not like you, as much as I long to be? By the time I make up my mind to act, the opportunity is gone. I never know what to say or how to help. Even when I know the good I could do, I don't do it. Why am I reticent, guarded, ready to sit back and watch rather than do?" As I talked, I heard my voice become more desperate.

John rested his heavy hand on my shoulder, and we walked that way. "I know, Jason. I've seen it, and I as well have wondered." He gave this some thought, and as I waited, my hopes rose. I anticipated the answer, the way to break through the barrier to a more meaningful life. His response was a letdown. "I don't know why, Jason—I don't know you well enough to say how this hesitancy came about." Great. That was disappointing. After a time, he continued. "One thing I can say with certainty: what is currently in the way is you."

A therapeutic counselor, John wouldn't make. "What? You're saying I'm the problem? How is that... helpful or encouraging? You might as well tell me to get myself out of the damn way! To go take a long walk on a short pier!"

"Yes, something like that."

I was speechless. So much for love. "John," I stopped on the road, exasperated, "you need to help me out! What on earth are you saying to me?"

We happened to be walking near a long beach at the head of a narrow bay. John detoured down to the sand, searching and soon finding near the water a small snail shell. He picked it up and tapped on it gently. In a moment, its resident emerged, wielding tiny but snapping claws. "He's a hermit crab," John told me. "This old shell is his home, which he carries about with him."

The crab had enough of us and squeezed back out of sight. I tried to anticipate John's analogy. "He carries around his shell like I carry around my social and emotional baggage, which holds me back from being the person I could be. Right?"

John sighed and put the shell in my hand. "You seem determined to place the blame outside of yourself. Why is that?" I didn't know how to answer, so he continued. "This little fellow sought a place to dwell. He wandered the beach, where he found many snail shells. But they were still alive, still full of snail. He continued his search until he found this one. The snail inside was dead, the shell washed clean, and our little friend was delighted to make his home in it." He looked at me. "Jason, you're not the hermit crab; you're the snail shell. And you are so full of you, there is little room for God."

I was confused. Of course I was full of me. What else could I be? "How is it bad that I'm full of me? God made me, gave me abilities and talents, dreams and ambitions. I've put my faith in him. What more does he want? Does he consider me worthless? am I in his way? I'm afraid I don't understand you at all this time."

"Worthless? No, how could you imagine you're worthless after the enormous price he paid to redeem you? My friend Peter wrote that you were not redeemed with transitory wealth but with the eternal precious blood of the Lamb of God. Imagine! That is the price tag placed on you. You're priceless, of infinite worth!"

"Then why does God want me out of the way so he can move in, like the hermit crab?" I set the shell back on the sand. After a few moments, the crab stuck out its legs and shuffled toward the water, his home on his back. John and I resumed our walk down the beach.

"Remember the call of Jesus to those who would be his disciples. If anyone would come after me, he said, that person must deny himself, take up his cross and follow me. The call to follow Jesus is a call to die!"

"I always assumed he meant martyrdom, or at least to be willing to die for him."

"If that were the case, I'm exempt. But here I am, still alive! Yet dead nonetheless." John became animated. "Do you see? Jesus spoke of a kernel of wheat, how unless it falls to the ground and dies, it remains what it is—a kernel of wheat. But when it dies, it produces many kernels." I struggled to keep up with him, both mentally and with the quicker pace of his long legs. "Yes, Jesus said this to show why he needed to die. But he spoke this truth about us as well. As long as we cling to the life we have, our life is all we will ever have. But if we die… well! There is no telling what crop we might produce! Do you see?"

"I wish I could say yes. Sorry, John, but I can't follow your wheat kernel analogy. I hardly grasped the crab idea. Would you please tell me what you want me to do?"

At that moment, we emerged from a narrow beach trail back onto the main road and encountered someone heading back the way we had come. We all stopped and stared, astonished.

"Tracy!" I exclaimed. "What on earth are you doing here?"

# 26

Tracy looked flustered. "Uh, I'm... What are *you* doing here?" She fumbled with the camera bag on her back, tried to close it up and set it on the ground. "I'm out exploring..." she started. More to herself, she muttered, "And trying to find someone I met before... this is bizarre." Whatever Tracy was up to, seeing us rattled her.

John broke through the awkwardness and hugged her. "Good to see you, Tracy. We're doing the same as you— exploring and seeking an old acquaintance. Were you successful?"

"Well, no. At least not in finding this guy... Who are you looking for?"

John looked at me. "It's this fellow I met in Skala," I began, noticing she didn't manage eye contact. "He's one of the locals, a bit of a scoundrel. But we're trying to help him. His name is Antonis."

That sent a shock wave through Tracy. Dissembling, she looked at something on her phone and replied, "Um, that's interesting. Because I'm also looking for Antonis." She looked up. "He doesn't seem to be here. I checked everywhere, and it's a small town."

"How did you meet Antonis?" I tried to keep it light but couldn't avoid an edge of incredulity in my voice.

"It was before I met you, at the market in Skala. He didn't seem a reliable source, as you would know, but I asked him to keep an eye open for me. I'm sure you would have done the same."

Something was missing. "Why are you trying to find him now?"

She didn't like my question. With a defiant glare, she answered, "To tell him not to bother. He's a persistent little chap, especially when there's something in it for him. I didn't want him stirring up trouble for John." We stared each other down for a moment. I broke first, and she smiled. "Is the interrogation over?"

"Tracy, I..."

"It's okay; I wouldn't trust me either." She picked up her bag, which was full of gear. "I have a long walk ahead since I don't want to offend anyone by hailing a ride. If you don't mind, I will be on my way."

I had nothing to say. But she gave John a quick hug before continuing down the road toward Skala. John wanted to go to Kampos even if Antonis wasn't there, and we walked in silence for a time. Finally, John offered, "You told me this morning that you have reasons not to trust Tracy. Are you ready to speak them, with grace?"

"I want to trust her, but it's difficult. I wish I knew what's going on in her mind." Why the camera bag? What was she up to? "I suspect that she's still chasing the story she told everyone she wouldn't."

"Love trusts and, if necessary, forgives. But it's not naïve. Let her prove herself, one way or another. I'm not afraid of her." What could I say? I had no choice but to take his advice, as disagreeable as it was to me. We walked up a steeper road through a valley. This was the greenest place I had seen on the island. I loved the many fruit trees and small vegetable gardens among the clusters of white houses. Imagine living in a place like this! I wondered how Jessica would manage here.

"Let's return to our previous discussion," John began. "I like your question, 'What do I need to do?' Many people, trying to please God, focus on a list of what they take pride in *not* doing. The religious elite in my younger years were champions of 'what not to do,' but they still failed at righteousness.

"Your question reminds me of the young man who sought an audience with Jesus. His question was similar: 'What must I do to inherit eternal life?' Jesus tested his resolve with the Ten Commandments—do this and don't do that. But the man was insightful and knew this wasn't enough. Jesus explained what would make him perfect. 'Go and sell all you have and give it to the poor,' he told him. 'Then come and follow me.' It was a gracious offer on Jesus' part, since many at that time clamored to be one of his disciples. But it was too much for this young man. He went away with a downcast face, his wealth a coffin hanging around his neck."

"Okay, I know the story. What does it have to do with the snail shell analogy or your death wish for me?"

"Wealth is material, but in this man's case, wealth had become quarantine. He had wrapped up all his identity in it—the man was a living bag of money. Jesus saw his dilemma and said, This has to die. Once washed clean of his wealth, there would be room in the fellow for me to bring new life." We stopped to catch our breath at the top of the hill. "Jason, who are you? What is your true essence? If you stood before Jesus, what would he tell you is the one thing that needs to die?"

Something came to mind immediately, but I wasn't ready to say it. "Can I get back to you on that one?"

"Of course!" John smiled. "But are you beginning to understand? One cannot follow Jesus without leaving his own life behind. And one cannot find his life without following Jesus."

"It's pretty mind-bending stuff, John. This will take time to process."

"How are you doing with reading through my Gospel?"

"I haven't read any of it these past few days. But I have read it through once. I'm going back over it more intently now."

"Good, good. May the Holy Spirit rest on your shoulder as you read! It's his word, not mine. Every time I look at it again, he reveals new wonders I never saw before."

We had arrived in what I guessed was the center of town, judging by a few commercial buildings strung along the road. No one at the *taverna* had seen Antonis that day. We ordered coffees at the *kafe* next door. A tall, dark man joined us at our table, and he and John talked fishing for a while. Unable to follow their conversation, I excused myself and wandered the street. There was little to see—a church, small hotels, a school—and few people were out in the heat of the day. But my thoughts were full, so I was glad for few distractions.

My conversation with John pinpointed the problem between me and Jessica. I had my life, she had hers, and there was no way either of us was about to relax our grip. Not only did we not surrender ourselves to God, we never surrendered to one another, no matter what vows we blubbered at our wedding. There were many clashes, and many times we went our separate ways, doing our own thing.

At the same time, I was always trying to impress Jessica. Our activities took the form of a competition to see who could do the more significant or smart or extravagant or adventurous or practical or daring thing. I hoped to win the approval of someone with glaringly different interests and values than me. It was always a struggle.

I remembered her reaction when I used my tax return and some of our savings to buy a motorbike. I knew she used to ride when she was younger, and she liked bikes. But she rolled her eyes at the idea of me having one. "Why, Jason?" I could hear her derision. "You, a biker? Why didn't you get that canoe you were talking about? I might have gotten into that. I'm for sure not riding behind you on that bike."

Jessica knew the real me. She daily witnessed my stupid attempts to be the guy I tried to pose, and she hated that guy. Rightly so. I was so full of that guy, there was no room for God. No room for Jessica. No room for the real me. I did it for a reward that was always out of reach, a carrot on a stick. My futile pursuit damaged not only me and my faith in God. I greatly regretted that I was also such a bad example to Jessica and many others in my life. I put on a great masquerade, but surely everyone could see there was no substance behind my words. So Jessica and I drifted away from God and from one another.

As I walked through a cluster of houses on the brow of a hill, I had the strange sensation of being watched. That wouldn't be unusual, being a stranger, but the street was empty. I once caught a flicker of movement out of the corner of my eye between two buildings. But when I looked, there was no one. John wasn't at the *kafe* when I returned. The proprietor pointed out a grocery store down the street where I would find my friend.

He bought a few small supplies he said were better quality than what Skala offered, and we started back. "I guess it was the waste of a trip," I commented on our way down the valley.

"Not what we expected, but never a waste," John replied. "I'm disappointed that we didn't find Antonis, yet not surprised. He doesn't want to be found. In the meantime, we enjoyed good conversation and blessed a few people on the way. Did you have some other pressing engagement today?"

I chuckled. "Not at all! I was glad to have you to myself today. I didn't mind when Tracy stormed off and didn't join us."

"Why is that?"

I was flustered about having said it out loud. "Well, I'm finding it hard, watching Tracy receive all this attention from you and Manos and Marianna—even that crazy bird! And I still find it difficult to believe she's a hundred percent genuine about being a believer and all. How do you know she's not faking it?"

"I could ask the same about you.'

"Granted. But in any case, it was nice to spend the day with just you and me. Sometimes, Tracy is hard to take."

"Again, you could be describing yourself. Think, Jason— why do you feel this way about Tracy? What's at the core of your attitude?"

John was praying for me as he spoke, I guess, because insight flooded me like a tsunami. I saw Antonis in the gutter and me weeping and confessing over him that he was my younger brother, the wastrel son I had resented. All at once, I saw that I was doing the same with Tracy. The prodigal daughter had come home. I was the older brother, questioning why we were slaying the fatted calf for her.

"John, I'm so embarrassed." I told him my thoughts, which of course he already knew.

"Embarrassment won't cut it. All you're saying is that you're distressed about getting caught with your jealousy against Tracy. What would it mean for you to confess this sin?"

"I'm not sure. Ask for forgiveness?"

"Still not enough! Why should anyone forgive you? What prompts forgiveness?"

214

I had never thought about that before. "Um, remorse? Feeling sorry for what I did?"

"More on target, but not the center yet. Feeling guilty isn't the same as confession."

"Is this a test?"

"Yes. Thus far, you haven't achieved a passing grade. But I have high hopes for you. Come now, we'll find something to which you can relate. What got you into trouble as a child?"

"That's easy. Next to my bedroom in the basement was a large freezer. My mom used to bake cookies, freeze them and store them in ice cream buckets. I was in trouble because she would go to the freezer for cookies and the bucket would be half empty. I was guilty as charged."

"Perfect. Let's say you felt remorseful about taking the cookies and wanted her forgiveness. What does she want to hear from you?"

"That I was the one who swiped the cookies."

"Good! What else?"

"Thaaat... I realize how frustrating it must be when she expects cookies and finds none."

"Yes! Well done! And...?"

"That I won't do it anymore."

"A promise you won't keep. What if instead you told her that you hoped not to disappoint her anymore?"

"Yeah, she would have appreciated that. This is what it means to confess my sin?"

"And if you do, God is faithful and right to forgive your sin and to cleanse you from all wrongdoing, to quote myself!" John laughed. "To confess is to agree with God about our sin—to say we're guilty, it was wrong and inexcusable—and to affirm that we don't want to do it anymore."

"You're right. That's more than feeling embarrassed. Let me apply this to my jealousy of Tracy and see if I have it right. First, I go to Tracy and..."

"Why to Tracy?"

"Well, because she's the one I sinned against..."

"Wrong!" He frowned at me. "You forget your previous lessons!"

"Help me out, John."

"Do you remember discussing the story of King David, when he took Bathsheba and had her husband killed?"

"Right. Now I remember. He said his sin was against God, not Bathsheba."

"Yes, and no. He had sinned against Bathsheba and Uriah too. But David understood that our sin is first of all against God. Why is this an important distinction?"

I thought back to John's beautiful and dreadful description of Jesus on the cross. "I guess because our sin affects him more than anyone."

"True, but we need to take a step back and see the larger picture. How is any action determined to be sinful?"

"In my society, people would say no one can tell them if their action is right or wrong. They alone determine this for themselves."

"And how is that working out for them?"

"Not well. It's because that view doesn't take into account the effect of our actions on others. I could decide for myself that abortion isn't a sin. But if the unborn child had a voice in the matter, what would they say?"

"Determining what is right and wrong, true and false, acceptable and despicable—it's a complicated task. When we take that responsibility on ourselves, failure is inevitable. The true and reliable measure of righteousness is God himself.

What is right and wrong in the universe is determined by his nature and character. That's why all sin is against him—it's against who he is."

"Okay, I understand that. I go to God and tell him I'm jealous of Tracy, like the older brother in the prodigal story. It's wrong because I care more about feeling left out than I do about encouraging Tracy's newly confessed faith. And I want to stop being such an idiot and accept her instead. Does that work?"

"If it's from your heart, it's music to my ears!" John smiled.

"My heart still lags behind a bit. But it's catching up."

"Your heart will catch up when you talk with Tracy. Even in confession, faith in God is expressed through action."

"Right. But I'm more afraid of admitting this to Tracy than to God."

We walked through Skala on the way back and stopped in to see Myrto. John seemed concerned about what she told him, but he didn't translate for me. Her granddaughter attempted to teach me a clapping game, which I was slow to learn. She was patient at first. But when I got the rhythm wrong the fourth time in a row, she went back to her grandmother's lap, crossed her tiny arms and frowned at me. I bought a ripe mango at a nearby stand, and thankfully, sharing it together brought her smile back.

As we left town, John asked, "Tell me, have you given thought to the one thing you need to let die, as I asked you earlier?"

"I have." I stopped to think about how to put it. "What needs to die is my need for recognition and approval. I want people to like me, to see me and appreciate my accomplishments. I want to be widely known, impressive, influential. When that thought immediately came to mind, I didn't want to tell you. I'm reluctant to let it go, as much as I know it hurts me and everyone around me."

"As was the rich young man reluctant to let go of his wealth. But this is interesting—I find in you a kindred spirit. When I first took you on, I saw myself in you. In my younger years, I also struggled with that very problem. Can you believe I asked my mother to go to Jesus and convince him to make princes out of my brother James and me when he came into his kingdom? I still blush to think of it! Recognition and approval were of such value to me, they might have disqualified me as a disciple. My arrogance damaged my rapport with my fellow disciples. It was our chief argument as we straggled along behind Jesus—who was the greatest of us all. And I was the most adamant!"

"Knowing you now, I find that surprising."

"Much has changed. The Father finally rooted out my arrogance by making recognition dangerous for me, both then and now. I'm not sure I would have had the moral fortitude to change from within. It required an external inducement to form my heart, like a clay pot in the hands of the potter."

"What do you think it will take for me?"

Once again, that weighty hand was on my shoulder. "I wish I knew, Jason. But I'm certain it will begin here on the island. This may be why you came. I will be here for you when it happens."

John's words were both comforting and disconcerting. A phrase came to mind: "Pride comes before the... fall." I wasn't too keen on falling. "Thank you, John. Much is changing for me too. I'm grateful for your grace and patience with me."

"And I for your friendship, Jason. More than you know." We ascended the hill out of Skala, the sky turning crimson before us. My heart was too full for words.

# 27

Once I was right with God, I was ready to take my heart the rest of the way and make it right with Tracy. John gave me a basket with some larger fish we caught that morning to go in Manos' freezer. He left on his rounds, and I made my way up the hill.

On the way, I rehearsed what I wanted to tell Tracy, changing it ten times. I wish now I had instead prayed my way there, but by the time I reached the door, I felt ready to make my confession. Marianna and I did the cheek kiss thing like experts now. I laughed inside, remembering my first clumsy attempt, which felt like months ago. With Tracy, it was still awkward—the butterfly kiss was something we would never do in the States—so I hugged her. She felt tense, and I guess she had good reason to be reserved with me.

"Tracy, can we go for a walk?" She nodded and got ready while I helped Marianna put the fish in the freezer. Tracy and I wandered down to the marina, hardly talking, and sat on the patio with a couple of coffees.

"What's the occasion, Jason?" she asked unenthusiastically.

I put it right out there. "I've been a jerk toward you, and I want to change."

Her eyebrows went up. "Tell me more!"

I did. The whole prodigal son story, with myself as the resentful older brother. How jealousy kept me from encouraging her in her exploration of faith; how I resented her stay at Manos and Marianna's and her participation in the community that gathered there. "And about yesterday, it was none of my business what you were doing in Kampos. It was wrong for me to pry. I hope you'll forgive me."

She looked at me, unsmiling. "I don't know whether to believe you. Why tell me you were jealous? And what am I supposed to do about it?" She set her cup down. "You still want to get rid of me, don't you."

I shouldn't have assumed she would simply forgive me. Or trust me. "I would prefer you weren't here, for the sake of my friends. But no, I'm not trying to get rid of you."

"Tell me why you're so protective of your friends, and I'll get on the next ferry."

"You know why. They believe—and I believe—he's the Apostle."

"So what? I'm sure you're wrong. Or delusional. And anyway, you have no proof. Nobody would ever believe it. Not even if he spoke a hundred languages and walked to the Mainland for the cameras."

In my mind, I pictured Manos' photo album, going all the way through the past to black and whites of my friend John before Manos was born. The man who hadn't changed a bit in all those many years. Pausing was my big mistake. I should have immediately replied, "Of course not!"

She instantly picked up on my momentary silence. "You don't, do you? Like, have any proof that John is the Apostle?" I looked up at her, appalled that I couldn't hide my desperation. "You do!" She sat back, smiling. "Well, well. And here I took you for a total dupe."

I stood to go. I was so angry with myself, horrified at what I had just betrayed without speaking a word. Before I gave Tracy anything else to go on, I walked away.

"I'm going to find it, you know!" Tracy called after me. "You could save me the trouble…" I rounded the corner and was gone.

For a time, I walked blindly, berating myself with every synonym for "idiot" I could conjure. But as I replayed that brief conversation in my mind, my divulgence seemed almost inevitable. Five seconds of silence told Tracy everything. Well, not quite. She knew there was evidence, but she didn't know in what form.

I decided to walk about and see if I could find John. I had to warn him about Tracy. And confess my blunder. I found myself in the vicinity of Sophia's home and turned off the road down the narrow path to her house. Imagine—a house with no driveway! I could handle having no need for a vehicle. Jessica loved her late-model BMW—that would be a hard sell.

Unable to bring myself to walk right in with a greeting as John would, I raised my hand to knock on the door. I stopped when I heard a man's voice inside, but it wasn't John. Through the window, I saw Sophia sitting at the table with a cold expression on her gentle face. Across from her, lounging back in his chair and dragging on a cigarette, was Antonis.

I didn't hesitate. Swinging open the door, I walked in with no greeting at all. Sophia looked relieved; Antonis rose up in surprise. "You! Little holy man! What you do here?" He sat down again, but like an animal ready to fight or flee. It must have been the expression on my face that cautioned him.

"Sophia, are you okay?" Of course, she didn't understand me, but I crouched in front of her and held her hands. She looked at me, a tear forming in one eye, and said, "*Kalá, kalá.*"

"See? She say all good, no worries!" Antonis exclaimed. He took a long pull on his cigarette and blew it in my direction.

"She doesn't look okay. What are you doing here?" No grace in my voice this time.

"I ask you first."

"Sophia is a friend. I came to see if she needs any help."

"Yes! Same me. But she is momma of my friend. May he rest in peace!"

"The man who died last week? You were his friend?" I said bitterly. "Were you one of the friends who left him in the garbage dump to die?"

Antonis looked at me with no pretense of friendliness. "I not sure what you say. I not like how you say it."

"You should leave now. With your hands empty."

Antonis laughed dryly. "Hey, not helpful to Antonis today! I should teach you. But no upset the dear momma." He stood, I stood, and we stared one another down. Something in the back of my mind warned me of my danger, but I was too furious to pay attention. Antonis broke first, grabbed his hat off the table and went out the door. Before he left, he leaned back in and said something to Sophia. His tone didn't sound threatening but the words must have been, from the look on her face. He slammed the door behind him.

I rushed to Sophia and, kneeling, held her close. She collapsed into my arms, weeping with great heaves of her little body. After a while, she calmed. She sat back and kissed me on the forehead. "*Efcharistó, sas efcharistó.*" Telling her she was welcome was as far as my Greek would take me. I couldn't find out from her why Antonis was there or what threat he was to her. Should I seek out John right away? What if Antonis returned while I was gone? I stayed and held her hands, listening to the pouring out of her heart that I couldn't understand.

"Sophia," I attempted. "*Iohannes? Edó?*" She shook her head. No, John hadn't been by to see her today. He might still come. Sophia puttered around her kitchen, offering me a share of the little she had. The day was turning to dusk, and John hadn't yet come. But I could do no good by staying. Even if Antonis returned, I was no match for him. John would be on his way home, if not home already. I needed to fetch him. I explained my plan to Sophia as best I could, and she again was relieved, so she must have understood. Kissing her cheek, I went out into the growing dark.

When I came to the road, I stopped and listened. I heard no footsteps in the gravel, no voices. Only a lonely nightbird with its repeated single call, like a smoke detector with a failing battery. Still listening, I heard another call further off, slightly higher pitched. Not a lonely bird after all. But the road was quiet and deserted.

Apprehension dogged my journey home. I jumped every time a branch brushed my shoulder. Each large rock and mailbox was a crouching marauder until I ventured closer. I was greatly relieved to see a single light as I made my way down the path to John's house. He was home.

"There you are! I was starting to wonder." As I came into the light, John saw my expression. "Whatever is the matter?" I told him about my encounter with Antonis at Sophia's house, and his face became serious. "The Spirit sent you to Sophia in her deepest need for protection. I must go to her at once, or she will never sleep tonight." I rose to go with him, but he asked me to stay. "I may have to spend the night. Accommodating the two of us would distress her. Find what you can for your dinner." And he was gone.

When John left, I began to shake. I guess it was the release of the tension from my confrontation with Tracy and from standing up to Antonis. And from watching for danger on my dark journey home. I prayed for John, for Sophia and—by the grace of God—for Tracy and Antonis. As I prayed, the trembling became intermittent and stilled. I was exhausted. What a day! Nothing in John's small larder whet my appetite, and in the end, I cooked up a bowl of oatmeal and stirred in a couple of chopped-up figs.

Sitting on the patio with the last light fading from the horizon, I wondered if Tracy was the reason Antonis showed up at Sophia's. I sure hoped not. That would be hard to forgive. Tracy was a work in progress, and I didn't know if I had the patience for her. But I thought about John and his perseverance with me. I too was a work in progress. Was the older brother indeed the one closest to the heart of God, or was it the prodigal?

I had my own prodigal to consider. Jessica was also a work in progress, and I longed for the opportunity to continue with her on her journey. I knew I was incapable of "fixing" her; all my years of trying did more damage than good. Would she give me the chance to be her encourager rather than her critic, her example instead of the hypocrite I had been? Would she be patient enough to "come and see" what I had learned about following Jesus? I knew only one way to achieve what I desired. I prayed for Jessica with all my aching heart until exhaustion finally won.

I must have slept in my chair. When I came to myself, the candle had blown or burned out. The patio was inky black. I could no longer see my hands in front of my face, and the sky was starless. Even the crickets were still that night. I groped about until I found a new candle and the matches. But once I had them, I was reluctant to chase away this utter darkness. It was comforting not to have to see or to know or to do. I lay on my mattress and looked up into nothing until nothing gave way to sleep.

I awoke to a gray dawn, gentle rain falling and the scent of ozone and damp grass. John hadn't returned, so he must have deemed it necessary to stay the night at Sophia's. I wondered what he had found out about Antonis and his threat. Weary of plain oatmeal, I tried stirring in some crumbled smoked fish. Yeah, not great. I ate it anyway. I thought about trying my hand at fishing on my own, but my curiosity about Antonis was too pressing. Taking the rest of the smoked fish with me, I started up the path toward Sophia's house.

# 28

John wasn't at Sophia's house at that early hour. I understood from Sophia's gestures that she expected his return and would like me to stay. We drank weak tea and did our best with the usual awkward conversation, which was mostly non-verbal. I broke and stacked the few branches in her back yard. She either didn't understand when I asked what other ways I could help her, or she was too distracted. Sophia sat at the table, looking out the small window, letting her anxious expression give way to a wan smile when she looked at me.

I took Sophia's hands, bowed my head over them and prayed. "Father, I place before you this godly woman and the threat that hangs over her. Whatever John is doing right now, please make it successful. Bring peace to this home. Bring peace and joy back into Sophia's heart. As for Antonis..." Sophia's hands tightened on mine when I said his name. "...soften his hard heart and work against his selfish ambitions until he turns toward home and you." I continued for several minutes, Sophia adding her "*Amín*" in trust of the words she couldn't understand.

Sophia prayed as well, whispering at first, then louder, defiant. The power of this little woman in prayer amazed me. I wouldn't want to be Antonis, on the wrong end of her petitions to God! But she began to weep, "Antonis! Antonis!" her voice pleading. I realized she was praying for him, not against him, despite his intrigues. Her battle wasn't against flesh and blood.

When she finished, she looked up at me, face beaming. "*Efcharistó! Alliloúia!*" I was glad to be a small part of raising Sophia's spirits and quelling her fears. It reminded me again of the power of our faith in Jesus. Even the oppressed are victors. We can be still and know he is God; stop struggling and recognize that he's fighting for us.

Sitting in the shack that Sophia called home, seeing her joy in the face of trouble, I had to wonder about my way of life, my discontented consumerism, and my complaints about first-world problems. It was hard to imagine how to take what Sophia had and translate it into life at home. Shopping was Jessica's favorite pastime. I was more inclined to research what I wanted and use the self-checkout when I picked up something at a big box store. We accumulated so much in the few years we were married. I would let it all go if I could just keep Jessica.

John showed up as we sat down for lunch. Sophia marinated the smoked fish I brought and broke it into a mixture of olive oil, spices and capers. She piled this on tiny pieces of hard bread, more like appetizers than lunch, but they tasted fantastic. John added cucumbers and fruit to the meal, and it was enough for the three of us.

After lunch, John talked with Sophia while she responded with nods and exclamations. As we left, it was reassuring to see her relief and gratitude. "Sophia has nothing more to fear from Antonis," John explained to me as we walked toward home. "He has relinquished the hold he had on her. Please don't ask me what it was—it's best you don't know. Once again, you'll have to trust me, my friend."

John stopped as we reached the path to his house. "The person I'm most concerned about now is you. Antonis wasn't happy about your interference, as he called it. He told me to keep my eye on you because he won't let you off easily next time he sees you. It wasn't an idle threat. It may mean it's becoming too dangerous for you to stay on Patmos."

"Seriously? After I tried to help him and called him my brother? Because I tried to help an elderly woman? That's a bit of an overreaction, wouldn't you say?"

"Most of what Antonis says and does are overreactions. We will have to consider. The time may have come for you to leave the island. I will be sorry to see you go, but I can't expect you to live here forever, like me." John smiled and did the hair-ruffling thing that was his form of affection for me, that I wouldn't tolerate from anyone but him.

The thought of leaving distressed me. I loved being with John—both the joy and the challenge. I felt I was making good progress toward being a man of God like him. The community I had come to love here would be a significant loss, and all because of that rat, Antonis. It wasn't fair. Just the same, I knew it was time to go back to Jessica. On my return, I would seek to be the man of God I was meant to be, whether with Jess or… without. I didn't want it to be without her.

Being mid-afternoon, we decided to visit Manos and Marianna. We found them at their individual tasks. Manos was in the garden. Marianna demonstrated for us the weaving of a rug, and Tracy was on the bench overlooking the sea, reading. When I joined her, she held up her hand for me to let her finish. Tracy had Manos' old King James Bible and was reading the first letter of John. When she finished, she closed the book and sighed.

"Is this a homework assignment?" I asked, taking the Bible from her.

"Yes. I'm to gain assurance of my faith in Jesus by reading this letter from John to I-don't-know-who. Something like that. Google Translate only takes us so far."

"And how is the assurance going?"

"I find the bar set quite high. Apparently, I should walk like Jesus and never sin." She found the places to which she was referring. "See? I can assure you, I'm as much a sinner as ever."

"Hmm. When I run into stuff like that, I ask John. Most often, I discover I have it all wrong. Not surprising when we're trying to understand a two-thousand-year-old book, translated four hundred years ago."

"Yeah, it's Shakespeare class all over again. Hasn't anybody bothered to translate this more recently?"

"Here, give me your phone." I searched for a Bible app and downloaded it, borrowing her thumb for the verification. I showed her the dozens of English translations, not to mention other languages. It felt strange to use a smartphone again. I found I didn't miss it.

"Yikes! Too many options! Which one do you suggest?"

"I grew up with this one, the New International Version. You'll like it—it has gender-inclusive language. See? It addresses 'brothers and sisters' instead of the generic 'brothers.'

"And that's okay?"

"I guess. Ask John."

"He's your one-stop source for everything Bible, huh?"

"Why wouldn't he be?"

"You're pretty certain he's the Apostle John, aren't you?"

"You know I am. You would be too if you spent as much time with him as I have. Sadly, it seems my stay here is coming to a close."

She sat up. "Why's that?"

"John thinks it may be time for me to leave." She asked the question with her eyes. "Antonis threatened me. Because I stood up to him at Sophia's house."

Tracy didn't answer right away and looked uncomfortable. "What was he doing at Sophia's?"

"I would like to know that myself. John knows but won't tell me. Don't deal with Antonis anymore, Tracy. He can't be trusted."

"Don't tell me what to do. I was trying to find him to call him off. I don't trust him either!" Tracy's eyes flashed, and I realized she would be a formidable adversary. "Antonis' threat has nothing to do with me."

"Tracy, I'm not your enemy."

"Neither are you my friend. You're still holding out on me."

"I wouldn't be acting as a friend if I told you everything I know. It wouldn't do you—or anyone—a bit of good. Please, Tracy, let it be."

"I've pondered what form of proof you might have…" Tracy smiled as I tensed to leave the bench. "It couldn't be empirical evidence, unless it was some form of DNA analysis. Very unlikely. So that means historical evidence."

"Tracy, I'm not going to…"

"Oh, it's fine. You don't have to. I'll still figure it out on my own. The very idea that there's proof of John's identity somewhere on this island is enough to fuel me for days." She laughed lightly at my distressed look. "What do you care? You're just a tourist!"

"Not anymore. These people are family to me now. I'll do whatever is needed to protect them." Tracy looked impressed with my assertiveness. Not that I cared. She picked up the Bible to examine it further, and neither of us said anything for a while. I may have drifted off, because I was startled when the bench beside me dropped a quarter-inch under a heavy weight. John.

"You're reading my mail!" John took the open Bible from Tracy's lap. "Has my letter made your joy full, as I intended? Or sleepy?"

"Hey, John." I scrambled for a chance to clear my head. "It's the warm sun making us sleepy. But Tracy had a question for you."

John looked at Tracy expectantly. She also needed a moment and opened the Bible app on her phone. "Um, what about this: 'No one who lives in him keeps on sinning. Anyone who keeps on sinning has neither seen him nor known him.' Hey, that's different from what I read in the book. Can I see that?" John handed her the Bible, and she found the same spot. "This one says, 'Whosoever abideth in him sinneth not: whosoever sinneth hath not seen him, neither known him.' That's quite a difference! Which one is right?"

John took on his teacher tone. "In the time when King James' scholars completed their translation, Galileo was trying to convince the church that Earth orbits the sun. That was ages ago. The translators did a good job with the resources they had for their day." I loved to hear John talk about his perspective on world history. "But their misunderstanding of the aorist tense has proved a stumbling block for people of the West ever since. Entire movements have hinged on the notion that followers of Jesus should never sin. The boasting about their extraordinary holiness is the greatest sin of all.

"Now you see, Tracy, in this more current and informed translation, it's a lifestyle of unrepentant sin that exposes the false believer. Did I not write earlier that the person who says he never sins is, ironically, a liar? He deceives himself. We all sin every day, and every day we confess and find forgiveness. Salvation by grace, not sinless perfection, is what sets us swimmers apart from a world drowning in sin."

"Yeah, that's helpful. Jason said you would clear it all up for me. Being the Apostle and all." She looked at him curiously, weighing the words she had said.

John laughed. I enjoyed his laugh. "Jason needs to remember I don't claim access to two thousand years of knowledge. I'm sure it exists in this large head of mine, but most of it rots on the shelves."

"Understandable," I countered, "but you haven't spent the last 2000 years with your head in the sand. You know of Galileo and King James."

"I would have enjoyed meeting Galileo. From what I heard of him, he sounded fascinating. King James, not so much."

During this exchange, Tracy looked from one to the other of us with a bit of a dazed expression. "Tracy," John chuckled, "it's okay for you not to know what to make of me. I don't expect you to extend your mind so far. You can take me for a quack for as long as you need."

"It's not that I don't think highly of you, John! But I can't..."

"And I'm fine with that. My age makes little difference in the here and now, true?"

Tracy sighed. I could imagine what was going through her journalistic mind. Did it matter to her whether the person sitting next to us was an ordinary guy or the Apostle John? No doubt she was still conjuring how to tell the world about the week she spent with a two-thousand-year-old man who had literally walked with Jesus. I vowed to make sure she never had the opportunity.

John stood. "Jason, before Marianna insists on feeding us dinner, we should be on our way." As we walked to the house, John turned back and called to Tracy. "We'll be occupied for the next couple of days, so we will see you here Saturday evening at our gathering. May the Father guide your thoughts and overcome all your fears!" She smiled and waved.

Walking away from Manos and Marianna's, I had sudden apprehensions about Tracy staying in the same house as the photo album. We walked a hundred yards, and I stopped. "John, I'll meet you at home. There's something I need to do." He looked at me questioningly, then turned and continued up the hill.

I jogged back to the house and came by way of the patio. Through the French doors, I saw Tracy talking animatedly with Manos, and my heart raced. As I entered, Tracy froze in her attempt to communicate with Manos and cast me a guilty look. Manos' face was set and icy. Marianna in the background had her apron to her face.

"What are you doing, Tracy?" I wasn't polite.

"I thought you left. Manos is pretending he doesn't know what I'm asking, but he's not fooling me. He has old photos, doesn't he?" She was reading my face. "Photos from his childhood of a man who looked the same then as he does now. Correct?"

"Get out!"

She raised her eyebrows at me. "I'm a guest here! Where do you get off…"

"You were a guest. You have outstayed your welcome. I'll help you carry your stuff back to the hotel." My voice was cold and firm.

Manos watched our interaction, then sagged heavily into his chair. Marianna rushed to him and motioned for the pill bottle on the table. I tossed them to her and grabbed a bottle of water from the fridge. Manos clenched tight to the arm of his chair, but he gradually calmed as the medication took effect.

When I glanced up, Tracy was gone. Her room contained no bags. As I hurried to the patio, I glimpsed Tracy pulling her luggage on the road below. She turned the corner toward the marina, where I assumed she would hail a taxi. I wondered if we had seen the last of her. Or if she scented blood in the water and would be all the more fixated on her prey. I went back to Manos and joined Marianna in praying for him. The color soon came back to his cheeks, and Marianna smiled her thanks at me out the door. All the way home, my mind sought to anticipate Tracy's next move.

# 29

When I arrived back at John's, I remembered I had promised to make dinner for us. John was teaching me the secrets of grilling fish to perfection. When he tried the filet I served him, he grunted his commendation. It was his recipe, but I added some capers, begged from Sophia, which set up the butter and lemon with a whole new flavor. "Keep this up and I won't do the cooking anymore," John threatened. I felt pretty good about impressing a guy who ate fish every day for the past two millennia.

John was less concerned with Tracy's bid to see the album than he was with Manos' heart condition and Tracy's unhappy eviction. "I'm sure you were right in asking her to leave their home, but you've disturbed a hornet's nest. She no longer has any doubt that such photos exist. Why Manos showed them to you, I'm not sure. He usually keeps the album locked in his safe. His confidence speaks of his regard for you; he hasn't revealed these photos to many others. I'm sure he now regrets doing so."

"I hardly know how this happened. Sorry, John. I've caused you trouble with my carelessness. How can I make this right?"

"The grace of God takes our errors and creates of them glorious victories. He has protected me until now. I'm sure of his faithfulness to come. I appreciate your remorse, but you don't need to punish yourself. You're accumulating enemies: Antonis, and now Tracy. How will you love your enemies and pursue their true best interests? That should be your first concern."

Love? Not the feeling that shadowed my heart. "John, will I ever be like you? Nothing fazes you! You pursue one straight course, unperturbed by circumstances. You believe in the undeserving, hope for the best and never give up. I know, you say it's all love, and you might remind me that we love because God first loved us. I know this in my mind, but living it out eludes me."

"I know, Jason. I know it from personal experience. Don't think that the fruit of love you see in me grew there in a day. Love has been a slow and often painful process for me. Much pruning was necessary for this love to develop, much cultivating and weeding and tender care. At times, in my clumsiness I've stomped it all down and needed to start afresh. But the Gardener is patient and kind and infinitely skilled."

After dinner, as we watched all the light seep from the horizon, John laid out his plans for the next couple of days. "How would you like to try your hand at line fishing tomorrow morning? You could bring in some larger fish for the market. I will visit Manos in the morning, and we'll go together to Skala in the afternoon. I would send you on your own, but I'm cautious about Antonis and his threats. We'll stick together the next few days, you and I." He lit the candle, which became our new focus of attention as the horizon disappeared. "Of course, we must be back and fed before the start of the Sabbath, so we won't stay long."

"Are we in need of cash?"

"Yes, I think so. I'm considering whether I should go with you when you leave, even as far as Kos."

I sat up at this news. "Really? When is the last time you left Patmos?"

"Let's just say, the last time I left, I caught a ride with a fisherman—under sail."

"Why now?"

"The purpose isn't mine, and it isn't clear. The Spirit stirs in that direction, and I must pay attention. To see you off? In case Antonis tries to follow? Because sometimes my eyes long for a change of scene? I'm not sure. We will make it known in Skala that you leave on Wednesday, and I go with you."

Wednesday! I went to bed feeling miserable and hopeful at the same time. Did I feel ready to leave the island? The larger side to that question was, had I come far enough along in my journey of faith to make any difference once I was out in the wide world again? Was I indeed a new man? Would Jessica appreciate the change, and was it enough to win her heart back again? I stared into the dark longer than I could afford, and morning arrived well before I was ready for it.

When we arrived at the beach, we could hardly distinguish the edges of the little swells as they swept up on the sand. The cold water swirling around my ankles made me sink a bit more with each wave. John's fishing rod was longer and more cumbersome than I expected, but he assured me I would soon have the feel of it. I cast too high on my first few attempts, and the bait sailed up and landed ten feet away. Then I cast too low, with the same result. But a few casts made it past the breakers. John had tied a piece of wood to the end of my line, not risking his tackle. Finally, my eyes and my arms came to an understanding. I made a cast that sailed far over the water, like John's. When I reeled it in again, he was ready with tackle and bait.

"What if I hook one of those big ones, the Queen of the Sea? I could never bring it in by myself." I made a cast with the bait. It didn't match my current record, but John said it would do.

"That's unlikely. I rarely catch *sinagrida* these days. Too many fishermen. More likely, you'll bring in *kefalos* or *gopa*, which can put up a fight but you will win. Good fishing!" And John was off to see Manos and Marianna. He told me I would have the best success leaving the rod alone, stuck in the sand and propped up with sticks. But I remembered how the rod took off from us last time. Plus, I felt more like a fisherman by holding onto the rod, so I stood in the water and waited, alert to any action at the other end of the line.

I waited a long time, feeling nothing at all. Gulls circled me in a half-interested way; the sun warmed my back as it came up over the hill. I had to keep shuffling my feet out of the liquid sand that sucked them down. John's words came to mind from the day I first watched him set his nets—how God either filled his nets or didn't, and that he knew what he was about. I told God I was okay with that. I admitted that part of me desperately wanted to catch something.

I had turned to take John's advice and bury the handle in the beach when the rod came alive. This wasn't the unbelievable weight of our last catch, but the rod still bent double. It was all I could do to reel in the line. Suddenly, nothing. The line went slack; the rod straightened. I reeled in, hoping this meant the fish was moving my way. But soon I saw the tackle trailing in the water, bait gone. Oh well. Rather than discourage me, the sensation of something big and alive on my line excited me all the more to try again. The story I had for John wouldn't be about the one that got away. I rebaited the hook and made a solid cast out into the sea.

There was no more action for a long time. John had said this was the reason he usually used a net, but I had no other pressing business that morning. I have nothing to do but fish, I thought comfortably to myself. Enjoy it while it lasts, before the swirl of life gathers me up back home. I thought about John's descriptions of Jesus and how he walked calmly through chaos and clamor. John also demonstrated this simplicity, the fruit of a lifetime of following the Messiah. Could I do the same?

In the middle of my thoughts, the rod bent double again. It was a good fight, and several times the fish leaped straight out of the water, trying to shake the tackle loose. I brought the fish up on the sand, a handsome specimen, several pounds at least, with silver scales and large fins. It was sad to dispatch it as John had shown me, but this was his livelihood.

As I continued fishing, a feeling that I was being watched came over me. I saw no one up or down the beach, which didn't make me feel better. Then I perceived that I indeed had a visitor. At first, I thought her interest was in the fish hanging from the tree below her. But as I watched, I saw that Zesi the eagle had eyes only for me. I panicked, having nowhere to hide. She stared at me, unflinching, as if I were some tasty morsel she could pluck any time she wished. I didn't want to turn my back on her for a moment, but with another fish on the line, I had no choice. Any chance I had to glance behind me, Zesi hadn't moved but continued to stare. The worst was when I had to go up to the tree to hang my next fish. My scalp tingled with the dread of being surgically removed by those gleaming black talons.

By the time John returned from his visit, I had four sizeable fish hanging in the shade. He brought with him three-quarters of a basket of small fish from the net. "Well done!" John was pleased. "These will bring a good price at the market. The restaurants might disdain the *kefalos* and won't serve them to the tourists. But the islanders love these. We need to take them to Skala while they're fresh. I say we leave right away." I stowed the rod in its usual place and lifted my stringer of fish from the tree where they hung. Ouch. All the way to Skala carrying these? It would be money well-earned. I was glad

John had a system—a shoulder sling that would make the carrying bearable. Carry them, I would!

John didn't notice Zesi until she drifted down from the tree and perched on the rim of the basket John had set on the beach. "My friend! Careful of spilling the fish, and you'll have your share!" He took the fish-killing club from the branch where it hung and coaxed Zesi onto it. "Should we take time for your favorite game? Jason, choose a fish from the basket and show it to her, but not too close." This didn't seem like a safety-approved game to me, but what was I to do? Hanging my stringer back on the tree, I showed Zesi a fish from the basket at what could never be a safe enough distance for a creature that can fly like an eagle. "Okay," John coached, "now go down the beach and hide it somewhere, but don't bury it." As he said this, he covered the eagle's eyes with his hand. It stood still, tense and alert.

Catching onto the idea, I jogged down the beach, looking for the best spot for this game of hide-and-seek. I wasn't sure how well to hide the fish, but I noticed a small piece of driftwood and tucked the fish underneath, only the tail showing. I ran back to John, and he took his hand from Zesi's head. The eagle glided down the beach and had both driftwood and fish in her claws in moments. Zesi returned, dropped them at John's feet and perched on the club again. "Give her the prize, Jason." Yeah, right! Expecting to lose several fingers, I proffered the fish to her. To my astonishment, Zesi took it with her beak as gently as a well-trained dog and proceeded to tear it to shreds with one foot while standing on the other. She ate the whole thing.

"That was too easy; she followed your tracks. Here, you hold her." I couldn't believe it when John handed me the club, bird still attached. Zesi didn't seem to mind this new arrangement. She looked at John with anticipation as he chose another fish. "Put your hat over her head instead of your hand—just in case." I did, wondering about fleas and other vermin, and John ran toward the water. When he was up to his knees, he turned and retraced his steps. Slipping past us (Zesi still turned her head), he hung the fish in a bushy part of the tree.

It was incredible to feel the eagle take off from my hand. She thrust away from me with marvelous power for such a weightless bird. I felt the wind from her wings as she glided away, sailing down the beach. When she reached the water, Zesi hovered, searching, wings beating hard to stay in place. She soared straight back toward us, circled once and braked under the tree. Talons up, she snagged the fish from the branch, twisted around and dropped it at my feet. I was too mesmerized to remember to hold up the club. She lighted on the sand and looked up at me expectantly. The whole game lasted less than a minute.

"That was amazing! Well done, bird!" I handed her the fish, which she destroyed like last time. I wondered about the sand she was consuming with her meal, but John told me it would help her digest. I was now in love with this gorgeous bird that once threatened to treat me like the fish. "Why do you think she's okay with me now, John?"

"As I told you, she's perceptive. On your first encounter, she sensed you were a threat." He took the club from me, and Zesi flapped up to it. "Now you're the friend of a friend, and Zesi tolerates you. Remember, she's not a tame bird! Take no liberties with her, and you'll be fine."

We left for Skala. Zesi circled over our heads until we reached the main road, then coasted back toward the water. I assumed the game had been her appetizer, and now she would hunt for the main course. I was glad not to be it. As we walked, John offered, "Your time here is short. I imagine questions have come to mind that you wish to discuss before you go."

My mind searched out my most pressing questions. "Okay, when you first started following Jesus, did you know he was the Messiah right away?"

"That was a process." John's eyes drew back into memory, and I hoped for more firsthand stories about Jesus. "We were all good Jewish boys, of course, with the usual dose of village *Mishna*. But we were no scholars. Not that it would have helped. Even the scholars could make nothing of this enigma named Jesus. He wasn't the sort of Messiah for which they watched and waited.

"But we had enough extraordinary experiences with Jesus to make us wonder. The most common phrase among us in those early days was, Who is this man? Common foot-washing jars he turned into chalices of choice wine. He healed the sick and lame and blind but shunned whole villages of skeptics. He called the poor among us blessed, and the rich cursed. What baffled me most were our times on the boats. I had spent all my life on the Lake of Tiberius. But never had I seen it go from squall to calm at a man's word or ever watched someone walk on it. We were often terrified of our own rabbi.

"We knew the rumors circulating about Jesus. People conjectured that he was a man raised from the dead, a man of old. Was he Elijah, or another of the prophets? Or was he my cousin John the Baptizer with his head screwed back on? We, as his disciples, had a growing realization that he was far above any of these. He was more of a King David than a Jeremiah. We were finally ready with an answer the day Jesus asked the all-defining question, 'Who do you say I am? What have you discussed about me among yourselves?' Peter was our spokesman, as usual: 'You are the Messiah, the son of the living God!'

"We had a sense of something imminent, something big. I assumed that Jesus would soon establish his kingdom on earth, with us as his ministers. But Peter's declaration on our behalf didn't have the result I expected. Instead, Jesus immediately began to tell us what it would mean to be the Messiah: Suffering. Rejection. Death. And the hardest to understand of all: Rising again. What was the point? This sudden shift in Jesus' pedagogy mystified us. Everything changed from that moment. We now had a King who was determined to die. He provoked the religious hierarchy. His enemies increased. The day he set his face like a flint toward Jerusalem, his doom was inevitable. We were once again terrified."

At this point, John shook himself from his memories and apologized. "Sorry, you had me going. What was the question again?" I laughed and assured him he had more than answered the question. How I would miss listening to this man! He spoke of Jesus as if he saw him just that morning. I thought of the introduction to his first letter: "That which was from the beginning, which we have heard, which we have seen with our eyes, which we have looked upon, and our hands have handled, of the Word of life…" Through John, I too saw Jesus and heard him and touched him.

"Let's work on your apologetics some more. Pose to me a skeptic's question, and we will discuss how best to answer."

What popped to mind immediately was an English teacher in high school who, as an atheist, loved to raise objections to the concept of God. "Okay, let's say someone was drowning, and you were present with the ability to save them, but you let them die. Would you be a good person, a bad person, or nonexistent?"

John considered as we walked. "A classic question! As in, where is God when bad things happen to us, true? I could offer you a theological argument for the efficacy of God, but it might not satisfy you and could miss the point of such a question. A demonstration is in order." We took the next road, which led up the hill toward the monastery, then turned down a little-used path.

Stopping at a worn and weary-looking rectangle of a building, John warned me. "What you will see here is not easy to receive. I come here often but haven't brought you because you weren't ready. However, your question demands it." A dank, fetid and all too human odor increased as we neared the building. John opened the door, and a new fetor assailed us. Death and decay resided here. It was all I could do to follow John through the door.

The only light in the room came from small, high windows. In that dimness, I made out several human forms, some on beds but others curled up on old mattresses or huddled against the wall. Two of them coughed, deep fluid barks that were as ineffective as they were involuntary. "Don't touch anyone," John whispered, "and don't breathe too near. Not that you'll catch anything from them—that's unlikely. But they will catch anything from you. They've lost all immunities."

John moved from form to form (I was having a hard time thinking of them as persons). He spoke gentle words, asking questions and hearing their labored responses. None looked at him as they talked; all looked down. They had differing conditions. Some bore red blotches all over, lesions that looked more than skin deep. One man's tongue was coated white, and another had a neck so swollen I didn't know how he (or she) could breathe. I was at a loss to understand what I could do. It didn't matter—none of them noticed me.

When he finished his rounds, John stood with me and spoke in a low voice. "Many of these are in the final stages of the AIDS infection. By now, all hope is gone. They will contract pneumonia, cancer and leprosy. All the worst of human diseases are out to kill them and find delight in taking their time."

"Why are they here in this God-forsaken place?" I whispered. I felt helpless.

"If they're fortunate, friends or family brought them. Some may have crawled here. Manos has tried most of his life to find a better solution for those who are dying of a feared disease. No one wants to listen; they close their eyes to this crisis. But God-forsaken? No, you're wrong about that. Look closer."

As I gazed into the gloom, I saw two that were sitting close together, and one was doing something to the other's face. That one stood, looking healthy and agile. As she walked up to us, I saw that she was a young woman in a medical uniform and mask. She greeted us and led us outside.

John spoke to her, but I couldn't follow what they said. He introduced me. "Jason, this is Dr. Chloe Demetriou, of Athens. She comes regularly—at her own expense—to do all she can. For the most part, she will only ease her patient's pain or clean their sores. But she has saved some who were brought here out of fear rather than necessity. She's a believer and is curious about how you found your way to me, so I explained. She says she would be glad to answer any questions you may have."

I was as tongue-tied as if I were in the presence of a celebrity. What did I want to ask? "John brought me to demonstrate the answer to a question," I stammered. "Why does God not step in when bad things happen, even when he could? These people are in a terrible plight. I'm wondering if John brought me to show that Jesus is here because you are here, in his name."

That took a few moments to translate, and in that time, her expression—fixed on me—seemed perplexed but compassionate. John explained, "She wants you to come with her, and she will show you." Dr. Chloe handed me a mask and led me back inside. John didn't follow. We went to a man who was rocking on his heels in one corner, weeping. She crouched next to him, indicating I should do the same, and began rubbing the man's back. She wanted me to take over. I was reticent to do this, but Chloe was insistent, so I took over for her.

Three things happened as I crouched beside him, running my hand over his back. First, the man slowed his rocking, and his sobs diminished with a great sigh. Second, he became human beneath my touch, not some creature in the dark. I realized this could be my father or my best friend—or me. Third was strangest of all. As I continued to quiet him with touch and gentle words, I had the growing sense that the person I soothed was none other than Jesus himself.

At that moment, the whole question turned on its head. Where is God when bad things happen? Here he is, disguised as the one to whom the bad thing has happened. He's so present, you cannot tell who is human and who is God. Why would anyone pass up such an opportunity! Dr. Chloe makes this hellhole part of her rounds because here she gets to rub the back of God.

The man lowered himself to his mattress and curled up. I tucked his scrap of blanket around him, and Chloe tugged my sleeve. Time to go. Once outside, I felt like I was exiting a cathedral, some holy place that leaves you quiet and thoughtful. John and Dr. Chloe talked for some time while I sat on a broken chair, struggling to make sense of what happened. As we were about to leave, the two of them put the fish from John's basket into a large pot with water and set it on an outdoor fireplace. Fish stock was a good source of strength for those who had lost all appetite for solid food.

I had to ask Dr. Chloe one more question. "You can't be more than thirty years old, and yet you're a doctor, bright and articulate—why here? Why these?" Dr. Chloe told me through John that she was thirty-seven and had an active practice on the Mainland. She made far too much money for a single woman, so she flew to Kos as often as possible. At her own expense, she made her rounds to all the islands in the vicinity, charging nothing for her services to people who could never afford the local doctors. As we walked back up the path, I asked God to multiply Dr. Chloe like the five loaves and two fish that—in Jesus's hands—fed the thousands.

Continuing to Skala, I thanked John for taking me and described my experience in the room. He was glad I understood his demonstration and summed it up like this: "Where is God when bad things happen? That is the wrong question. The correct one to ask is, Where am I when bad things happen? For thirty-three years, God walked about on this earth. During that time, he resolved few of the world's problems—other than bringing about forgiveness, of course!"

"Right," I agreed. "I've often wondered about that. Jesus didn't free them from the Romans or end slavery or speak out against abortion and infanticide."

"True. Instead, Jesus demonstrated what God would do if he were one of us. He would heal the sick, feed the poor and come alongside the oppressed. Everywhere Jesus went, he preached the good news of the kingdom and called people to faith and repentance. He brought light into the darkness and set people free—even those who remained slaves. But then God the Son departed again, leaving us to continue his good work, in his name and by his power. He gave us his Spirit for this purpose."

"He could fix things himself, couldn't he?"

"Yes. And far more often than we realize, God intervenes directly against evil. But either we never know about it, or you hear those stories because they're exceptional. You and I are God's usual strategy for when bad things happen on earth."

If anything, his debrief made me more uncomfortable. If I was God's strategy, I was hardly in the game. I thought back over my younger years as a journalist—how many times I ran across incredible people who were in the places where bad things happened. Or who were trying to bring good where it was lacking. Like the time I was on a bus in India, trying not to puke on the narrow, winding roads at the foot of the Himalaya. The driver stopped for chai, and he suggested I go see what I would find in a nearby cowshed.

I expected cows, and when I looked through the partly open door, many eyes gleamed back at me. But they weren't cows; they were little boys, dressed in identical black pants and blue sweaters. Coaxed by someone I couldn't see, they stood, turned to me and said in English, "Good morning! Welcome to our school." Their teacher came out to chat, a diminutive blonde woman who was from a town less than a hundred miles from where I grew up.

She had approached the nearby village with the offer to give their children a world-class education, and they in turn offered her the cowshed. She said she cried for a while, then got up and started shoveling manure. That spring, she expected her first graduating class. These students would excel in any college or university, with the advantage of fluency in Hindi and English. I realized now that experiences like these didn't simply reinforce my faith in human nature. These stories told me of the pervasive activity of God through the actions of countless good people.

John was happy with the price we received for my fish. We picked up a few groceries but didn't stay long. I was glad, as I didn't want to run into Tracy, who I was sure hadn't given up her quest. John chatted with several people in the market about our travel plans. I also heard him use the name "Antonis" a few times, so I assumed he was still concerned about his whereabouts. I was not. Let him hide, as long as he stayed away from the people I cared about. We hurried home—our day having grown longer than expected—and arrived at the start of the Sabbath. As usual, we ate a simple meal, and John disappeared into his room for the evening. I didn't mind this time. I had much to process from this day, which felt more like three.

My days here were coming to a close, and I had no idea what to expect when I got back home to Jessica. But hope overflowed my heart that evening. My mind projected ahead to the day Jessica and I would return to the Greek islands, not to soak up the sun on a beach but to introduce her to John and Manos and Marianna and all the others. We would explore the market, join John on his rounds, listen to his stories and feel on our shoulders the hands of the local believers as they prayed for us. I wanted to show Jessica the place where my life took a whole new trajectory. I prayed that she might follow my example as I sought to follow the example of Jesus.

# 30

It was quiet in the house. I had eaten my breakfast oatmeal several hours earlier and hadn't yet seen John this fine Sabbath morning. My mind kept straying to all manner of tasks I would rather do that day than rest. I was trying to deflect those thoughts because of something John told me the previous Sabbath. "Yes, God made the Sabbath for your benefit, as Jesus warned the Pharisees. But don't take that to mean the Sabbath is all about you. It's a day set aside by God for a purpose: that we would honor and trust him with our time."

"What do you mean?" I had asked him.

"Can you afford to take a whole day off? No! And that's the point: the Sabbath means you have to trust God to see all your work done in six days. In the same way, he requires your tithe. Why? Because he's in need? No! The tithe means you will have to trust God and manage on ten percent less than your income. Your faith in God is more important to him than your prosperity or sense of security. God gave us the Sabbath and the Tithe as rhythms to live by, so to increase our faith, and more, to prove him faithful. It's what the poor of this world learn by living, and the privileged must learn by giving to God until it hurts."

I could see his point but was still not sure what to do with all this downtime. I read, prayed, drank cocoa and went for a walk to the beach. That took me all the way to 9:00 AM. I thought of visiting Manos and Marianna but couldn't think of a good enough excuse. I would see them tonight anyway. Then I remembered that I had brought home Manos' English

Bible since Tracy had the app on her phone. I settled into a chair on the patio and wondered what part I should read. John's Gospel I had read twice and his letters once. That left his Book of Revelation, which he encouraged me to read, but I hadn't yet tackled. With some misgiving, I turned to the last book of the Bible, not expecting to understand much of what I would find there.

The introduction was fascinating. Unlike his shadowy appearance in the Gospel, John talks about himself in the first person. "I John, who also am your brother, and companion in tribulation, and in the kingdom and patience of Jesus Christ, was in the isle that is called Patmos, for the word of God, and for the testimony of Jesus Christ. I was in the Spirit on the Lord's day, and heard behind me a great voice, as of a trumpet."

Thinking about these words, I had an inspiration. Where better to read the Book of Revelation than in the Cave of the Apocalypse? I had all day. I collected a few items for my lunch and started out. As I walked up the path, I realized I should leave a note for John. But I remembered he wouldn't be able to read my English anyway. Plus, he might be away all day himself.

It was a pleasant morning, on the cooler side and free of the haze that sometimes spoiled the view. The sea below me was a dazzling aquamarine, the sky dotted with clouds in which you could imagine any animal or shape. I wrestled with the thought of leaving all this in a few days. Though I was excited to get back to Jessica and hopefully reboot our relationship, I desperately longed to stay on Patmos. Which brought to mind John's admonition not to go off on my own in case I had a run-in with Antonis. My bad. But it wasn't like I was going right into town. I would be fine.

It hadn't occurred to me that the Cave might not be open. When I arrived, I found the door locked and no one around.

Disappointed, I took the doorkeeper's chair in the warm sun and opened the Bible again to the first chapter of Revelation. John's encounter with Jesus in all his glory mesmerized me. "I was in the Spirit on the Lord's day, and heard behind me a great voice, as of a trumpet, saying, I am Alpha and Omega, the first and the last: and, What thou seest, write in a book, and send it unto the seven churches which are in Asia; unto Ephesus, and unto Smyrna, and unto Pergamos, and unto Thyatira, and unto Sardis, and unto Philadelphia, and unto Laodicea.

"And I turned to see the voice that spake with me. And being turned, I saw seven golden candlesticks; and in the midst of the seven candlesticks one like unto the Son of man, clothed with a garment down to the foot, and girt about the paps with a golden girdle. His head and his hairs were white like wool, as white as snow; and his eyes were as a flame of fire; and his feet like unto fine brass, as if they burned in a furnace; and his voice as the sound of many waters. And he had in his right hand seven stars: and out of his mouth went a sharp twoedged sword: and his countenance was as the sun shineth in his strength. And when I saw him, I fell at his feet as dead."

I wished for Tracy's phone app and a more current translation as I encountered some formidably archaic words. "Girt about the paps with a golden girdle." I found this description of Jesus hard to imagine. But whatever John saw was beyond awesome. He had once witnessed the glorified Jesus on the mountain, glowing and robed in white, chatting with Elijah and Moses, and that was astonishing enough. Now Jesus had flaming eyes and a sword for a tongue. Not the picture of Jesus you imagine with children on his lap.

It turns out that the first reason Jesus came to John on the island of Patmos was to convey a message to a group of nearby churches. The colorful map at the back of Manos' Bible showed me their location in what is now the nearby country of Turkey. I always wondered why we didn't have any of the writings of Jesus. The Bible is one of the main ways God expresses himself to us, so why doesn't it contain the written words of Jesus, the Son of God? As I read Revelation 2, I saw that Jesus had indeed written something—seven letters to seven churches—dictated to John.

What would it be like to receive a letter from Jesus? What would he say? As I read those seven letters, they sounded like Jesus in the Gospels but more formal, and I could relate to some of what he was saying. One church had lost its first love for Jesus. He wrote about perseverance, about remaining faithful and holding on to what the churches had. Another church was dead, despite its reputation for being alive.

Greeted in English, I looked up from my reading. A young man in a white robe approached—not an angel, thankfully— but one of the young monks who tended the door. "Welcome! You wish for a tour? Is the host inside?" When I explained that the door was locked, his face fell. "Oh, that is not good! Someone has slept in or forgotten his place in the schedule." He looked flustered, and I assured him I was okay and no other visitors had come. "I must go retrieve the key. I will be right back!" And off he ran before I could assure him he could take his time. He returned before I finished reading the letters of Jesus. I wound my way down into the coolness of the cave and took John's seat.

The hardest letter of Jesus for me to read was the last one. Jesus could have penned this letter to my own church back home—or to me. I cringed inside as I read it: "I know thy works, that thou art neither cold nor hot: I would thou wert cold or hot. So then because thou art lukewarm, and neither cold nor hot, I will spue thee out of my mouth. Because thou sayest, I am rich, and increased with goods, and have need of nothing; and knowest not that thou art wretched, and miserable, and poor, and blind, and naked."

The word "spue" was particularly explicit, especially spelled that way. That's what happens when you take a drink expecting one thing and find another. I remembered as a kid watching a show in an Old West tourist town. The barmaid hands a glass to the piano player, who chucks it down and then spews it all over the floor. "What in blazes was that?" he yells (it was a family show), and she tells him it was water. It might have been lukewarm, as well as not the whiskey he expected. And that is how Jesus feels about... me.

What would make someone revolting to Jesus? According to his letter, it's not our character flaws or what we would think of as gross iniquity. Instead, it's the same quality Jesus saw in the Judaism of his day and which was now showing up in his newborn church. He cannot stomach the attitude that we're self-sufficient and don't need a thing, when in reality, we are "wretched, and miserable, and poor, and blind, and naked."

In one sense, this appears strange. Everyone knows Jesus for his compassion toward those who are wretched and miserable, poor and blind and naked. He's not offended to find us in this condition. And he's no stranger to squalor and poverty and impairment. These are the circles to which he gravitated throughout his time on earth. Instead, he cannot tolerate the pretension that we have it all together, in denial of our actual condition. This self-deception is what makes us unpalatable to him.

As I sat in the very place where Jesus dictated these words to John, my heart cried out to him for mercy. This was me he described—I was the one who made him ready to spew. As I had admitted to John, the one thing that held me back from following Jesus was my obsession with approval and recognition. I did everything possible to maintain the image that I'm independent and self-made. I'm a witty and insightful journalist who exposes corruption and injustice but is himself far above such disgraces. By no means was anyone permitted to see my inadequacies. My self-doubt and depression. My misperceptions and shame. No one, not even myself.

In despair, I scanned Jesus' letter for any sign of hope—and found it. "I counsel thee to buy of me gold tried in the fire, that thou mayest be rich; and white raiment, that thou mayest be clothed, and that the shame of thy nakedness do not appear; and anoint thine eyes with eyesalve, that thou mayest see." Thank you, Jesus. I didn't know what these purchases from the store of Jesus represented, but I wanted them desperately. If I could admit my spiritual poverty, there was the hope of spiritual wealth. Jesus would lift me out of my pitiful condition, as he did with many people during his days walking around Israel.

I loved Jesus' intentionality in his letter to this sad excuse of a church. "As many as I love, I rebuke and chasten: be zealous therefore, and repent." He loves me. That's why he brought me to Patmos; that's why it was heart-wrenching every day. He loves me too much to leave me in the condition in which he found me. His discipline, painful in the moment, was for my reformation. It would be worth it in the end if—with all my heart—I put the praise of others behind me and chased after his approval alone. In the end, only his commendation will satisfy: "Well done, good and faithful servant!"

If I could. The appeal of Jesus was loud in my ears in the very place where he said these words. "Behold, I stand at the door, and knock: if any man hear my voice, and open the door, I will come in to him, and will sup with him, and he with me." That's all he asked. Open the door! Stop shutting me out! I want in! And so I did—I opened the door. I can't tell you what happened after that. It's not like I'm trying to hide anything. But this—this was too close to my heart, too inexpressible to put to paper.

I don't know how much later I startled out of my profound meditations, wondering where I was and what was the time and what I should be doing. Dazed, I made my way to the door, surprised to find the daylight fading outside. I thanked my white-robed host and didn't care that I staggered a bit as I made my way up the path. The end of the Sabbath. We would be meeting at Manos and Marianna's, likely soon. Hopefully, no one was worried about me and my long absence.

# 31

I stumbled in deep snow. Not the light fluffy stuff, like traipsing through a cloud, but as if I were slogging through freshly poured concrete. More was falling and melting down the back of my neck. Every step was painful, and I wished Jessica would take over the lead, except I was too proud to admit I was dying. She kept telling me to go faster or we were going to miss her appointment with the doctor. I couldn't lift my feet any longer. My whole body was too heavy, like I weighed five hundred pounds. I was frozen beyond shivering. And that ringing in my ears—it had been there a long time.

I wanted to stop and sink into the snow and let it cover me. But Jessica's insistent voice wouldn't let me quit. I'm not a quitter, I told myself. I tried to say that to Jessica, but the words hardly passed my dry, parched tongue. Why was my speech slurred? I'm not drunk. I'm not drunk. It's this damned snow, up to my chest now and no way will we make it through. Jessica laughed derisively, which I would have thought unkind if her laugh didn't sound like a man's rough guffaw. And her ridicule was in Greek. I forced open one snow-encrusted eye a crack to see what was the matter.

"See? You okay. I think, hit you too hard. Come, wake up!"

I wanted to wake up because something was wrong. Who was speaking? The light was too great—my head throbbed, and I closed my eyes again. I was cold except for one leg, which had a warmth that crept toward my other parts but didn't make it. I must have drifted off again because the next time I came to, I was warm all over. The snow was gone. I opened my eyes, and several moments passed before I could take in my surroundings. In front of me was the sea, but as if I was looking at it through binoculars held the wrong way. I slowly realized I was in the back of a cave, not like the Apocalypse Cave but a narrow one with rough, jagged walls and a dirt floor.

I was alone. My body still felt numb, yet I needed to move and find out where I was and why. My arms were behind me, and I tried to push myself up to a sitting position. But I couldn't do it. My mind took time to register the reason my arms wouldn't obey me. They were bound with something that hurt when I tried to move. How did I end up here? I was fishing with John... when? And games with Zesi the eagle. I slowly remembered a sharp blow to the back of my head. My whole world turned crimson, and there was a loud buzz in my ears. Before I lost consciousness, someone lifted me over their shoulder. I recalled bouncing as they ran down the road. Nothing came to mind after that. Why was I here, tied up and alone?

No, not alone. I remembered a voice, mocking me. I had thought it was Jessica, but it was a man. A Greek man. That thought sent a shudder through me. Antonis. He did this to me. But he wasn't here now. I tried to yell his name but little came out, my mouth was so dry. I swallowed down the lump in my throat several times and tried again. "Antonis, what's this about? Hey! Antonis!!" No answer, no movement at the mouth of the cave. He had left me there.

What *was* this about? I already knew—it was me standing up to Antonis at Sophia's house. But this seemed over the top even for a rascal like Antonis. Would he leave me to die because I protected an elderly widow? Or did he have something new against me, some fiendish scheme in mind? Didn't he realize I had powerful friends on the island? Or was it my friends he intended to hurt by kidnapping me...? That seemed the most likely of all the possibilities. What did he hope to gain?

Now that my mind was clearing, I assessed my situation. I was too deep inside the cave for anyone to hear me yell, and besides, it faced the sea. I twisted around enough to make out how my hands were bound. Strong, dirty white zap straps cut into each of my wrists, and several more straps bound them to a large iron ring in the cave wall. I knew the nylon was unbreakable, even if I could maneuver to a position that would allow me to try. The iron ring looked old, and I wondered if any other prisoners had languished in my cell with a view. The warmth was from a rag of a blanket that half-covered me. Many donkeys must have benefitted from it before me.

Antonis. Where was he, and would he return? I vaguely remembered him trying to wake me up. Would he have bothered if he intended to leave me to die? It wasn't much to cling to, but it was my only hope. I tried to remember what day it was. I had been bound in the cave long enough to be constantly uncomfortable. That meant John and the others were already worried about me and on the search. Sunday. It must be Sunday. There was no spot on this island that John didn't know. I hoped they found me before Antonis returned.

I had to change my position. My arms kept falling asleep, and I had no room to get anywhere near comfortable. Could I move my arms out in front of me? Not up over my head, that was for sure. Down under would be the only way. There was limited room in the cave behind me—the iron ring was near the end. Lying on my side with my back to the ring, I tried to scoot backward between my arms. At the worst possible point, I found I couldn't move, backward or forward. The nylon straps felt red hot on my wrists. With a desperate effort, I pushed through, legs following, and my arms were out in front of me. My wrists bled pretty badly, and I could do nothing to stop it except raise them as high as possible. Great. I tried to remember when I last had a tetanus shot. It might not matter. At least I could position myself more comfortably now, with the blanket under me and my back against the wall.

When my wrists calmed down, I realized how much my head hurt. I remembered Antonis saying he had hit me. A concussion would explain my spells of fuzzy thinking and wandering memory. A person could die of a concussion, but that might be preferable to dying of thirst in this cave. And I was desperately thirsty. I prayed someone would show up soon with something to drink. I later wished I had been more specific. On the other end of the spectrum, I had to pee. Let's just say it was no easy accomplishment, but at least the cave floor was absorbent.

John would tell me that God was with me in that cave. If so, he was currently not much help. I talked with him about that for a while, but dozed off again. When I woke, the light was brighter in the cave and the air stifling. Antonis was a foot away from my face, staring at me. I tried to kick him, but I was too slow and he fell back out of reach.

He laughed scornfully. "Hey, little man has life in him. Is good." He drew near again and inspected my bloody wrists. "How? No good. These covered in the fish gut, I think. Maybe bad for you. Oh, well!" He returned to the mouth of the cave and brought back a metal pail. It was half-full of water. John didn't even drink the water straight from his well without boiling it. What would this bucket from who-knows-where do to me if I drank from it? I wasn't that desperate yet. Antonis shrugged off my refusal and dumped the water on the ground, turned the pail over and sat on it.

"Antonis, why?"

He regarded me dispassionately. I was sure my life meant nothing to him. "Is easy question. Money."

That surprised me. "Why do you think kidnapping me will bring you money?" He didn't understand me, and I gestured at the cave and my bonds. "This—how is this money for you?"

He took on a crafty look. "Is good plan, no? My own idea. Newspaper friend of you, is for him."

What? Who could he be talking about? "You don't mean Tracy?"

"Yes, Tracy. Pay me much. Manos, if I make him give me old pictures of John. Then she pay me."

"I don't believe you!"

Antonis shrugged off my protest. "Whatever. You see." He took his pail to the entrance, likely for the breeze. I could have done with a breeze.

How could this be? Tracy was relentless, but not ruthless. Or willing to risk her career for a story. Surely she couldn't be behind Antonis' plot to kidnap me. "Antonis!" I needed more info from him. And the means to survive this. I realized I was a bargaining chip; I had some value to Antonis. How could I convince him that he had to treat me better? If a person could saunter while bent over in a cave, Antonis sauntered his way back to me. "Antonis, tell me the plan. Does Tracy know you kidnapped me? When does she pay you? And what happens next?"

My assertiveness surprised him, but he remembered I was his prisoner. He gloated, "Why tell? You live, or you die. That all." Antonis looked smug. Despite his haughtiness, he gave away details of his scheme over the next hour or so, and I could piece the rest together. I had to admit, as stupid as the plan seemed, he had covered himself fairly well.

For a small sum, a boy Antonis didn't know was on his way to Manos' house to deliver a message demanding the photos. The drop-off was a fishing boat in the harbor in Skala. In exchange, Antonis would release me and sell the photos to

Tracy. If Manos didn't comply... Antonis didn't tell me what would happen next, but his chortle made me think the worst.

"You didn't answer my question—does Tracy know you kidnapped me?" He glanced at me sheepishly, like a child caught misbehaving, and shook his head. That was a momentary relief, but then I remembered that this meant that only Antonis knew what had happened to me. I wanted to tell him that his plan stunk, that there were much simpler ways to extort or steal the album from Manos. But I wasn't about to help Antonis make improvements to the scheme. I would have to go with it and hope for the best. In the meantime, I needed to protect myself.

"Hey, Antonis, you realize this might take a while. Until then, you have to keep me alive. I need water—not from a dirty bucket; I need bottled water—to clean up my wrists and to drink. And food. I'm no use to you dead." My head swam with the effort of this speech. "And more blankets. You hit me too hard. I could die if you don't keep me warm." I said this while I was sweating, but I knew it would become cold when the sun set.

He seemed to be weighing my demands against how little effort he could get away with. Finally, he said, "Okay, maybe." He pulled a few euros from his pocket. "You already pay," he laughed. He must have cleaned out my pockets. I wasn't sad to see him leave. Immediately, I inspected the straps that held me captive. I could create no friction on them with the metal ring, and the cave walls were too crumbly to be much help. Any rocks that might be useful were well out of reach. I wasn't going anywhere soon.

Antonis was gone for a long time. As a journalist, I'm conditioned to people's capacity for cruelty. Yet I had never been so mercilessly the victim. How could one person do this to another? From John, I was learning what it means to love; from Antonis, it was a lesson in hatred. John would die for me—if he could. Antonis apparently wouldn't think twice about killing me. The extremes of love and hate. But how does one arrive at that place? I remembered what John wrote, echoing Jesus, that the one who hates his brother is a murderer. Love, as demonstrated by God himself, means to lay down our life for our brother. All love is in the direction of self-sacrifice, but all hatred follows the course of murder.

Thinking of John's words, I wondered what happened to Manos' Bible when Antonis grabbed me. It might still lie on the road; it could give John a clue about my location. The light was dimming inside the cave, and the bit of sky at the entrance faded to a rosy gray. They would have to give up the search until morning. The thought of spending another night here filled me with dread. The nylon straps on my wrists made them tingle, and when I moved my hands to help the circulation, they bled again. Being here was torture. I didn't know how much more I could handle.

Antonis returned, stumbling under the weight of a 24-pack of water bottles. Thank God. He stumbled for other reasons, too—the essence of cheap alcohol was potent. I downed an entire bottle of water before caution stopped me; the next one, I sipped slowly. I hoped Antonis would drop everything off and leave again. No, he was settling in. With two more trips, he brought food and blankets and other supplies. I realized he wasn't only hiding me in the cave; he was also hiding himself. Antonis tossed me an old sleeping bag that smelled like an entire summer camp had peed in it. The night would have to become pretty darn cold before I resorted to climbing into that thing.

We ate cold lamb, beans and rice—not enough—and we didn't talk. He wouldn't unbind me but put in my hands a styrofoam container of food that I had to wrestle to my mouth as best as I could. Antonis was always pulling at his bottle, which after a while loosened his tongue. Fortunately, it was all in his own language and I didn't need to pay attention. He seemed pleased with himself and happy to spend a night in the cave with his very own prisoner. I did what I could for my poor wrists with some of the water. I wasn't sure what I would do to Antonis if my hands were free. It was too easy to go down the road of hate.

I looked up when he paused his monologue. I saw he had a book—Manos's Bible. His dim flashlight would make it difficult to read, even if he was able. He examined the thin pages and carefully tore one from the middle. This he ripped in half again. He took a pouch from his pocket and proceeded to roll a couple of joints with the torn page. He offered me one, but I refused. I would inhale enough, I soon realized, captive in the hotbox he fashioned of our cave. I never did like the smell of pot. It didn't help me relax at all.

I guess I slept. When I woke, it was because Antonis was snoring. I couldn't see my hands, it was that dark. The cave was bitterly cold—at least for a Mediterranean island—and I pulled myself into the rank sleeping bag. I tried to think of any lower point in my entire existence and could not. What would tomorrow bring? Would John give in to Antonis' (or Tracy's) demand? Or would they find us first? Or was this my last night on earth? With that unhappy thought, I sought out the least uncomfortable position and tried to sleep. But I looked long into the blackness before sleep came.

# 32

I was awake again before the first light trickled through the narrow cave entrance. Antonis still slept the careless sleep of the uncaring. He sometimes snorted himself half-awake and rolled over again with a snarl at his discomfort. Every part of me ached, having run out of options for a satisfactory posture. I was positioning myself to pee again when Antonis spoke. "Hey, no! Stinks! Here, come." He reached out with a wicked, rusty knife and sawed through the straps attached to the iron ring, leaving my wrists bound. "Come!"

I struggled to rise to my feet, dazed by the sudden flow through my veins. Bracing myself against the walls of the cave, I followed Antonis to the small entrance. Though it wasn't long after dawn, the light was blinding. I was glad Antonis stopped me when he did because—not two feet from the entrance to the cave—the cliff dropped away to rocks and ocean more than a hundred feet below. The thought came to me that I could push him over the edge, though more likely than not, I would go over with him. Antonis must have had the same thought—he kept well ahead of me along the narrow path. We arrived at an opening in the cliff where grass grew and a stream might sometimes run. I relieved myself under Antonis' baleful eye, and he made me go ahead of him back to the cave. The entrance was low, and we had to crawl to get inside. A person could pass right by on the path without ever noticing the cave.

We ate cold, greasy pizza for breakfast, far from fresh. Likely from a restaurant dumpster, by the looks of the box.

We said little to each other, as we hadn't much to say. Antonis seemed anxious, often looking at a watch with a broken strap that he kept in his pocket. About the time the heat from outside was finding its way in, he rechecked the straps that bound me and told me he was going out. "Pay day, I think! Better hope, hey? No more bad pizza for Antonis, hey?" And he was gone.

This day was a hundred days long. I couldn't help wondering if Tracy would pay a guy like Antonis to extort photos from Manos, with me as collateral. I didn't want to believe it, but here I was. Antonis wouldn't go to all this bother for nothing, as little as he liked me. Money was involved, and where would it come from besides Tracy? The idea made me sad, not angry. I wondered how I could possibly love Tracy as my enemy. I grew more depressed as the day became warm and breathless, then orange and dim with sunset. Antonis hadn't returned.

I was dozing when an angry shout startled me awake. "Get up! Damn..." Antonis rushed up to me and held his knife so close to my throat, I could feel the cold. I was terrified. He was drunk and out of his mind with fury. Antonis glared at me, shaking, his knife sometimes touching me, for what seemed forever. He leaned back, spat in my face and put the knife back in its sheath. For several minutes he raged up and down the cave passage, using language I was glad to not understand.

Finally, Antonis calmed down enough to grab me by the shirt and speak tersely into my face, "Manos—he say no! Say is big mistake." He threw me back against the wall and continued expostulating in Greek until he ran out of foul words. I was trembling so badly, I could hardly wipe my face with my shirt. I'm going to die here, I told myself.

"What about Tracy? Did you tell her what you did to me?"

He growled at me. "Tracy—she gone! Left! No money for Antonis." He sneered at me. "Bad for you!" The thought that John was safe from public exposure was some consolation, but this wasn't the way I wanted to go. I had hardly started a whole new life; it wasn't yet time to die.

I heard a scraping sound and looked up. Antonis was a silhouette sitting at the cave entrance. He alternated between tipping a large bottle into his mouth and honing his rusty knife on a small boulder. I guessed both actions were in preparation for slitting my throat shortly. I wondered what to say to him that might buy me more time. In my despair, nothing clever came to mind. "Antonis, what are you going to do?"

He laughed and became more deliberate with his knife sharpening. "You know."

"You don't have to do this, Antonis! Killing me won't make you rich. You won't get away with it."

He got up and sat on the water pail in front of me, feeling the edge of the knife. I could hardly see the expression on his face in the fading light, but his voice was crafty. "You got better plan, maybe? You make Antonis rich?" His bottle was empty, his speech slurred.

"If I promise you money, will you let me go?" He raised his eyebrows, head tilted back, and clicked his tongue. Greek for, "No way, Hosea." My heart sank. "Why not, Antonis? What's the point?"

"No promise. You give money, take Antonis to Mainland, maybe I not kill."

"How am I supposed to do that?" It was the wrong thing to say—the difficulties of that plan were occurring to Antonis at the same time. He began sharpening the knife again. My brain scrambled in desperation. "Okay, you send another message to Manos. Tell him you'll let me go if he gives you money. He will do it."

"Manos, I hate. No want his money."

"Well, you already took everything I had in my pocket. Manos will give you money and I will pay him back. It will ultimately be my money, not his." This was too much for Antonis' inebriated grasp of English. I tried to explain, but he threw his head back again. "You, shut up. I think." He returned to the cave entrance and clicked off his flashlight. Though I could hardly see him, I heard the uncorking of another bottle. How that would help him think, I couldn't imagine. My prayers were wordless, my mind frozen. I had little hope of surviving this night in a cave with a drunken monster.

I once called that monster my brother, during a time when he deserved it no more than he did now. Here was a twist to the story. The prodigal son returns, enjoys the party, and throws the elder brother into a cave with the intention of killing him if he didn't get what he wanted. What would Jesus say about that scenario? Would it still be self-righteous to complain about my sibling's behavior? Would the father finally wash his hands of him? Or did the hope of forgiveness remain? Antonis was still alive, despite all his bad choices in life. I had to assume the possibility of redemption. Nuts. That meant I had to at least try. It might be my last chance.

"Hey, Antonis!" He ignored me, but after my third try, he got up and staggered back to see what I wanted. Where to begin? "Hey, do you remember when I called you my brother?"

His bleary eyes flashed annoyance. "No remember. No care."

Antonis started to rise, and I put a hand on his arm. He pulled away, but I persisted, "It's okay. It doesn't matter about me. I want to talk with you about your father."

"Is dead!" he rasped. "Thank God." Since I wouldn't leave him alone, he sat on the bucket. "I hate father."

"You thanked God just now, but God is your father." Antonis' face looked quizzical in the beam of the flashlight. "God is your father, and he is good. He loves you." A tear formed and glistened in the corner of one eye. "All your life, Antonis, you have run away from God, who is your father. You have made him sad, but he always, always watches for you to come home. Do you remember the story I told you?" He looked down and nodded. "I want you to know... it's not too late for you to come home to him. Never too late."

I watched him, wondering. He said nothing, and for a moment I thought he had gone to sleep. He looked up, and I will never forget the sadness in his eyes as he said, "Is too late. I let you go, I go to jail."

I should have jumped at this chance. Antonis was softening. Instead, I heard myself say, "I forgive you, Antonis. Whatever you decide to do, I forgive you."

We held one another's gaze, unspeaking. Antonis stood and carried the bucket to the cave entrance and sat down. I didn't know what I expected, but at that moment, I knew I had said and done all I could. Now each of us was in the hands of God, for better or for worse. Accepting this, I collapsed against the side of the cave in exhaustion. In moments, I fell into a troubled sleep.

I was climbing with a heavy pack. Every step up the snowy slope was agonizingly slow and painful. I wasn't wearing gloves, but was afraid to put my hands in my pockets for fear of losing my balance. Jessica was a dark form behind me, hardly visible in the blinding blizzard. She struggled to follow my steps, which were too long for her. I turned to say something, but nothing left my mouth. Jessica became smaller, and I realized she was sliding backward and the whole pitch of snow with her. Her terrified cry reached my ears as I watched in horror. Then the entire scene cut off like the power went out at the movie theatre. My eyes flew wide open, and only by touch did I know I was still lying bound in the cave.

Not simply dark, but the cave was also silent as a tomb. My dream about Jessica lingered, vivid and undivided from my waking consciousness, and her shriek still reverberated in my ears. I called out to Antonis, and as my senses anticipated, received no reply. Antonis had left me again, and I was still alive. What was he up to now? I didn't care, as long as he brought more food and water. Weariness dragged me down, down, and I drowned in it for a long time.

When I came to life, the sun was already on the ocean. The bucket lay on its side at the entrance, but no Antonis. I prayed that this time they would apprehend him and force him to tell where I was. How much more of this could I take? Every bone and muscle ached with inactivity. My wrists, red and burning, were getting infected. This had to end soon. But as the day rolled by, nothing happened. No rescue arrived, and Antonis didn't return.

I was sipping one of the few remaining water bottles when the thought occurred to me: What if Antonis doesn't come back? What if this is his solution to a reticence to kill me outright? Has he abandoned me to a conveniently pre-dug grave? Surely not, but the idea made me replace the cap on the half-finished bottle. Or he might have used all my money and was waiting for the next dumpster pizza. He might be too drunk to navigate the narrow path to the cave.

Considering the latter explanation, something more alarming emerged from the corner of my mind where I had pushed it. That shriek last night in my dream—when I imagined Jessica caught in an avalanche—could it have been real? Antonis was plastered last night. Was he capable of getting up before dawn and making an excursion into town?

What if the scream was real? Could Antonis have toppled from the cave entrance to the rocks and ocean below?

This was a far worse scenario. Not only might no one ever find me, but they would also never find Antonis so they could find me. If Antonis fell, the cave would be my end, and a slow and agonizing one. I replayed the dream again and again. Each time, I become more convinced that the shriek I heard, and could still hear, didn't come from Jessica's throat, not even in a nightmare. The possibility of Antonis' death brought no relief to my anxiety. Nor could I find it in my heart to mourn his loss. All I felt was abject horror.

Dusk came, then dark. I was sure Antonis wouldn't return, for whatever reason. A deluge of emotions ran through me. How could a wretch like Antonis decide my fate? What justice was that? I knew my friends sought me in prayer and in person. Why did God not answer? I had an acquaintance who never picked up his phone when I called. The phone would ring again and again until it went to voice mail. All the while, I knew he was there but ignoring my ringtone. It was such a helpless feeling because I could do nothing to make him pick up.

God, do you see me? I raged and wept. Does it not matter to you that I'm already dying and that my death will take a long, long time? If you want me dead, do it! Not to mention that my demise is needless and makes no sense. I'm not sick, I've committed no crime, this is no accident. But if you require my life in this cave, make it happen. Please, please don't let it drag on until I'm crazed with infection and thirst. The reality of the suffering ahead of me ripped at my heart and soul. I wouldn't be the first to die this way, I was sure, but I didn't want to be the next.

What will death be like, I wondered? Will I go mad first? Will I fall asleep and wake in another realm? Or is heaven only an illusion and will I cease to exist? Will I have a funeral? Who will come, and what will they say? I thought about places in the world I have been where death is a familiar companion, where people talk about death and have long-established ceremonies. In my own culture, we save death for the TV screen and newsreel, as far removed from our personal experience as possible. Death only happens to other people. When it touches us personally, it's as much of a surprise as if we made it on TV ourselves.

And when death does touch us, we sometimes break away from our fabricated reality and remember what matters the most. Temporal stuff—wealth, recognition and things on a screen—fade to their proper, obscure place. We long for the people in our lives, the ones who give meaning to our existence. I knew my loss, realizing I would likely never see any of them again. Even if someone discovered my remains, it would bring relief to no one. I prayed for them, for comfort and grace. I hoped they would remember me kindly.

And then I became angry again.

# 33

I hardly slept, being in too much pain. I alternated between shivering in my thin rag of a blanket and sweating until my shirt was damp, which made me cold again. My mind was often too numb to think, too full to pray. I could no longer calculate how many days and nights I had suffered in this cavern. But I was down to two bottles of water that I sipped only when I couldn't help myself. When it was gone, I would have at best three days to live. It seemed too long.

My greatest regret was Jessica. Languishing in that cave, I comprehended how precious she was to me—the best of gifts and one I had long squandered and neglected. A couple of days ago, I was afraid of losing her. Now it seemed she would lose me. Memories of Jessica often came to me, clear and lucid as if I were there, and my mind brightened and the sweating or shivering stilled. It was like God rubbing my back. As much as I wondered how he could abandon me to this open grave, I was grateful for this assurance that he hadn't forgotten me.

I remembered Sophia's vision and was confident that God had shown her Jessica in real time, sitting in the window seat with her coffee. My heart ached with sadness and joy over her tears about our marriage. I was certain that if I could just get home, we would sort things out and make it work. It was maddening to be trapped here, unlikely ever to get that chance. Bitterness against Antonis took root easily. Keeping it under control was a constant effort.

How does one love an enemy? I prayed for Antonis' soul, prayed that—in his drunken stupor before toppling from the cave—his heart came home to his Father. God, have mercy on his soul, I pleaded. Father, forgive him because he didn't know... didn't know... I can't remember what he didn't know but the mercy of God stoops deep and low and the fact it's underserved is the whole damn idea... no, not damn, quite the opposite, but you know what I mean and I don't think Antonis is hopelessly lost because God heard—like me—the sadness in his voice when he whispered that it was too late for him and God you don't need much time and only a minuscule seed of faith and you reward the one at the final hour the same as the first...

My mind strayed like this for an interminable while. When I next came to myself, my prison was dark again, and I panicked. I flailed hard against the restraints on my wrists and the pain was incredible, but it reminded me that I was still alive, and if I was still alive, I had hope. An idea formed itself, which I immediately rejected, aghast, then pondered again. A fine, strong string can be a cutting tool. I had two of them attached to my wrists, and my wrists were a matter of meat and bones and sinew. Could the nylon zip ties cut through my wrists? Would I die of blood loss before I made my way to help—if I could make my way at all? It was such a drastic measure to saw through my own wrists to save myself. Unthinkable, but better to lose my hands than lose my life.

I drank an entire bottle of water. It glided down my throat like John's best wine, and as John came to mind, tears I couldn't afford fell from my eyes. John. Manos and Marianna. What were they going through, wondering if I was alive or dead? Did Jessica know I was missing? I thought of Tracy, the other enemy I must love, and wondered again if she knew Antonis kidnapped me, and if so, whether she regretted her part in it. The bottle of water cleared my aching head long enough to pray for them all, and that the grace of God would carry them, his peace would guard their hearts and souls. That they would place me in his hands and leave me there.

My mind reopened the discussion with John about the God who doesn't act to save, even when he could. What about me, John? Why does God hold me in his hands but leave me bound in this cave until I'm ready to remove my own hands to secure my release? A fraction of an inch of nylon is all that keeps me from freedom. It would be nothing for God to breathe it away, yet he doesn't. I couldn't see John, but I heard his compassionate reply: God is at work even when it seems he does nothing, he said to me. That you're unable to see what he's doing in this cave is no fault of his. Or yours. It's simply too dark for you to discern the love of God in action. I know. I too have languished hopelessly in a cave.

The night was endless, and the coming day held for me only the horror of my plan to amputate my own hands. I wasn't sure if I was sleeping and dreaming, or if my waking mind saw visions. I was in a massive hall made of stone of many colors: walls and pillars and a high-arching roof. Wall to wall, it was full of creatures like from a Star Wars scene, some animal-like and some human or nearly so. They all faced one point in the room: a throne raised high above the floor with a towering human figure seated on it.

Every throat in the room—mine included—roared with a deafening but harmonious resonance in a language I didn't recognize. Not a brutish babble but something bright and articulate and intelligent, and always toward the Person on the throne. We stood with our hands raised high and fell on our faces. All of us were in front of the throne, yet we filled every corner of the room. The joy was too immense for my heart. It burst from my chest and merged with the flood that swelled around the throne. When the vision faded, I wept and my heart beat fast, now back inside my chest again.

The words continued in the one language I know. These words may have been coming from my own mouth—I wasn't sure—but they rang against the walls of the cave and filled my mind. "Worthy is the Lamb that was slain to receive power, and riches, and wisdom, and strength, and honor, and glory, and blessing. Holy, holy, holy, Lord God Almighty, who was, and is, and is to come! Blessing, and honor, and glory, and power, be unto him that sits upon the throne, and unto the Lamb forever and ever."

And it came to me that, in the end, the praise of God is all that matters. Even the people I love the most find their best orientation in that throne room, facing their Maker, worshipping him forever. Not one has any thought of praise or recognition for themselves, only for Him. Brilliant glory there makes every trouble here fade to black, never remembered again. Every tear wiped from our eyes, every ache soothed, our mortality swallowed up in immortality. No one is ever alone again. My heart yearned for eternity. When daylight finally came, it took everything I had left to return to the cave and my scheduled self-surgery.

I contemplated my hands for a long time, feeling surprisingly sentimental. These hands were formed in my mother's womb. They had been kissed, wiped clean, held, bruised, clapped, high-fived and taken for granted. Many good deeds—and some bad—were accomplished daily by my hands. I would miss them. What a wonder it was to watch them open and close! I imagined them lying lifeless and twitching on the ground. How could I possibly do this?

It would have to be quick. I would likely pass out, and it wouldn't do to come back to consciousness with the job half-done. If I leveraged with my feet on the wall and pulled with my back... But how would I navigate the nylon straps through the many bones and sinew that made up my wrists? I wouldn't know until I had tried. What if I got halfway and couldn't finish?

For a long time, all I could manage was nothing—my feet on the wall, muscles poised to extend—but I could not commence the operation. It was a desperate plan. My mind reasoned I must do this or I will die, while my heart felt that dying might be preferable, and my body glanced from one to the other and did nothing. It was like standing on a cliff above the water, and all my friends are yelling for me to jump, and I... just... can... not.

Without warning, my mind took over. I lunged backward, pushing with my legs, screaming before the pain registered. Pulling with all my strength, everything I had left, I knew right away it wasn't enough. I fell forward, shaking, bleeding—and ashamed. Because I knew my plan was workable, but I didn't have the heart to follow through. I was desperate, but not desperate enough. Trouble was, by the time I was that desperate, I would likely be too weak. I might be so emaciated that setting myself free this way was no longer an option.

Which left one other: I would die here.

Sometime in the night, in a fever of thirst, I drank the last of the water. I once thought I might last a few days after the water was gone but no longer thought so. Every movement was agony, as well as every non-movement. Sometimes if I closed my eyes and calmed down enough, I didn't feel anything, and that was best. I had a taste of what was coming, and I didn't blame Jesus for his request in the Garden to avoid death. Yet my suffering was nothing compared to his. Like him, I was in physical torment, but Jesus took on himself all the shame and guilt of our sin, the full wrath of his Father. When he died, he crossed the finish line after an unthinkable race.

By faith in him, the death that approached me was all bark and no bite. Dying alone in a cave was the worst, but the best was yet to come! Sometime soon, this scruffy world would roll back like the lid of a sardine can, and the real adventure would begin! My body would be free—not only from the restraints on my wrists—from every limitation, imperfection, ache or pain. Sooner than expected, yes, but what were a few years in comparison to eternity?

I wasn't always clear in my mind about what was real and what was not. I wanted to sing my last hours away, as I could think of nothing better. Old songs from my childhood, the occasional classic, a few hymns of which I remembered only the first verse. The cave had excellent acoustics; the reverb was remarkable. I sang at the top of my lungs, which wasn't very loud. As I sang, I saw a bird glide by in the distance past my window. Every time it passed, it circled closer. At one point, it must have heard me sing because it faltered as it glided by. This happened several times and then it flew by no more. It was such a joy to be acknowledged again after all this time, even by a bird.

I dozed again and someone nudged me awake. Zesi the eagle had kindly brought me a fresh mug of coffee and donuts. As thirsty as I was, I held the cup under my nose, inhaling the rich fragrance. Zesi was an accomplished barista; I never enjoyed a better cup—mellow and fruity and deep. She declined a sip but took a donut, starting at the end where the jelly was injected so it didn't squeeze out everywhere. Mine was a maple glaze, my favorite. It was a kind gesture, but Zesi was a busy eagle and soon excused herself to her next appointment. I appreciated her thoughtfulness in taking time out to see me. I wished I could pay forward her courtesy, but I didn't seem able to move my legs anymore.

I don't know if it was dark again or if I could no longer see. No matter. Eyesight is overrated, and I saw now with my eyes closed.

# 34

We were nearing the summit. Jessica was leading because for some reason I had to drag myself by my arms through the snow. She was yelling something, but the blizzard whipped her words away before they reached me. I didn't think I would make it. Why again were we climbing this mountain? And what would happen when we reached the top? Jessica retraced her steps to where I lay helpless and exhausted. Her strength amazed me as she put me over her shoulder and labored up the steep face. For a moment I panicked, fearing it was Antonis who carried me again. Then I remembered that Antonis fell, which brought me sadness and relief in equal measure.

The light was blinding after many days in the storm. We had to be above the clouds, higher than the wind. There was no oxygen, but that was okay because I stopped breathing hours before. I wanted to open my eyes and see the view, but they were frozen shut. Jessica laid me in the soft snow at the summit, and I felt the warmth of the sun on my face. I could have stayed forever. But I wanted to see—what was the benefit of making it to heaven and a person couldn't see anything? Soft lips kissed my frozen cheek, and it thawed. I know, because when a tear fell on my face, I could feel it rolling down. If she would kiss my eyelids, I was sure the frost would leave for good. As if hearing my wish, she did, and I opened my eyes.

I'm glad that the first person I saw wasn't Moses or the prophet Habakkuk or the Apostle Paul. Not that I have any objection to meeting any of these excellent people and many others when I die. But if the first face I saw would be my anchor in this new world, I'm glad it belonged to...

"Jessica." My voice was quiet; I could hardly hear myself. Her face was blurry, yet I had no doubt it was Jessica. How could this be? She smiled at me with affection and anxiety. My eyes tried to scan our surroundings, as I couldn't move my head. Not a mountaintop. And, judging by the presence of Jessica and a growing awareness of pain everywhere, not heaven either. Nor a dark cave. I would have shaken my head to clear it if I had any inclination to move.

"Hey, Jason, it's okay. You're safe. You're with friends. I'm here, and I'm not going anywhere." My body was too deflated to relax anymore, but her words would have done it. I was still alive, and I was free. And Jessica was here. I felt tears rolling down my cheek again and could do nothing about them. Jessica dabbed them away and kissed me on the forehead.

"Where... is this?" I managed, blinking.

"One of the best places in the world. Manos' and Marianna's home." Her voice was tight with emotion. "Hush now. You don't need to figure it out. All is well." I guess I drifted off again because the next time I opened my eyes, my entire circle of vision was full of people. I looked at each in turn. Marianna, wearing a white uniform. Myrto and her granddaughter. Jessica. John. And to my amazement, Sophia.

It was John who took my hand. "Good to see your eyes open, my friend." I managed to make eye contact. "You have been here for some time, and you must give yourself more space to recover. We have much to tell one another, but it can wait. Rest well. You're in good hands."

It was like this for a while. I would drift off, drift awake and find someone there. Always someone there. Often Marianna, sometimes John. Usually Jessica. Never Manos. I wondered about that, and after some time it became a worry.

One time when Marianna was with me, I found her hand and said, "Manos..." Her eyes filled with tears as she smiled back at me and almost imperceptibly tilted her head. No! The possibility proved too much to manage. I drifted off again.

I have vague memories of that time, of people moving me around, warm sponge baths, some spoon-fed broth, voices speaking but not to me. I had many dreams and some nightmares, but I can remember none of them after the ones about climbing the mountain. The worst was when I woke up at night and thought I was back in the cave. Panic was always barely under the surface, ready to take over. But always, someone was present to take my hand or stroke my hair, like I was a puppy who had recently left the litter.

And one day, all at once, I was awake. Jessica was in the room at the time, reading something on her phone. I watched her for a while before she became aware of me. Jessica looked different. Everything, from her expression to the way she sat in her chair, spoke of peace, like the war was over. When she glanced up and saw me watching her, she gasped and came to my side.

"Jason! You're... you have the light back in your eyes! How do you feel?"

She looked delighted, and I managed a quiet laugh. "I'm awake. I hope so anyway. This is better..." I had to catch my breath. "Better than I could have hoped." She sat on the bed as I looked around the room, which looked like a hospital, with an IV stand and chairs and a table with various medicine bottles. "How long, Jessica?" Jessica shook her head, but I needed to know. Panic was knocking.

Finally, she told me. "You disappeared about two and a half weeks ago. You've been here about half that time, unconscious until recently. And that's all I will tell you right now." Jessica's last words were tearful. She bent down and held me close, smothering me with her hair. I wanted to hold her too, but my arms still felt like lead. Two and a half weeks! All I could think of was how much Jessica and my friends had suffered on my account. More than me.

"Jessica, I love you." She smiled and I smiled back and that lasted a while until I woke up again and she was gone and John was in her place. My eyes fluttered, and he was looking right at me, and I knew from his distant expression that he was praying for me. No doubt, this is how he had spent much of the past few weeks.

Several minutes passed before his eyes refocused and he spoke to me. "Jessica tells me you're more awake. Thank you for not leaving us. It must have been tempting, but we would have missed you around here."

"I didn't seem to have any choice. I have a stubborn spirit. Wouldn't let go."

He smiled at that. "And you haven't lost your wittiness. That's a hopeful sign. But rest now. You still have more healing to come. God is faithful, but the restoration of the body is slow. You will need to be patient, my patient!"

It felt good to laugh, good to be alive and in this room with the man whose far more tenacious spirit held him these two thousand years. I thought I might have a few more years left in me too. Over the next few days, I drifted off less often in the middle of conversations. My wife and my friends bolstered me with their presence and laughter. Not to mention some strange and strengthening concoctions from the hand of Sophia. She insisted on spoon-feeding me long after I was sure I could feed myself. I went with it. It was too exhausting to fight her.

The story came out in bits and pieces with a different perspective from each person. The synopsis goes something like this. When I didn't show up for the gathering at Manos' and Marianna's house, the group prayed and broke up and went searching everywhere. The crew and captain of the ferry insisted that only one American had left the island that day, and it was a woman. When everyone regathered and had found no sign of me, they all joined Manos, who stayed back to watch for me and pray. After praying for some time, everyone went home. John contacted the local police to report me as missing, and continued searching.

Late the next morning, a boy arrived at the house with a message but disappeared before Marianna could detain him. The search became a manhunt, as Antonis proved to be elusive. They set up a sting to catch him when he went to claim the ransom. But a relay of little boy messengers took the bait—which was Manos' refusal to give him the photo album—and disappeared, foiling the efforts of the police. Now everyone feared for my life, and with good reason.

As time passed with no sign of Antonis or me, John and many others searched every corner of Patmos. The days must have been exhausting. The authorities suspected that Antonis had fled the island, and I was likely dead. They were pretty close to the truth on both counts. Tracy's departure at the same time seemed to them suspicious. But though it was clear she had told Antonis about the photos, she might have known nothing of his consequent actions. They had no other evidence to indicate her complicity. John was confident I was still alive. He kept up the search while the others prayed night and day for my safe return.

Manos was in a constant state of prayer. That alone told me how much he had come to love me. He also felt responsible for Antonis and wished he had done more as a judge to bring him into line with the law. But of course, he wasn't to blame for Antonis' failure at rehabilitation. Marianna worried that her husband's devotion to prayer was too taxing for him. She was right. One morning, she found him in his chair facing the sea, head bowed and hands folded, in the presence of God as never before. His funeral took place the day after my rescue. My heart broke for this man who prayed himself to death for me.

Eight days after my kidnapping, John was on his patio, mapping out his search plan for the day. A rush of wings startled him, and claws pulled at his shirt as if to pluck him off his chair. He tried to calm Zesi, but the eagle wouldn't leave John alone. "So, I had a conversation with her," John told me, laughing at the memory. "I told her that if she had something to show me, we better start off. But to remember that I can't fly and she will have to be patient. She studied me as if listening to every word, then lifted from the back of my chair and began circling in the direction of Skala."

John kept her in sight and happened upon several friends on his way. Soon a small crowd was tracking the eagle over every hill and outcropping, field and terrace, picking their way through the coarse brush. Zesi brought them to the brow of a long bluff overlooking the sea west of Skala, where she dropped from the sky and out of sight. Everyone rushed to the edge and spotted her a distance below, perched on a goat path high above the rocks and waves. The group scattered to find their way down. Of course, Zesi was waiting at the near-invisible entrance to the cave. Even a bird had learned to love her enemy! Though she hadn't brought me coffee and donuts.

I was near death. One fellow ran for his truck while the rest took turns carrying me like I was a crate of eggs. They initially took me to the medical clinic near the monastery, which would have transferred me to a hospital on the mainland. But Dr. Chloe happened to be visiting, and she decided that moving me again was too risky. I could get all the necessary treatment there under her management. When I was out of immediate danger but still unconscious, they took me to Manos and Marianna's house. Marianna had been a nurse at the clinic, and Dr. Chloe helped her collect the equipment and medication that was needed. They also brought Sophia, the healer. Between them, they set to work to preserve and strengthen the thread of life remaining to me. It was a near thing. But I began to show signs of improvement.

Using the call history on Manos' phone, John contacted Jessica soon after I was kidnapped. She immediately booked a flight back to the Mediterranean and had an anxious few days joining the others in the search. Of course, Manos and Marianna welcomed Jessica into their home and sustained her in every way, and God began his work in her. While I was dying in the cave, she was coming back to life. They told me that Jessica buried herself in prayer while I was gone and hardly left my side when they found me.

The transformation in her was astounding. Hours and hours of prayer were fertilizer for the seed of faith she had in Jesus. Now it was evident, confident, flourishing. If following Jesus was a race, the tortoise had passed the hare by a landslide. We talked and talked throughout my convalescence. Not about what happened or what was next, but about here and now.

"I love Marianna. I want her life," Jessica pondered, gazing pensively at the bay below us. Marianna was allowing me several hours on the patio each day. "Did you know she has always lived on Patmos, except when she went to nursing college? I guess you don't have to travel the world to become wise and passionate and strong."

"She is all that."

"Marianna discussed with me—through John—how Jesus interacted with women. I found it fascinating, especially after John told me what it was like for women back in the days of Jesus. I wouldn't have survived." Jessica sat up and searched the notes on her phone. "Marianna told me about a nameless someone who had three strikes against her. She was a woman, she was a Samaritan and she was a social outcast. Having one husband is a lot of work—sorry!" She put her hand on my arm. "She had gone through five husbands by that point. Can you imagine? That's why she was drawing water at the well by herself in the heat of the day instead of in the morning with the other women. Jesus' disciples were upset to find Jesus talking with her. But he changed this woman's life, and in turn, she changed her whole town."

Jessica's interest amazed me. "What other women did you talk about?"

"Um, the Mary's. All of them. It seems everyone called their daughters Mary in those days." She searched for another spot in John's Gospel. "This one. She has a sister named Martha and a brother Lazarus, and John says the family were special friends of Jesus. But very different from one another. This Mary I don't understand. She sits and listens to Jesus while Martha does all the work."

"Which of them is like Marianna?"

"That's a good one. I kinda think Marianna is a blend of Mary and Martha. She would sit at Jesus' feet. But a side table of moussaka and grilled fish would appear, and no one would notice how she did it."

"Nice! That's pretty accurate."

"But my favorite is when Jesus rises from the dead, and the first person he appears to is a woman, another Mary. And it's on purpose. This Mary goes to Jesus' tomb and it's not only open, it's also empty. She finds Peter and John, and they go running off without her like a couple of boys, to find everything exactly as she told them. When Mary arrives, they've already gone home. So she's left at the tomb, crying her eyes out. And that's when Jesus shows up. I love that!"

"You make Jesus sound like a feminist."

"I know, right? Who would have thought it? I'm dying to study more about this man who wanted women to be free from suppression."

I couldn't stop looking at her. "Jessica, how did we go so long doing the Christian thing and missing the whole point? It's like we had just enough Jesus to vaccinate us against the real him."

"It's how we grew up, Jason." She returned my gaze. "I always struggled with believing in Jesus, and I didn't want to miss out on everything the world had to offer. I think it was because I couldn't see the reality and relevance of Christian faith in my family, in my church, and—I'm sad to say—even in you." Tears ran down her cheek. She sniffed and swiped at them. "I'm not trying to excuse myself or lay the blame on you. But to me, the world was real and Jesus was only a fairy tale for children, with little evidence in real life. Why would anyone expect me to choose differently?"

I took her hands. "Jessica, I hope someday you'll come to forgive me. First, because I agree with you entirely—I haven't lived out what I claimed to believe. My faith in Jesus became an unreasonable code of ethics. As much as I spoke and acted like I despised the world and its ways, inside I was full of pride and judgment. I was intolerant and thoughtless. When I told you I loved you, my actions said that I only loved myself and what I got out of you. I was of the world but not in it, which is the exact opposite of what Jesus taught." She reached forward and kissed me on the forehead, which melted me because I didn't deserve it.

But I wasn't done. "Second, I hope you'll forgive me because I have changed and will continue to be different. I came to the island out of curiosity and maybe to show you I can be adventurous too." She laughed, and I loved the sound. "But it was God who brought me here. He wanted to turn my life around, whether here or at home. I don't know what will happen with us, Jess, but either way I want to be a child of God, a follower of Jesus, a man of love in action and in truth.

There's no turning back for me now. I hope we can follow him together."

She didn't say anything for a while. It had been a long time since she looked at me this way, like I was a real person, maybe someone she wanted to be with. It gave me a thrill of hope. "Jason, I... I can see what you say. I want this kind of faith for you more than anything. But you'll need to give me time to process what's happening here. It's a lot to take in. You wear sandals now, and you like oatmeal! And there's this island-full of new friends who are ready to die for you. I met a man who is apparently a couple thousand years old, who I'm coming to love more and more each time I talk with him. And an eagle listens to him and saves my husband from a kidnapper. I feel like I'm in a movie."

"I'm so glad you're here, Jess. So many times I wanted you to see and hear and smell and taste what I was experiencing. It almost—not quite—makes it worth nearly dying. I will do my best to be patient, like John was patient with me. This will be God's job, not mine. Take all the time you need."

She rested her head on my shoulder, and we soaked up the sun and the scent of blossoms and the birdsong so different from home. The ever-changing tones of the sea below were mesmerizing. Jessica filled me in about her time on the island, when I was lying unconscious. Many of her conversations and new food tastes and language frustrations and fresh experiences sounded comfortably familiar. I understood exactly what she meant when she described it all as unforgettable.

"I want to die like Manos did," Jessica concluded. "I can't think of anything better—to be in the throne room of God in prayer, open my eyes and I'm in his throne room for real. Can you think of anything better?"

I shook my head, but it was as much in wonder of this transforming Jessica as it was in agreement with her words. "I miss Manos so much. His apologetic shrug with the wry little smile. His approval when I did the yard work right. I even miss his coffee!" I looked ruefully at the cup Marianna had attempted for us. "Our loss, heaven's gain. And if it were not for Manos—and everyone—I'd be with him in heaven myself right now. I'm not sure I should thank you."

Jessica smiled at me. "Do you think we wouldn't miss you and your interesting sense of humor? You also would have been a great loss. I'm glad to have you back. Though I am perplexed about what to do with you."

We gazed at one another, not saying anything. That was also the question at the back of my mind. I loved this time of healing of body and soul; I almost didn't want it to end. Could we take home with us what we gained here? Could we start fresh our life together? I desperately hoped so.

# 35

It was a perfect fall day, cool enough for a hoody but still warm enough to stay out on the deck of the ferry. Jessica had her head on my shoulder, but we weren't talking. We had far too much to process since leaving Patmos that morning.

Neither of us wanted to leave, yet we knew it was time. More importantly, John told us it was time. And he felt it was no longer necessary to accompany us as he once thought. I hadn't yet regained all my strength, but my bad days were few and infrequent. We could tell that Marianna needed time to grieve for Manos and think through what life would look like without him. We moved back in with John, which meant tight quarters, and he introduced Jessica to Zesi, my rescuer, who took to her right away.

But John was also grieving. "I haven't much to offer you right now, Jason," he told me one morning as we were washing the nets at the shore. "My heart is too full and too empty. It's time for you to gather all you have learned here and take it back out into the world. You have powerful voices at home, and you will need to use them for the sake of the kingdom of the heavens. I won't hold you back."

"What should we tell them, John?" I wanted to hear how John would sum up his message for our people back home.

"That the kingdom to which they belong is not of this world. The church of the West has long preoccupied itself with establishing Jesus' kingdom on earth, politically and socially, and it has never gone well for anyone. Instead, teach your people to *be* the kingdom of God—living out his commands by faith—in a world that they should expect to become increasingly hostile. Love audaciously, preach the Gospel of the kingdom. Serve the undeserving. All in the name and power of Jesus. Keep in step with his Spirit."

"And what will happen?"

John smiled at me. "From my experience, some will love you and others will hate you for bearing the name of Jesus. Yet his kingdom will advance as it has these two thousand years, relentless and unstoppable. Wherever faithful disciples of Jesus go, more disciples will appear. We will take them under our wing and teach them—by word and by deed—the obedience that comes through faith. And they will do the same."

"Like you have done with me, and now with Jessica. I can't thank you enough."

"You're welcome. You have filled up my joy in these past weeks, as difficult as it's been." He reached into his pocket and pulled out my phone. It felt strangely heavy and foreign in my hand. For a moment, I wanted to turn it on and let the world flood back in. Then, with a flick of the wrist, I launched my phone and skipped it many times across the still waters. John laughed, and squeezed my shoulder.

They never found Antonis and concluded that he must have fallen, as I guessed. I found myself praying for him anyway, just in case there was still hope for him. Or because there's always hope that the prodigal will find his way home. Zesi loved me when I was once her enemy—and she was a bird! No eagle was going to outdo me. I would love and forgive Antonis for the rest of my spared life. I had a great pair of reminders—the scars on my wrists remained. I later had them worked into a couple of tattoos, with eagle feathers and the words from Psalm 91, "He will cover you with his pinions; and under his wings you will find refuge." They look pretty cool.

Jessica and I prayed for Tracy often, yet we never heard a word from her. We thought about tracking her down—for the sake of closure, not accusation—but in the end, we decided it was best to let her go. I was nervous that someone like Tracy knew what she did about John and the existence of the photos, but John was unconcerned, so I let that go as well. My prayer was that God would continue to lay siege to the gates that held Tracy back from faith, that he would overcome and she would surrender, and she would find fullness of life. Forgiveness does wonders at relieving us of emotional burdens. John said it was like dropping an anchor with no chain attached—nothing to hold us back from moving forward.

We spent the final few days like my first on Patmos, with some notable differences. Jessica joined us on our rounds, showing amazing ability to come alongside those who were hurting, despite the language barrier. And John more often followed my lead. "Myrto told me of a family where a man left his wife and four children..." I would say, or "Can we go check on Aegeus? I haven't been back since Antonis..." and so on. We always found ways to help, larders to fill, hearts to encourage. I loved this way of life and grieved it days before we were to take the ferry away from there.

"We don't have to stop, you know." Jessica cheek-kissed a new friend goodbye, and we turned toward Marianna's house, where we were to meet everyone for a farewell dinner. "Needs are everywhere—this was a dress rehearsal. We can do this at home too." I tried to picture myself showing up at some guy's door on 42nd Avenue with a basket of fish. Jessica didn't appreciate my cynicism. "Idiot! I'm not talking about dispensing fish! We'll get to know our neighbors, for a start. I don't know one of their names, but we'll make the effort. They might find us strange, but we can love them, no strings attached. The deserving and the undeserving." I loved hearing her quote John. I loved hearing her say "we."

Nearly every person we had met on the island came to Marianna's house. Happily for Marianna, they all brought food and drink and bright laughter to her home. I wished Manos was with us, welcoming each one and hearing their news. I noticed his chair remained empty, though there was limited seating. Finally, Marianna led Sophia to it and helped ease her old bones into the soft leather. Sophia hadn't yet returned to her own home after I was no longer in need of her spoon-feeding. Since she slept a good part of the day, I imagined Sophia was the right balance between the solitude and companionship Marianna needed.

I was amazed at how many connections we had made on the island during our short stay. John crowded everyone into the living room. He opened the floor for words of appreciation, encouragement and hopes for us, as he translated. Their praise would have inflated our egos if they were not just as ready to offer their guidance and advice. Marianna spoke of her hope that Jessica would surrender her independent spirit and rest in Jesus and the care of his people. Thoughtful words, not easy to swallow but full of love to make them palatable.

Myrto told me she loved my wry sense of humor, but more than that, she wanted to see me laugh. Life had robbed me of my joy, and I needed to seek it out again like I was hunting for buried treasure. This was true, and it brought tears to my eyes. John gave me the words of Jesus: "Abide in me, and I in you. As the branch cannot bear fruit by itself, unless it abides in the vine, neither can you, unless you abide in me. I am the vine; you are the branches. Whoever abides in me and I in him, he it is that bears much fruit, for apart from me you can do nothing." His gaze told me this was more than mere advice; it was his prayer for me.

As we sampled Marianna's creamy chocolate eclairs and more wine, someone called out to me. John interpreted,

"What will you write when you're back home? Will my name be in your newspaper?" Everyone laughed.

I looked a bit dejectedly at John. "I guess I have nothing to write and everything to write about. I don't think I will ever get over it—the story of my life at my fingertips, and I can't write it up!"

John shrugged off my dilemma. "It's no problem, Jason. You should write a novel, telling of your adventures on Patmos and what you learned and became. That way, no one will believe a word of it!" When John translated this, the idea both amused and excited the group. They offered many suggestions, each more ridiculous than the last. The food and wine had put them in a merry mood.

Later that evening, John and Jessica and I sat on his patio and looked out at the stars—so full and ripe, you could pluck them. He offered many other words of his own. "You will leave here," he warned, "and the world will try to pick you up where it left off. It wants to swallow you whole and convince you that what happened here was unrealistic and insignificant. Don't listen. Don't let the counterfeit reality devour you. The world moderates and polishes its ways until they're gleaming, but beneath the surface, they're full of decay and dead men's bones. You've found truth here, and the truth will set you free—if you reject the half-truths and outright lies of the world."

Jessica stirred uncomfortably. "I've spent my whole life listening, telling myself the world was right when I knew deep in my heart I only wanted the world to be right."

"So now, Jessica, do not love the world or the things in the world." John's voice was gentle, entreating. "If anyone loves the world, the love of the Father is not in him. For all that is in the world—the desires of the flesh and the desires of the eyes and pride of life—is not from the Father but is from the world. And the world is passing away along with its desires, but whoever does the will of God abides forever."

"You're quoting yourself again, John." I recognized the words from his first letter.

"Ironic, isn't it, that I should tell you not to love the world when in my Gospel, I wrote that God so loved the world. But he is God, and you are not. He can touch the world in its filthiest condition, and it won't soil him. Love the people of the world by hating its system. The way of the world promises pleasure with one hand while choking the life out of them with the other. Go and save them, Jessica and Jason! Be rescuers, never victims."

John stood and placed his hands on our heads. "Go, without fear. You have come back from the dead, Jason, and those who have tasted death no longer need to fear it. You have suffered in your soul, Jessica, so—as my friend Peter wrote—you are done with sin. Your people back home won't know what to do with you; they may fear you because you no longer fear what they fear. You have a second life—make it worth more than the first. Live in a way worthy of the good news of Jesus, the Messiah, the Lord, your King. Never again live to impress your fellow travelers in this world or to seek their petty pleasures. Live for the next! *Marana tha!*" Our Lord, come!

With many similar words, John built up our hearts. It wasn't until later that I found the word everywhere in the Scriptures for what John was doing: *admonition*. How had I missed this before? John loved us as he found us, yet loved us too much to leave us there. He spoke words of his longing and his hopes for us. I love this about you, Jason, yet... this I want to see in you. This would be good for you, Jessica. This would bring glory to God. Never said from the standpoint of disappointment in us, always said with love and anticipation of what we would become. We decided that our life's ambition now would be to speak truth into people's lives this way. To love them too much to leave them as we found them.

Two days later, we were at the dock in Skala. Marianna and Sophia had said their farewells at their house, but many others came to see us off. Myrto administered her barrel hugs. Her granddaughter wrapped herself around Jessica like a cloak. And the cheek-kissing was profuse. John laid his heavy hand on my shoulder one more time and spoke to me with no words. The horn sounded, we boarded the ferry—and it was over.

After our long, sad silence, Jessica sat up, stretched and twisted around to watch the yellow hills of Patmos fading away behind us in the morning mist. "Unbelievable. It already feels like it never happened, like we were never on an island with the Apostle John as our dearest friend. Not to mention Marianna and—Manos—and all the rest." She turned to me. "Did it happen?"

"I don't know. How can you tell?"

Jessica's gaze made the world fold back on itself. "I can tell here..." she put her hand on her heart, "...and here." And she kissed me.

Also by Jim Badke:

# The Island and i
### Nelson Dunkin of Copper Island

**How do you love
your neighbour
when you live alone
on an island off the
wild coast of
British Columbia?**

Nelson Dunkin lived on a remote West Coast island more than three decades ago. Yet he remains well remembered and loved by the many visitors whose lives were gently altered by his generous hospitality, example and influence.

*Available from Amazon*

Jim Badke writes from
40+ years of church and
camp ministry. He and his
wife Sarah live by the lake
in Honeymoon Bay on
Vancouver Island.

www.ingramcontent.com/pod-product-compliance
Lightning Source LLC
Chambersburg PA
CBHW020341180626
46812CB00001B/292